Anna

# THE COLOUR OF SNOW

RENU PARMAR

Thanks for celebrating
this
Love
Renu

*Life is not a series of gig lamps symmetrically arranged; life is a luminous halo, a semi-transparent envelope surrounding us from the beginning of consciousness to the end.*

*– Virginia Woolf, The Common Reader, 1925*

# MAYA
## 1976

LOOKING BACK, my first memory of Canada isn't really a memory – it's a colour. Before I had left India at the age of nine, *Papaji*, my grandpa, told me it would be cold in the new country and I would have a better life. Those were the two things he told me. But he didn't tell me about the colour white. I remember standing outside on a porch looking at the white blankets of snow around me on the grass, rooftops, and trees. They were shimmering and glistening diamonds in the sun dancing around me, and I started to move with them. I bent down and grabbed at this special powder – so white and clean – it numbed my fingers. I laughed and grabbed more, put it in my mouth, and let it dissolve. When I breathed out the air was like a haze of smoke, and I was filled with wonderment. Yes, he told me it would be a better life, but he didn't tell me about all that white.

WE HAD ONLY BEEN in Canada for a few months, but it felt like forever. My brother, Jeevan, and I would tire from standing at the window, waiting for Mom and Dad to come home from work as the light from the cold sun faded in the afternoon. When it got dark there was only one source of light – or so we were told as a means to save electricity – a hideous elephant lamp with menacing eyes that glimmered a pale pink light among the shadows cast from the trees outside. Even in the day, the image of the snow through the curtainless windows would sometimes alarm me. Perhaps it was the enormity of the front yard; a shiny, untouchable sheath of white that I wasn't allowed to play in, because apparently, in Canada, going outside could be dangerous. The contrast was the thing that scared me the most during those winter afternoons; it was so bright and white outside yet so dark inside. In comparison, India seemed neutral to me – a series of browns and greys that all merged into one colour – one expectation. My overall conclusion of the place after two months was that there was too much time and too much space here.

Prince George was the name of our town. No one ever told me who he was. Even later as an adult, I still didn't really know anything about him. All I was told was that they made lots of paper here and that's why it smelled so funny. Paper here was white too; white like the snow and white like the people. In the mornings, I would see people wearing fancy clothes (suits and high heels) getting in cars, or I would see mothers trudging off to school with their children wearing big puffy coats and weird fuzzy things around their ears. But after that, hours would go by and I wouldn't see anyone through that window, and even more disturbingly, I wouldn't hear anything. I ached for the sound of a rickshaw driving by or of *Bibi*, my grandma, pounding spices with her rolling pin. I missed the sound of people just laughing and shouting over the price of mangos, grabbing and clambering on top of each other to get the best deals. The depth of silence made me shake sometimes, and I clung to Jeevan, as much as he clung to me, telling him it was only because I felt cold.

What surprised me more was that this was supposed to be a better life. I guess children don't idealize things the way adults do. I saw our new home for what it was; a dingy two-bedroom apartment with walls that smelled like sour milk and stained shaggy, brown carpet that smelled like smoke. There was no furniture other than a worn tweed couch and a plastic side table that held the only decorative piece my parents had brought over from India – the drinking bird.

The drinking bird was everything to me: my pet, my friend, and the only relic that reminded me of home. More importantly, it helped me pass the time. It consisted of two glass bulbs, one for the body and one for its head, joined by a glass tube filled with fluid. Everything was held together by two plastic legs with a pivot connection. After initiating a few swings, the bird would dip its beak into a glass of water and then continue swinging all on its own. So, for a distraction, we would sit and watch the drinking bird's blue top hat bobbing back and forth, back and forth.

"It's going to bend down and drink after three more dips. . . . Watch . . . three, two, one!"

I tormented Jeevan by pretending to psychically know when it would take a sip even though I could guess fairly reliably from counting.

"How did you know that?" he would ask in Punjabi, pulling at my arm. "Do it again!"

"Dippy Bird told me," I would say. "He doesn't talk to you but he talks to me."

The dippy bird took on a life of its own, becoming my sad little imaginary friend. I still don't understand how it worked exactly, but back then it was magic, and it was all I had. When Jeevan took naps, I would look into the dippy bird's felt eyes and speak to it. I would ask it to tell me that I shouldn't miss the hot dry soil prickling at my feet, and I shouldn't miss carving pictures in the dirt with Rupi, my best friend. I would ask it to come to life and replace Jeevan as my sibling.

I didn't mean to hate Jeevan. I really didn't. I was just like any other daughter in an Indian family plagued with the harsh realities of having a younger male sibling. Resentment was merely a natural response to an inevitable future of Jeevan getting the bigger roti, the more expensive shoes, and the later curfews. Often Mom would put more toothpaste on his toothbrush, and when I called her on it she told me I was being silly. But I knew.

I eventually got to start school. Mom and Dad made friends with the only other Indians in town, and they looked after Jeevan so I didn't have to. My job was to pick him up every day after school. Sometimes I took him to the park and pushed him really fast on the merry-go-round, cussing and swearing the few bad words I learned: "Fuck-face, Paki, faggot." He didn't know what they meant, but he was scared. I always felt bad after I did this, but it seemed like something larger than myself would take over me. I couldn't help it. I needed to purge everything that I experienced during the day: the mocking of my thick accent and mispronounced words, the rejection at recess time, and the loneliness of having coloured skin which Jeevan didn't quite grasp yet. I also used the words because they gave me a false sense of power. I didn't know what they meant. I assumed the word "fuck" meant kick or hit. I imagined when someone used that word it was like they were hitting someone with a rolling pin. I assumed "Paki" meant someone from Pakistan, and I didn't understand why they kept calling me that when the teacher had clearly announced that I was from India.

If I could erase one day in my childhood, it would be the day Jeevan robbed me of the dippy bird. That was the worst. I had just been turned down for the Mother Mary role in the Christmas nativity play. I had practised my lines the night before in a perfect Canadian accent and used a towel to mimic holding a baby at just the right angle. But Tammy got the role. Tammy with her thin, golden-blonde hair.

Jeevan stood by the kitchen door and waited for me to notice him while I rolled roti in perfect round circles. I could always feel his presence every time he entered the room. He had a watery, needy current of energy that seeped from his pores.

"Jeevan, what's your problem?" I turned to him, pushing my hair forward into my face. I didn't want him to see I'd been crying.

His eyes stared back, big and round.

"What?" I said.

He had something in his hand. It was the dippy bird.

"I was playing," he said. He held it up.

I grabbed it out of his grip and examined it. Nothing seemed amiss. "What is it?" Then I noticed. A felt eye was missing. I could feel my voice tremble. "Where is it?"

He opened his other hand, and there was the felt eye staring solemnly up at me. Before I could think, I brought up my palm and slapped him across the face. He fell into the wall next to him, hitting his head and falling to the floor. I stared at my hand accusingly, removed from it, bewildered that it would commit such a heinous act on its own – at the same time curious about the sheer force of it. Jeevan lay slumped on the floor, shocked by the momentum, looking at me quizzically. Scared. There was blood on his forehead. I ran over to him, scooped him in my arms, and held him to my chest.

"It's okay," I said, "We can glue it back on. We can just glue it."

He sobbed quietly while I rocked him back and forth, silently begging his forgiveness. He was pure. I wanted to tell him that I was jealous of this the most. His heart was simply more open because he was a boy. It had not been, and never would be, as hard for him. He didn't suffer the armour that I was required to wear and the baggage that I carried. He could walk steady, unassuming, open and inviting to all.

In the spring, Dad gave up his factory job for a better paying job in a pulp mill outside of town. It was the place they made paper and he was earning a good reputation for himself. They said he could find and fix problems other people couldn't, and that he was smart for an immigrant. I didn't know what that meant, or what he did there, but I imagined he knew the secret formula for making the paper really white.

I never saw him for weeks at a time. I didn't really mind. He wasn't the kind of Dad that sat around and played with me anyway. Mom minded though. My most consistent memory of my mother is the expression on her face – the perpetual surly frown – of someone who's been given a raw deal in life from the moment she was born. All her life experiences began with the phrase, "You don't know what it's like . . ."

"You don't know what it was like to work in the fields in India at four in the morning with your grandfather. You don't know what it's like to scrub floors in Canada with less breaks and less pay than all the other white people."

Often, she would come home from work crying, her eyes puffy and swollen. She worked at a hotel, cleaning rooms. There was always a story of some injustice.

"I got a warning for using the bathroom. Of course, Margaret sits around smoking and laughing with the boss for an extra twenty minutes, but she's white so it doesn't matter. And I know they're talking about me, Maya. I know they are. They think I don't understand English enough, but I can hear them saying my hair smells like onion."

Sometimes she would shout all of this at me as if I were her boss standing in front of her. I would flinch and listen. I'd console her by telling her that the kids mocked my smelly hair too and my rolled up rotis filled with mango pickle, while they all ate peanut butter sandwiches. She'd then remind me that if we were in India I probably wouldn't even get any mango pickle, and I should be grateful. There were other things I wanted to tell her about too, like how a group of white boys threw me down and rubbed my face in the ground – calling me "curry-muncher" – while girls laughed hysterically nearby. I would never forget the taste of cold granite in my mouth as I picked dead leaves from the braids in my hair. But I didn't tell her that stuff.

Instead, I taught myself how to make curries, learned all the spices by heart, and brewed chai after dinner every night. Jeevan would try to make it better for Mom too. He would jump on her lap and hug her tight. She hugged him back, but I knew, as Jeevan did, that most of her hugs were empty or diluted. Jeevan clung to me in those days, inherently knowing that despite my vague resentment of him, I was still capable of more than her.

Our mother passed the time reading Hindi romance novels. This was the only time I saw her truly content. She would sit with her red paisley shawl wrapped around her on the couch, and I would watch her while she read. She had the most serene look on her face, with even a smile sometimes curling at her lips. I would gaze at the front cover of her book and wonder about its contents. There would always be some ridiculous image on the front, like a beautiful long-haired woman standing on the edge of a field looking up at a man on a horse.

One day she said to me, "You don't know what it's like to be married to someone so much darker than you." In her mind, this was the ultimate shortcoming. Mom was quite white – I mean really white – for a brown person. She told me she was so fair that she could have married anyone she wanted. She often lamented about when she was nineteen and she looked at our father's photograph for the first time. "Everyone in the village laughed. All my friends mocked me because they said he looked like a Negro."

"But you're really short, Mom. How about that?"

Mom almost smacked me when I said that. "Yes, that makes it even worse – that he's so tall!"

What was romance for her? I imagined a very fair-skinned Indian man dismounting from a carriage being pulled by a white horse, strolling through the village as all eyes gazed upon him. He would exude strength and wealth, with his mother walking idly behind him as she waited for him to choose the woman he would save from poverty. Of course, he would ultimately pick the unassuming girl who wasn't paying attention; the one fervently trying to get water out of a well for her elderly parents and siblings. He would stroll over to her and tell her to stop her efforts and then whisk her away without any mention of a dowry.

The only book Mom ever read to me was *Snow White*. She read it over and over again, probably because she identified with being treated so unfairly because she was so white and beautiful. I was pretty white too – not as white as her – but I somehow didn't have the same expectations of being rescued.

If she wasn't reading, she would be out in her garden. She was amazing at cultivating good soil and knowing how much water it needed. Plants gave her a sincerity that people never could. They flourished under her and nourished her. She gazed at them in a way she had never looked at any of us. She opened her heart to them bit by bit, each year as the plot grew bigger and more abundant.

Sometimes when she wasn't home, I would wrap myself up in her paisley shawl and try to feel into the parts of her I didn't know or fully understand. My mother: the martyr, the diva, the overlooked one – full of hope and despair.

The day she got fired from the hotel she didn't shout. In the evenest voice, she said to me, "You don't know what it's like to be a young girl ripped away from your family or working for people you don't understand while they stare at your lunch. Your dad brought me here, but where is he now?"

1978

"Okay, it's quite heavy. Move out of the way, sweetie," said Uncle G.

He placed the box on the centre of the lounge floor and we all marvelled at it – our first television. It was a gift from Uncle G, who was the highlight of our existence back then. Uncle G wasn't really our uncle, but he was someone who grew up in my dad's village in India and worked in a nearby mining town. He was much younger than my father, trendier, and seemed to have a lot more money. Tall and clean-shaven, he wore a pungent aftershave that always made me cough. I suppose Indian women may have found him handsome.

I imagined Uncle G might have been a more polished westernized version of the man I envisioned in Mom's Hindi novels. Because of my father's frequent absences, Uncle G's presence was never unwelcome. He was our Indian Santa Claus. He would bring goodies for the whole family: a bottle of scotch for my father, chocolates for my mother, and rattles for my baby sister Sarika. The gifts he gave to Jeevan and I were infuriating. I would get a bag of Hershey's Kisses and some sort of doll. He would give me the Hershey's first and say, "I have given you lots of kisses, now give me a kiss," and he would lean down and point to his cheek. Then I would have to sit on his lap and open the box containing my next doll.

The whole ceremony was distasteful. I hated dolls. I found them artificial and frightening in the way their eyes looked at you dead on. I was never really sure what to do with them, so I gave them to Jeevan, who loved them. For Jeevan, Uncle G had an array of gifts: cars, planes, trucks, you name it. In the end, Jeevan had every form of transport you could possibly imagine.

I never particularly liked Uncle G, not because of the gifts, but because of an unsettling quality that, at the time, I couldn't quite grasp. His overly friendly demeanour combined with his matted, side-parted, and gelled hair (he didn't need gel, nor did he need a side part), gave him an overzealous persona you could never quite trust. That, on top of an overriding sense that we were indebted to him in a way that could never be repaid. In truth, he was simply lonely and had nothing better to do. I knew this and Mom did too. Nevertheless, she cooked for him: perhaps because he was alone, or because he was charming and brought gifts, or because she had to.

Uncle G spent that Christmas with us. I had no memory of a previous Christmas since we had never celebrated it. He insisted that we had been in Canada long enough and he bought us a tree with red and green baubles and lots of gold tinsel. We were living then in a house with pale yellow siding, the colour of a worn-out sun. It was not much better than the apartment, really. Just bigger. The carpet was still ugly and a bit stained, but it still went well with the elephant lamp. Most importantly, I had my own room. It was strange, though. It felt even lonelier and more isolating than the apartment. At least in the apartment, I could hear voices next door and pretend we were in some sort of makeshift village. I tried to decorate my room, but it was a strange concept to me, this idea of decorating. In India, such a thing

didn't really exist. You had what you had. I bought a tattered poster of
Stevie Nicks at a garage sale across the street for twenty-five cents and
taped it to my wall. I had no idea who she was, but she seemed glamorous with her feathery hair.

Our Christian neighbours were pleased to see the tree in the
window and brought over a huge hamper of food. We didn't know
what to do with the pantry items it was filled with: cranberry sauce,
canned corn, stuffing and gravy mix. In the middle of the hamper,
wrapped in red cellophane, was a great big Mother Mary figurine to
put on top of the tree. She had on a white dress with a red scarf over
her head, and she had kind eyes. I liked her and thought she might
replace the dippy bird. Uncle G lifted me up and I put her on top of
the tree with pride. When he set me down he patted my bum and said,
"You like your dolls, don't you? Wait until you see the one I got you
this year." His hand lingered there for a moment as he smiled down
at me.

"I like that doll," I said pointing to the tree.

"You can't have it," he said. I shot him a look that suggested what I
thought of him. It was fleeting, but it was enough. I went and sat on
Dad's lap while Jeevan opened the mammoth box in front of him.

He ripped the shiny, reindeer paper off in one go. "Look! It's a big
train set. And it's red, just like I wanted."

Of course, this wasn't just any train set. It was a freight set with
over a hundred parts, with dozens of little workers, trees, shrubs and
an assortment of wagons, with a massive track that looped around
half the room. Jeevan jumped up and down, leapt onto Uncle G's lap,
and threw his arms around his neck. I looked sideways as Dad's face
fell. Dad had asked me to wrap a smaller gift earlier that sat shyly
under the tree; it too was a train set but less than half the size with a
small linear track.

I shouted out, "Why did you get him that, Uncle G? You knew Dad
was getting him one!"

"Don't be rude, Maya," said Dad. "You should be grateful for all the gifts your uncle buys you. Let's pour some drinks to celebrate our new holiday." He pushed me off his lap and went into the kitchen.

"I know what you want," Uncle G. said to me. "Come and open your gift."

Grabbing the rectangular box from under the tree, he sat down in an armchair and motioned for me to come over. I glanced enviously at my baby sister Sarika, who was lying next to the tree playing with a trinket. She didn't have to participate in these contrived scenarios with Uncle G.

"Have some manners. Go over to your uncle," my mother demanded.

I wondered how she might feel if she had to sit on his lap.

I walked over and stood reluctantly at the armchair. I was not looking forward to the next addition to my doll collection. He patted his knee, and I continued to look at him woodenly. He grabbed me by the waist and pulled me onto his lap, kissing my cheek as I choked on the smell of whisky and curry.

"Open it," he said. I tore off the silver paper and threw it to the ground.

He was right. It wasn't just any doll. It was a Barbie doll. She had long blonde hair – of course – and wore a pink miniskirt, pink high heels, and a shiny low-cut, black top that showed her midriff. I stared at her for a long moment, speechless.

"Let's take it out of the box." He removed it from my hands, opened the box, and took her out by carefully unfastening her plastic body from the cardboard. He held her by the waist, his thumb just under her left breast. That was all I could see. His thumb there.

"Isn't she lovely, Maya? You're getting older now, aren't you? So, I got you a big girl doll. She's pretty, isn't she?" He was looking at her and then looking at me. His other hand was around my waist, squeezing my side. I was suddenly conscious of what I was wearing, a blue V-necked sweater. My own breasts were just starting to develop then. I jumped off his lap and ran to stand by the window – feeling exposed – wanting to run out and jump into the mounds of cold snow outside.

Later that night, when I was lying in bed, I could hear the rain outside. It was a heavy winter rain; the kind that mixed with snow. I didn't like winter rain. It melted half the snow and made it icier and harder – too compact. I knew I wouldn't be able to play in it tomorrow. Then I heard footsteps coming down the hall and the faint creak of my bedroom door as it opened ever so gently. Mom never came in, and the man was too short to be Dad. As the silhouette became clear, I could see that it was Uncle G. I looked up at him curiously, wondering if he was so drunk he had confused bedrooms. He had something in his hand. It was the Barbie doll.

"Sweetie," he said, as he perched next to me and leaned forward, his breath inescapable. "You forgot something."

I looked at the Barbie – at her breasts, at her legs – and I hated her. I hated how she resembled Tammy in the Christmas play, and how she bore no similarity to me. But it was easier to look at her. I didn't want to look at him. He lay the Barbie next me on the pillow as if she were my friend. Then he brushed the hair out of my face and caressed my cheek with his thumb. My gaze rested on Barbie's bright blue eyes as he pulled back the blanket. I probably should have screamed or shoved Barbie in Uncle G's mouth, but I couldn't seem to summon the courage to do anything; so I just waited for it to be over, the way I used to wait at the window for my parents or wait for Mom to comb through the big tangles in my hair.

I don't remember much of those ten minutes, though I remember thoughts that raced through my mind: how I had kept trying to glue the dippy bird's eye back on but it wouldn't stick; the Mother Mary figurine guarding the Christmas tree, gazing out the window, sending her invisible love to our neighbours and the houses beyond; and my best friend, Rupi, in India. *Did she learn how to make roti yet? Did she still carve images of animals in the dirt?*

I also thought of another day when I was playing with my neighbour Angela outside, and she taught me how to make snow angels.

My arms flailed with excitement as I looked up at the infinite grey sky. I thought about how I pricked my finger on a twig, and I stood in awe of how much blood came spurting out. How beautiful it was – droplets of red – against the stark white snow. I will never forget the smell of Uncle G's breath; that dark combination of whisky and curry. I still can't say his name.

# SARIKA

## 1986

WHEN I THINK about my childhood it's always in a series of moments. I wonder if it's this way for everyone: my father's crinkly fingers reaching for the chutney bowl; my big sister, Maya, applying blush to her fair skin; and Jeevan, my teenage brother, spinning me around the room.

"Whoo-hoo! Come on kid, fly!" he'd say. That was the best.

I remember the day I truly became a bird. I was eight. Jeevan picked me up as usual and spun round and round as I squealed with delight. When he finally put me down the room kept dancing and spiralling around me. I rolled back and forth, laughing hysterically, as I grabbed the kitchen counter for balance.

"Do it again." I clutched at his leg and pulled at it until he picked me up and held me upside down with one hand, tickling my belly with the other. I laughed and screamed some more with glee. "Spin me! Spin me!"

"Okay Birdie, you asked for it!" But this time he lifted me over his head.

I spread out my arms and legs and closed my eyes: imagining myself up in the clear blue sky, swooning around over the trees, finding the highest one and swooping down and claiming it as my own. I didn't know it then, but it was in those moments that I harnessed my natural instinct to disconnect myself from the earth to embark on a search for something more. I began indulging in fantasies of forming a new community in the forest, living off nuts and berries.

I felt my foot knock into something. It was Maya's head.

"Oops, sorry sis," said Jeevan.

"Go do that somewhere else!" Maya's shrill voice ripped through my moment in the wilderness like a forest fire.

"Oh, we gotta stop, Birdie. She's getting mad."

He placed me gently on the ground. I grabbed his leg again for balance and looked up at Maya, who was carefully scooping lasagna noodles out of the pot, placing them neatly in a casserole dish row by row. Her checkered apron was tied tightly against her heavy bosom and it matched the checkered slippers she wore. Bits of tomato sauce had splattered on both her apron and her left slipper. She seemed to be out of place – from another time – someone from my Social Studies books. She constantly had a look of being inconvenienced, like an old maid cooking for unexpected guests.

"Why don't you actually do something useful? Like help do dishes? Or sweep the floor?" Her lips were pursed and her eyes ripped straight through Jeevan – a look she reserved only for him.

"God, you're heavy. You've been hanging around Mom too long."

He returned her gaze evenly, deciding whether or not he could be bothered to take her on. Instead, he grabbed a used glass from the counter, filled the glass to the brim and downed it one go. He was fluid in his motions. Then he filled it again, just halfway, and bent down to give it to me. "Here Birdie, gotta fuel up when you run around." I took the glass and nodded in agreement, clutching the bottom of his shirt and attempting to drink it fast like him, spilling it down my Scooby Doo nightie.

Maya's eyes shifted to me. "And you, why don't you go change? You've been in your pyjamas all day."

I switched my gaze to Jeevan's yellow socks. I could never really look at my older sister in the eyes. They were an unusual colour – a hazel that should have been beautiful – that changed depending on the intensity of the light. Instead, they seemed to change with her mood – sometimes stormy, sometimes glassy – and frightfully clear. Secretly, I thought she was a witch. Not necessarily a bad witch, but I was sure she could read my mind. She knew Jeevan was my personal hero, my favourite. She was more like a distant relative that lived in the house. Nevertheless, she was cordial to me, polite like a school-teacher.

Jeevan leaned over the pot on the stove and stuck his finger in, scooping out the sauce and putting it in his mouth. Maya brushed his hand away, "Gross. Ever heard of a spoon?"

Jeevan scrunched up his nose. "What did you put in here? Ginger? Why does it taste like a curry?"

"Yeah, and masala."

"Why? Why would you do that? In pasta sauce? How about oregano or something? Even I know that."

"Because Mom and Dad won't like it then." Maya convinced our parents to let her experiment with food as a celebration of their assimilation into Canadian culture. They were integrated enough to have pasta on a Friday night. They had made it; they were Canadian.

"Well, they're not gonna like this." Jeevan grabbed the glass out of my hand and filled it up again. "It's disgusting. Maybe stick to what you know for now."

Maya sighed and grabbed a spoon and began to layer sauce onto the noodles. "If you're not going to do anything, then get the hell out of here and get her changed before Mom and Dad get home."

"Can't we get chicken instead?" I asked Jeevan. We could afford take-out once in a while. Sometimes we would get Kentucky Fried Chicken. Mom didn't eat meat, but she picked the crunchy, salty skin off the chicken and gave the rest to Dad. Every time we ate it, Dad talked about how skinny the chickens were in India and how lucky we were that one piece of chicken here was so juicy and big.

"I don't know, Birdie, but look who's home. Bet Dad got something good for ya."

Jeevan winked at me and pointed out the window at the old yellow Nova parked outside. It looked like a bruised banana. I ran to the window but could only see Mom slipping and sliding up the wet ice, her face puffed up and red. She was sporting a big puffy, purple ski coat that she bought on sale at Woodward's. She looked like a blueberry that might burst any second.

The door handle turned. A crisp burst of winter air came through the opened door as we heard Dad's voice through the foyer. "Jeevan, come and get these bags."

Dad came sauntering through with grocery bags and a big grin on his face. He was my other hero. He wasn't contained and overly dignified like the other Indian dads in the community. He wore baseball caps while he cooked curry so the smell wouldn't get in his hair. He was awkwardly too lanky and stooped over sometimes, but he had a presence. He was a tree that you never took down because it had some other ancient quality that made it dignified and untouchable.

"Guess what I got?" He held up a large elongated object wrapped in foil. "Salmon – fresh! Dimitri got it for us."

Dimitri was Dad's Greek friend at work. Dad was intensely proud of this friendship he sustained with a non-Indian. Every once in a while, he'd come home beaming with some sort of parcel we were required to cook and eat as a confirmation of their friendship. Whatever it was, Dimitri always claimed to have hunted it, fished it, or risked his life in the depths of the Canadian wilderness for it. Jeevan always thought Dimitri was lying and got it from some Greek butcher or fishmonger downtown who had good deals. Another time, to our disdain, it was moose meat. "Here Maya, put some tandoori masala on it and cook it for us tonight. We'll have it with the dhal I made yesterday."

"Actually Dad, I'm making lasagna for us," said Maya, taking the parcel.

Dad ignored her and picked up the mail, while I went over to him and pulled at his leg. "Hi, Dad." He smiled and scooped me up in his arms, and I contemplated my position as the favourite child. His eyes were like Jeevan's, but they were just starting to crease at the edges.

"I bought you rainbow ice cream," he whispered. "Your mom said it was too expensive, but I snuck it into the cart when she wasn't looking."

I clutched his neck while he carried me into the living room. I looked back at Maya, who stood there woodenly with the parcel of salmon in one hand and pasta spoon in the other.

He put me on his lap as he started opening the mail. This only happened occasionally, so I'd try to make the most of it. Sometimes he'd tell me stories about going to school in India; how the teacher slapped his wrist with a long, slim ruler when he spoke out of turn, and how bruises would get covered with layers of dirt. This was the only time I had with him. Otherwise, he was slightly more formal, going about the business of working around the house and meeting his friends at the Sikh temple. I was certain he never shared any of these secrets with Jeevan or Maya. I was the chosen one; the keeper of anecdotes from foreign lands. I didn't enjoy most of his stories, but I put up with them. They were dark and meandering and disrupted my hunger for a joyful, predictable life. I was aware of my neediness but couldn't control myself.

Dad opened one bill after the other, tossing them onto the floor. "Get a good job Sarika, or marry a rich boy. Things are getting more expensive." I nodded in agreement as I watched him open the last envelope and read it. His eyes darkened. "What's this?" he said. I glanced at the page but all I could make out were some letters next to words: *D, E, B,* and *E.* "Jeevan!" He pushed me off his lap, and I followed him into the kitchen. Jeevan was handing Mom jugs of milk to put in the fridge.

"What?" Jeevan looked at Dad with an empty expression. It was amazing to me how people's eyes changed depending on who they were looking at.

"What the hell is this?"

He held up the letter.

"What?"

"Your report card!"

"Oh yeah," said Jeevan. He continued emptying the bags and carefully placing tins of chickpeas in neat rows in the cupboard.

"Oh yeah? Look at your grades. Look at me." Dad shook the open letter at him.

Mom stopped. "What's going on?"

Maya paused from grating cheese, vaguely interested because Jeevan might be in trouble.

"He got a *D* in math and he's failing all his science subjects. That's what's going on."

Dad threw the letter at Jeevan and it fell to the floor.

"I got a *B* in English and an *A* in art," said Jeevan, leaning against the counter, arms folded.

"Who bloody cares about that? What's that going to do for your education?"

"We're immigrants, Dad. You always said English was important," said Jeevan with elaborate patience.

Dad's lip started quivering. "Don't talk back. How are you going to become anything? You're sixteen years old. What university is going to take you? You're either stupid or just lazy."

"I'm no scientist Dad. I keep telling you that." There was a sharpness to Jeevan's voice.

"You're not much of anything as far as I can see." He was shouting.

My heart started to race and I felt slightly ill. I hated when my favourite two people fought. It was like Superman and Spiderman at war against each other. I loved them both and didn't want either to lose.

"Why, because I don't want to be a dentist or doctor like Maya? Because I don't want to stare at teeth all day?" He looked over at Maya, who was pretending to stir the pasta sauce.

Mom finally piped in. "What do you want to do then? Sit around and draw pictures like an idiot?"

"What if I do? Or what if I want to do a trade? What's wrong with that? I want to be a plumber." Jeevan had a big grin on his face. He had picked his strategy. He would belittle his father and win by default.

"You think you're funny?" Dad stepped forward, almost knocking me over as I stood between them. I went to clutch Jeevan's leg again. "Your Mom told me how you go out every night with your stupid friends. Those kids don't know anything about how hard it is for us. You think it's okay making me work this hard just so you can bring shame on this family?"

"So what's shame then? You working with your hands to feed your family?" The smile was gone and Jeevan had fire in his eyes. "Your own dad working in the fields? Are you ashamed of yourself and your own dad?"

Dad leaned forward and cuffed the side of Jeevan's face, missing slightly and hitting the side of his ear. Jeevan flinched, and I screamed, "Stop it, Dad!" I knew what would happen next, I had seen it all before. I tried pushing him away by pressing my little hands into his knees, but Maya grabbed me and pulled me up into her arms, something she normally never did. She pushed my face into her chest so I couldn't see.

"Try again, go on." I heard Jeevan say. "Or why don't you join in, Mom, and get a stick or something."

Mom began to raise her voice. "You don't know anything about respect. You . . ."

"That is enough!" Maya's voice permeated the room like a loud whisper of a ghost. I turned my head and saw that everyone was looking at Maya in surprise, especially Jeevan. "That is enough," she repeated quietly. Jeevan pushed past Dad and ran through the foyer and out the front, slamming the door behind him.

Maya gently put me down and said, "You go change now, and then I want you to help me make salad." I looked up at her. Maya's eyes were bright and a little scared. She let me see that.

Jeevan didn't come back for dinner. I was worried about him. The lasagna tray sat virtually untouched on the centre of the table, with a piece on Maya's plate and a piece on mine. I picked around pieces of hardened cheese, chewing on bits of dried pasta, and wincing silently when my tongue encountered bits of ginger. Mom seemed unaffected by the whole drama. I stared at her hardened jaw as she scooped up bits of dhal with a spoon into her mouth.

Dad sat with his shoulders hunched forward as he picked at bits of his salmon. He knew he'd lost his superpowers. He'd abused them. "You girls need to understand that we came here so you would have opportunities that we didn't so you could have an education, so we could buy this house. I work bloody hard to give you those chances."

Maya stood up and grabbed the lasagna tray. "Anyone want any more?"

I stood up too with an immediate urge to find my brother. I was too young to know much of what was going on, but I did know that he was becoming more and more distant with each one of these episodes. He was starting not to care. I ran up to his room and decided to wait for him there in the dark, crawling beneath the duvet adorned with images of the solar system. I turned on the lava lamp next to me. Bubbles of pink exploded onto the array of heavy metal posters on the wall. One wall was painted black with graffiti; Jeevan's name printed over and over again in different fonts. I traced his name with my finger in the air as the cool breeze from the open window touched my face. There was faint rustling from outside.

"Jeevan?" I called out as I crept over to the window. He was sitting out on the ledge with his legs crossed and hands folded neatly in his lap as if he was meditating.

"Do you want to come out, Birdie?"

I nodded.

"You better not tell anyone I let you out here sometimes." He leaned across and gently pulled me out the window next to him, holding me close as the strong odour of marijuana filled my nostrils.

"Look at the moon, Birdie. Do you see its face?"

"No," I said, shivering slightly.

"Look harder. There's two eyes and a nose and a grin."

The moon was full and enormous with just a shadow of black cloud around it.

"I can see it," I said.

I couldn't really see anything but I didn't want to disappoint him. I buried my head in his lumberjack shirt and he squeezed me tighter.

"Do you know why I call you Birdie, Sarika?" I looked up at him feeling slightly alarmed. He never said my name.

"Because you spin me round and round?"

"No," he said, turning and grabbing my face. He looked unhinged; his brown eyes glazed and intense.

"Because my name means *bird*?"

"No," he said. "It does mean bird, but I call you Birdie because I want you to fly. Do you get me?"

I didn't respond. I wasn't quite sure what he wanted from me, but I could relate to his need to connect – to get inside others and affect them deeply.

"You see, Maya isn't going to fly. And I'm not going to fly. We're stuck. But I think you can. You can go and fly wherever you want to when you grow up. You can leave this dump and go do whatever you want. Don't let anyone stop you. Remember that. Know what I'm saying?"

I nodded in complete acceptance because that's what he needed, but I knew that I didn't fully understand his sermon. I only knew it felt like one of us should say goodbye.

He pinched my cheek and smiled. "Just don't ever go flying off this ledge."

"Well, well, well. What's going on out here?" Maya popped her head out, banging it on a protruding awning. Jeevan's body stiffened immediately.

"Move over," she said as she gathered up her skirt and climbed through, knocking over Jeevan's beer. As much as Jeevan was fluid and weightless, Maya was equally cautious and deliberate to the point of clumsiness.

She had a Tupperware container and fork in her hand. "Here," she said, handing it to Jeevan. Jeevan opened it carefully, bewildered by her uncharacteristic act of generosity. It was the lasagna. "I thought you might be hungry."

"Thanks."

Jeevan bit into it as he looked at Maya curiously.

"I didn't poison it. Leave it if you want." Maya linked arms with me. "Look at the snow, Sarika. Look how it sparkles against the light from the moon."

"Can you see the eyes and the nose and the grin?" I said.

"I don't know. Maybe. How's the lasagna?" she said, looking straight ahead.

"Mmm, good." Jeevan had a little grin on his face.

"It's shit, isn't it?" said Maya. She mirrored him and smiled too.

"Kind of, yeah. But the ginger really works." And then they both burst out laughing. The fever broke between them. Jeevan threw the lasagna onto the snow below and they laughed some more. I pretended to laugh too, but my elation was too much for me to fully participate. They didn't see what I could see. There we were – the three of us, together – as solid and luminous as the moon before us.

I NEVER GOT to say goodbye to Jeevan. Not long after that night, right at the beginning of spring, I got pneumonia. I vaguely remember being in the hospital. I was in and out of consciousness with a high fever and an IV drip stuck firmly in my hand for two weeks because it wouldn't take to my arm. I was scared in the hospital. It was odd being an eight-year-old and having hardly any visitors. Mom and Dad came a couple of times looking ashen and sullen. I remember them telling me that I would be taken care of. I spent days and nights staring at shadows of the IV drip, an evil parasite that lurked over me. There was a nurse, Lisa, who would sit by my side sometimes and put a cool cloth on my head. She was pretty, with long red hair, and she smelled like strawberries. The few times she saw my parents she looked at them with curious disdain.

Jeevan had been drinking and driving. That's all I was told. By the time I got home, it was over. I had missed the funeral. It was like he was a season – a guest who had come and gone. Sometimes, in early September, there would be a sudden temperature drop and that would be it. Overnight, the grass would be covered with frost and Mom's garden would be destroyed. She would make us run outside to save it, anxiously handing us buckets to pick raspberries and peas, only to find everything soggy and wilted. She would look stunned because she never saw it coming. She had that same look again.

Apparently, I was physically fine, but for the next few months I still felt how I did in the hospital – like I was in a dreamy, fever-like haze – with snippets of moments so defined I could taste them: watching Dad through the window as he stood out on the front lawn every night, just standing there in the centre until his limbs grew weary and he had to go inside; hearing the sound of Mom's crying when she sat on Jeevan's bed with the door closed – that loud, echoing guttural pitch that touched the insides of my belly; and Maya's eyes, which became more eerily translucent and green with each passing day.

I didn't know what to do with myself in those days. Sometimes I would go off to the park on my own, but there were strangers and shadows everywhere, much like the corridors of the hospital. Often, I would go into Jeevan's room and wait for him, crying silently with the lava lamp on as I etched my name next to his in the graffiti. Sometimes if I opened the window, I would see him sitting out there. I would apologize to him for becoming ill and for leaving my careful watch of him, recognizing my own responsibility of sustaining his existence in some vital way. Most of all, I would speak to the moon. I would apologize for lying about not being able to make out her face. I would stare and squint and plead, begging her to reveal herself to me.

# MAYA

## 1988

AT THE END OF WINTER, Mom and Dad renovated the house. The red shag carpets were replaced by a pale blue. In fact, everything turned blue. They got rid of the brown curtains and replaced them with blue blinds, put in blue and grey marble kitchen countertops, and stripped the yellow wallpaper. They painted the walls the colour of summer sky. I didn't really like it; it seemed sterile to me. I only bring up this day because nothing had happened in so long it seemed. Nothing but the seasons marked the passage of time. And even those were boring. I felt like we hadn't even had a remarkable storm in so long. So we got new blinds.

The morning after the last of the workers had finished in the kitchen, Dad stood in the centre looking satisfied as he wiped dust off the new counters. "We needed to modernize. Move with the times. Change like everyone else."

Sarika sat sulking in the corner of the kitchen on the floor with her worn out Cabbage Patch doll.

"I liked the purple flowers on the yellow wallpaper."

Dad looked at Sarika with resignation. She'd become an enigma to him. Playful chats and banter didn't work for her anymore – not that he really tried. "Sarika," I said, "You look ridiculous with that doll and it smells. Grow up. You're ten years old." She stuck her tongue out and pulled her hair over her eyes.

"Let's all get ready to go to temple," said Dad. "We have to help cook."

"You mean me and Mom have to cook."

"Maya, help me today."

It was a simple statement. His eyes were pleading and tired, and the lines around them so creased.

I leaned over and touched his arm. Something I never did.

"Okay."

"What are all of you doing just standing there?" Mom's clunky gold bangles rattled across the room as she hurried into the kitchen and opened a drawer to get safety pins. "Maya, pin my scarf to my suit." She wore a simple lavender Punjabi suit that shimmered in the light with a long, sheer, lavender scarf. I tried reading her face as I pinned the scarf to her shoulder. I wanted to know how she was doing, but I couldn't really tell. Her eyes shifted back and forth like she needed to keep going. There was too much foundation on her face that was a couple of shades too bright, even for her, so it looked like it had chunks of bleached flour rubbed into it.

"What are you going to wear?" she asked, almost accusingly, as she caught my gaze. She disliked being observed.

"Does it matter? It has to be a pale colour, right?"

"Actually, it does matter. Lots of people are going to be there. The Grewal family is coming."

"The who?"

"The Grewal family. I told you about them. The mother called a few months ago asking about you for their son. He's the one who's a dentist. I thought it was too soon before but now enough time has passed. You can maybe look at each other today."

"Look at each other?" I threw the safety-pin box on the counter and they all spilled onto the floor. "What? You want me to check out guys at my brother's memorial service?"

"What is a memorial service? Stop making it sound like we are going to church for whites. And anyway, Maya, it's time to move on."

"What the hell does that mean?"

"It means it's been two years and we have to try. And you're not getting any younger, you're twenty-one now." Her eyes started shifting again. "Go put on your green suit with lines that go up and down. It brings out your eyes and makes you look skinnier."

I was about to respond with a clever comment about how paisley wasn't exactly making her look like a rail, but as always, I swallowed it and went upstairs.

The parking lot was packed when we pulled in. The dome at the top of the rectangular temple looked like a big, yellow pumpkin with a giant, gold stem. Loads of people were chatting out front, shaking hands, and hugging like it was some big old family reunion even though they had just seen each other the Sunday before. Although the Indian community had grown over the years, *everyone* knew each other. You couldn't stand at the bus stop without someone calling your father to raise concern. Mom and Dad mingled into the crowd, greeting people as they went in. Sarika ran after Dad, tripping through the crowd of men until she caught his attention. She stood next to him with her stupid doll while he chatted to his friends. He looked a bit embarrassed.

I stepped into the main foyer, straight through into the dining hall, catching a whiff of butter and sugar. Plates of Indian sweets – diamond shapes of every colour and size – lined long rectangular tables. It looked like a school cafeteria hall. The old people sat next to each other, sighing into their chai cups as they commiserated over their poor knees and unhelpful daughters-in-law. Everyone ignored the children who ran around picking up chairs and swinging them around as if they were in a playground. A few of them had rolling pins they must have stolen from the kitchen. There were some people my age, feigning respect in their Punjabi suits while they quietly milled around, checking each other out and having discreet conversations about what they got up to the night before.

I didn't know what to do. I had nothing to say to any of these people, and I felt hot and uncomfortable. I grabbed a *gelabi*, a bright orange, pretzel-shaped sweet that burst liquid sugar into your mouth when you bit into it. It was good – crispy on the outside. I sat down on the bench, grabbing two more sweets off the table.

"Hey Maya, is this yours?"

I looked up. It was my archenemy from school, looming over me in a sparkly, tight-fitting bright orange Punjabi suit with inappropriate sequinned spaghetti straps. Her hair was perfectly curled all around her face so that she looked like a peacock. Her bright pink lipstick glistened under the neon lights. She handed me my scarf, which had been on the ground and had footprints on it.

"Oh hi, Sarina."

"Hey! How are you?" Her voice was sweet and patronizing, just as it always was. She looked at my oily hands as the sweets crumbled in them. I grabbed a few napkins to try and manage the situation.

"I'm fine, I guess." What did she want me to say? I was gorging on sweets to celebrate the two-year anniversary of my brother's death.

"That's good. I'm just here with my friends. Do you remember them?"

I looked over at the group of them standing in a circle. They all looked the same. I couldn't tell them apart with their identical hair, pink lipstick, and shiny suits.

"Yes, of course."

I did indistinctly remember all of them. When I was a kid they used to run circles around me in the playground and call me "white wannabee" because of my pale skin and light eyes. In high school, they would glance disapprovingly across the lunchroom because my clothes were always two months behind in fashion. I always bought them when they were on sale. Every morning they would pose on the steps at the front of the school dressed completely in black while they waited for the Indian boys to arrive. I knew they talked about how odd I was when I walked by wearing my bright yellow flip-flops and matching windbreaker with my nerdy white friend Anna.

But Sarina's father was good friends with mine, so she forced her insipidness on me. At traditional Indian gatherings, she would smile sweetly at me and offer to do my hair. The adults loved her because she knew how to play them, craftily serving food and doing dishes when she knew they were watching. At school, she hid in bushes to make out with boys.

"So, sorry about your brother, hey? I mean . . . I guess you miss him?"

Taking a deep breath, I oddly remembered something Jeevan used to say. You can't get angry at stupid people because they can't help themselves. You just have to breathe through it.

"Yes," I said, smiling vacantly at her. "Yes, he died two years ago so you don't have to say sorry *now*, and yes, I guess I miss him."

We looked at each other blankly for a moment. "Do you want a sweet?" I asked. "They're really good."

"No, I better go actually." She looked down at my top. There was a perfectly rounded oil stain right in the middle of my breasts from a dissolved crumb. "I'm just here with my Mom and Dad, and guess what? My fiancée is here. I'm getting married!"

"Great." I should have got up and hugged her. I should have asked questions. I grabbed another sweet instead and looked at her. "Congratulations, Sarina."

"Okay then . . . I better go." She scuttled away back to her friends as if I had sneezed in her face. Skinny bitch. I wished I could will myself to be better at those things – to be less paralytic, more graceful, and full of wit.

I caught Mom coming into the temple with the same urgency she had been carrying with her all morning. Waves of frenetic energy seeped out of her as she ran towards me. "What are you doing sitting here?"

"God, mother. Calm down. I was waiting for you."

"Let's get in the kitchen." She grabbed my arm and took me past Sarina's friends who observed us in mild amusement.

The kitchen was small and packed with a few little old ladies. They were wiping sweat from their brows with their scarves as they stirred dhal and made roti. It stunk of onions and there was flour everywhere – on everyone's faces, arms, clothes. It shone against their brown skin. I wanted to crack a joke about Asian skin-whitening techniques but thought better of it. They looked like a tough crowd.

They all hugged my mother and offered their condolences about her only son. "It is karma, having to lose your son out of everyone, and we will pray for you today." In other words, *It would have been better if you'd have at least lost one of your daughters. You must have done some serious shit in your past life to deserve this.*

I was instructed to roll roti, which was fine by me. I was good at domestic Indian chores. The ladies praised my speed and the perfect roundness of the flatbread. In a parallel universe somewhere, I could see myself in India as a good subservient wife doing the same thing – rolling roti – but stretching my arms out as far as possible to reach the rolling pin because I was eight months pregnant with my fifth child. I was content in that parallel universe, where I didn't have dark imaginings about wishing death upon skinny girls with fake voices.

"What is that around your neck?" One of the ladies broke me out of my reverie.

I looked down to see the cross that had been nicely tucked into my top had come out. I had bought it at a charity shop ages ago. I don't know why. I knew little about Christianity, but my obsession with Mother Mary had become a constant fixture in my life in a way that I couldn't quite explain. Dad said it was fine and that all paths led to the same place. Mom was horrified I wore it and forbade me to wear it to any Indian gatherings. I surveyed the woman who was ready to have an aneurysm over my jewellery. She was the feisty one, the ringleader of the kitchen who told everyone what to do. I focused on the coarse, prickly bits of grey hair coming out of her chin.

"Um . . . oh, it's a cross. I just like it."

Mom stopped chopping cauliflower and looked up, mortified. "Maya, take it off now."

She explained to the ladies that a poor Christian lady down the road gave it to me and I felt obliged to wear it.

"So, she's not Christian?" said the woman.

"No. No, of course not." Her jaw was slightly clenched as she tried to dissolve the necklace with her eyes. "Maya?" I tucked it into my top and resumed my rolling duties. There was no way I was taking it off.

Eventually, I was instructed to go sit upstairs where the service had already begun. At the top of the stairs was a sea of people with their heads covered. The men sat on the right all wearing orange handkerchiefs on top of their heads, while the woman sat on the left wearing their sheer scarves. Dividing the men and women was a long, skinny, crimson-red piece of carpet that led straight down the middle to the altar, which was covered in a red and gold decorative material. Behind the altar stood the *giani*, with a long white beard, reading from the *Guru Grant Sahib*, the holy Sikh scripture.

I walked up the aisle tentatively. I hated doing this. Everyone watched and there was always the strong possibility that I would fall and trip over my scarf – a fear that was validated many times throughout my childhood. When I reached the front, I bent down on my knees with my five-dollar bill to offer at the altar. The scarf fell off my head, and as I stood up I could feel the leggings of my suit slipping down. It wasn't my fault. They were only held together by a piece of string that kept untying on its own. What was I supposed to do? Why couldn't Indians move with the times and start sewing proper zippers and fasteners on these things? I pulled them up as I tripped over to a spot on the carpet. When I looked up, I could see a picture of Guru Nanak staring down on me with disapproval.

There were pictures of the gurus everywhere. Quite frankly, I didn't find them very welcoming. When I was a kid, Mom would send me to the cold, dismal basement to get tins of food from the pantry. Down there was a picture of one of the gurus, looking fierce, with his big black beard and long sword. Sometimes when I snuck a bag of chips to eat, the boiler would suddenly roar and hum at me; and I would look into the guru's eyes and know it was him telling me to put them down.

Right then, Guru Nanak was telling me to pull my pants up. I looked around, already restless and awkwardly sitting closer to the front than I would have liked. There was a large cohort of second-generation people that clearly had no understanding of the songs or hymns. Some were tracing pictures in the plush pink carpet as they tried to pass the time. Others sang along devotedly, especially the little groups of old biddies sitting against the wall with their legs propped up. Towards the end, I caught on to the one prayer that *Bibi* taught me when I was young. It was one of the few prayers that I actually understood all the words to:

*Ik onkaar* (There is only one God).
*Satnaam* (Truth is his name).
*Karta purkh* (He is the creator).
*Nirbhau* (He is without fear).
*Nirvair* (He is without hate).
*Akaal moorat* (He is timeless and without form).
*Ajooni sabhang* (He is beyond death – the enlightened one).
*Gur prasad* (He can be known by the Guru's grace) . . .

It brought me back to the hot stone steps in India where *Bibi* would clutch my hand and make me recite the prayer ten times every morning and every evening. Sometimes she would preach the virtues of Sikhism; pulling out stories from the scriptures, while I sucked on a sugar cane. She told me how, despite it being such a new religion, it was a strong one. The warriors of our faith fought hard, with endless bloodshed against the Muslims, to make us who we were. And I should have been grateful for that. Late at night, when I climbed the steep steps to the rooftop terrace to have a pee in the ground, I would recite the mantra over and over again, petrified by the howls of stray dogs and potential snakes that could overtake me at any second.

"Go on," *Bibi* would say in Punjabi. "You'll be okay. The guru energy is one of protection."

The words that I so easily digested as a child became fickle to me. What was "the guru's grace" and what did they know about protecting women from suffering? Where were they when I needed them? And where were women represented in this religion anyway? Did it say anywhere in the scriptures how the women selflessly stood back on the sidelines like silent cheerleaders at a football game, while men decided to go slaughter each other in the fields? I clutched at the cross around my neck and then I had a thought. Maybe I could have a baby like Mary too.

The group threw me out of my reverie and started chanting, *Waheguru, Waheguru*. It was perhaps then that I realized I was prone to madness; that I could sit there in a Sikh temple and mourn my brother's death and dream about Immaculate Conception all at once. The most rebellious thing I could do at that moment was to wear an illicit cross around my neck and not even have the courage to display it openly. I was a disengaged onlooker pretending to fit in. I chanted louder and harder, reminded that I was here for my brother. I had to honour him sincerely if for no one else but myself. And then all at once – I don't know what happened – I was a participant, and my head started spinning and I looked into Guru Nanak's eyes. I felt like I was asking his forgiveness for something. I wasn't sure for what.

After the service and lunch, people milled around downstairs as they said goodbye to each other. Sarina's friends stood with a group of boys that were similar to them, middle-class mama's boys who arrogantly drove around in their Mercedes-Benzes even though they still lived at home. Mom came over and gently grabbed my arm as she introduced me to some woman. She had a high forehead and was wearing a *bindi* that was slightly out of place.

"This is my daughter, Maya." Mom's voice was alarmingly higher pitched and more animated than usual and she had an inane grin on her face.

"Oh, how old is she?" The woman looked me up and down and set her eyes on my tummy, which was slightly rounded and pressed against the tight, shiny fabric. Then her eyes went higher to the oil stain on my chest. Suddenly, I realized I was being presented to this woman who must be Mrs. Grewal.

"She's twenty-one and she's almost done school. Dental hygienist!" I didn't like this side of my mother I was seeing. She sounded like a guide for some cheap tour bus. I wanted to undermine her by mentioning I wasn't smart enough to be a dentist.

"Okay, we should be in touch then."

The woman looked at me carefully before walking away towards the group of boys Sarina was chatting to. She grabbed one of them, pulled him aside, and whispered in his ear. He looked straight over at me. He was the least attractive of the group, with hair that was too long and slicked back which gave him a greasy appearance. But he was really tall, which according to my mother, was hard to find. His eyebrows merged into one, and his nose was porous and oily. He looked like a villain in a mafia film that gets killed early on – a side character – undeserving of a mildly important role. Our eyes met briefly and I turned my back to him to face my mother.

I sputtered out the words quietly. "How could you do this to me here?" Without letting her respond I pushed past her, running into Sarika as I escaped through the temple doors.

"Where is everyone?"

There was my sister, cute as a daisy, in a pink dress she chose to wear. She was unfettered by the business of potential arranged marriages taking place at memorial services. Her big milky eyes were like Jeevan's, searching mine as they always did for that something Mom and Dad couldn't give her, some sense of purpose or hope. Her impending beauty coupled with her lack of dignity made me cringe. I lost track of myself and I grabbed the Cabbage Patch doll out of her hands.

"Maya, what are you doing? Maya!" Sarika followed me as I ran across the parking lot towards the massive green garbage bin that was almost twice my height. I lobbed it in and turned around.

"You look like an idiot carrying that stupid thing around. Grow up!"

"Jeevan gave that to me." She started punching at my legs with her fists, tears streaming down her face. "Jeevan *gave* that to me!"

"Yes, and Jeevan is gone!"

People were looking at us. The Grewals stood by their cars paralyzed by the image of their potential daughter-in-law, who they thought might bear their grandchildren, grabbing a doll from an innocent child and throwing it into a garbage bin.

Mom and Dad wouldn't speak to me for the rest of the evening. I sat in my room munching on a bag of ketchup chips. I licked the salt off of them one by one and let them dissolve in my mouth so they wouldn't run out too quickly. They said what I did was out of character. What was in my character? I had no idea. There was something wrong with me. I had known that for a long time. I seemed to lack some inherent ability to connect. I looked around my bedroom and nothing in it made sense. There was a framed photograph of the family from years ago when I was ten pounds skinnier, an outdated poster of John Travolta (who didn't even look that good anymore) right next to Stevie Nicks, and a bowl full of random jewellery that I didn't wear – everything from Indian gold to water pearls. It was cluttered in a way that made me arbitrary.

My actions were the same; my inappropriateness was arbitrary. I didn't need to throw away Sarika's doll, but I *did* need to. I didn't need to laugh at Jeevan's funeral, but I did. I had been standing there in the crematorium that day completely sombre, and as I looked around, I saw Dad's pale, drawn face as he pushed the button that reduced Jeevan to ashes. Everyone started crying. Mom was wailing. But to me, it all seemed absurd – the efficiency of it all. We could put him in an oven and that was it. Those funeral directors made a small fortune just like that. That's all I could think of – how much money those people were making – and the ridiculous jar we'd be given afterwards. Jeevan's life was summed up in that.

So I started laughing. I laughed and laughed. Everyone looked at me in horror, but I couldn't stop, even though Dad's face was growing paler by the second and my aunt started shouting at me. I ran out of there eventually and spent a good portion of time in the bathroom until I sorted myself out. I tried to make myself cry. I thought that would make things better; if I could produce tears as a display of my guilt. Because I did feel really bad about what I had done. Because I did love my brother. But I couldn't. I am still waiting.

# SARIKA

1994

MARCY OPENED the window as she let out a big drag. The cold wind blew ash onto her glittered blue nails and all over my bedroom floor.

"I can't believe he's dead. I just can't believe it."

"You're gonna get me in trouble." I wiped the ashes on the floor with a tennis shoe, rubbing them in rather than rubbing them out. "You can smell that through the floors, you know. My parents will kill me."

"Who can smell anything other than garam masala and onions in this house anyway? It's embedded in the walls." Marcy jumped up onto the windowsill, her short denim skirt riding all the way up so I could see her red underwear.

"Does that mean I smell like curry too? I thought you told me I don't smell like curry."

"I lied." She leaned over to hand me the cigarette. "Give it a go."

I reached forward but then pulled my hand back. Who was I kidding? I didn't know how to smoke. Every time I tried I coughed and turned into a blubbering mess.

"No, I suck."

"That's the problem. You don't suck hard enough. God, I can't believe he's *gone*. Are you not upset by this? Do you not see what that man did for music? Grunge will probably be dead now."

Marcy was talking about Kurt Cobain, who was found dead the day before. I was into the angst of it all at first but then I got tired of the endless dissecting of why he did it and where he ended up and how this would impact our lives. It made me feel tired.

"We still have Pearl Jam. We'll be fine."

Marcy was my badass friend. We met three years ago, when I was thirteen, at the roller rink. She was a tall, blonde, slovenly princess hanging with the cool kids, laughing and skating around while holding hands with Graham Stevens, the hottest boy in eighth grade. It all went downhill when blood started dripping down her leg and I caught sight of it. I nudged her while she was tying her laces, pointed to her leg as I handed her a tampon, and walked away without saying a word. None of the snotty girls understood her unshakeable loyalty to me from that moment forward, or why she ditched them for the nondescript Indian girl with glasses, whose bangs were too long and thick.

"I decided those girls know nothing about loyalty," she said. "They'll take your weed when you're not looking and blame you for it if they get caught with it."

Marcy lived on Bleak Street, literally. We used to laugh about it in the beginning. Her dad died in a mining accident when she was a kid. The few times I went to her house, her mom was wearing the same peach robe with ketchup and coffee stains on it, smoking one joint after another, occasionally peeling her eyes from the television screen to pour herself a gin. Marcy called herself an Indian too because her Mom was half First Nations and constantly affirmed we were united in our plight against the world. She wanted to make a poster of the two of us wearing outfits from our respective backgrounds that read, "What kind of Indian am I?" to address stereotypes. I openly took offence to this. "You're blonde. No one can tell you're a minority and everyone worships you."

Marcy inhabited my bedroom more than I did, lining her colourful shoes against the wall, in various corners, and leaving hints of lavender body spray on my clothes. If she wasn't at bush parties in the woods or out with college boys, she was divulging her stories here with careful precision while I lived vicariously through her. Both of us thought that if we lived our polarized lives simultaneously, we would become one balanced person – if nowhere else, here in this room.

Mom would look at her suspiciously, wondering what it was that brought this tall, white girl to our house. "She eats our food. She could take our jewellery," Mom used to say.

"No Mom, she brings her own sandwiches and nobody wants your ugly Indian gold."

Marcy actually found my home comforting, she told me. It was the routine smell of cardamom and cloves simmering in a pot for chai every morning when she slept over – which was often – and the incense that Dad lit as he listened to his Indian prayer hymns and mopped the floors. To me the routines were a farce; a series of domestic chores that had collected like dust over the years to console the living and validate time. The pounding of spices rhythmically buried things and the smooth to and fro motion of the mop on the floor covered stains that could rise up beneath the surface at any point. A torrent of things that people didn't say could crack through the floors. Dishes and people could break and shatter. Mom did yell a lot, but it was distant and hollow, like the clanging of pots and pans. It didn't touch the sides of anything in this house.

"Everyone's quiet today, including you."

Marcy had the quality of knowing something was up without really knowing what it is was.

I didn't want to talk. I reached over to my bedside table and opened the bottom drawer and gave Marcy a sly grin.

"Let's do divination cards."

"Ooh, she's gonna get all witchy." Marcy stubbed out her cigarette and crawled over to sit across from me on the floor.

I looked through the array of cards I had: angel cards, tarot cards, and goddess cards. It was my new thing. It gave me a sense of control and power over my own future and made me feel hippie and cool.

"I say we go traditional this time." I grabbed the deck and removed it out of its box ceremoniously, held it up to my nose, and took a deep breath. They still smelled quite new.

There was a knock on the door.

"What do we do now?"

Marcy looked stressed.

Last time this happened Mom was showing around one of her friends just as we were chanting to invoke our guides and angels. Of course, Marcy got blamed. Mom yelled for ages about my non-religious, white friend teaching me bad things. *These white people have no values, nothing guiding them but television and cigarettes.*

"Don't worry. It's just Maya," I said. "I can tell." Maya's knocks were firm and hesitant at the same time. "What do you want?"

Maya opened the door wearing a ridiculous ruffled, blue apron covered in big tea kettles. She surveyed the room suspiciously. Her eyes roamed from the cards to the plate with the stubbed-out cigarette.

"Hey, Maya. You're just in time." Marcy grabbed the cards and smiled at Maya as she shuffled the deck. "Do you want a reading? I'm really good now." Marcy loved to freak out Maya any chance she got.

"You know I can't stand that stuff," said Maya.

"Why, because Christ might get angry?" I said.

"Sarika, where is my curling iron? And I'm missing half the stuff in my make-up bag." Maya shifted her gaze to Jeevan's lava lamp which sat on the floor next to me. I switched it on. What bothered me most about my sister was that she pretended to like me because it was the polite thing to do.

"Oh, come on, Maya," said Marcy. "Stop being a grump. Come and shuffle the deck. I heard you're getting married. Let's see how it all turns out."

Maya was getting an arranged marriage. Well, I thought it was an arranged marriage but Maya and my parents would disagree. They all said it was just an introduction. After years of protesting against being set up with someone, Maya finally gave up on her love life at the age of twenty-seven and agreed to meet some guy at Starbucks that Dad's aunt had known. I met him and he was actually kind of good-looking, for an Indian, and he had a pretty good sense of humour. He was a dentist, so that helped.

"Do you think your sister's finally getting laid?" Marcy asked, "Or is she waiting until the wedding?"

"Gross. I don't know. Ask her yourself." Overall, Maya seemed relatively pleased with the whole thing. She had a bit of spring to her step, and she had lost fifteen pounds in the last three months. She even smiled occasionally in a way that suggested something like happiness.

"Come on, pick a card." Marcy patted the floor next to her. I stared at Maya intensely, impelling her to leave with the force of my desire, but to my surprise, she slowly crept over like a pigeon sussing out scraps of food and then eventually sat down with us in a circle. She looked expectantly at Marcy while she played with the fabric of her skirt, bunching it and folding it repeatedly. I felt no sympathy for her eternal awkwardness; only a strong desire to keep as far away from it as possible so I wouldn't catch it.

Marcy fanned out the cards in the shape of a *U*. "Here, we'll do an easy one. One question, one card. Shall we ask about your marriage? How do you wanna phrase it?"

"I don't know. Let's ask how it's going to turn out? Is that too vague?" She tried to keep her voice even but I could detect a hint of girlish nervousness.

"No, that's cool," said Marcy. "Go ahead and pick one."

Maya ran her fingertips over all the cards and then stared at them as if she were in a forensics lab.

"Oh, for God's sake," I said. "Just pick a card."

She grabbed one and quickly turned it over like she was ripping off a Band-Aid.

"Oh," said Marcy. It was a big red heart with three swords piercing through it.

"What the hell does that mean?" asked Maya.

"Don't worry about." Marcy looked at me for help. "They're just stupid cards."

Maya glared at me with icy eyes, as if it were all a set-up – a mean joke. "Thanks a lot."

"What's your problem? You don't even believe this stuff." I did feel a bit bad for her and fully believed the card was a bad omen.

"Make sure you give me back my curling iron." She stood up and walked to the door, slamming it behind her.

"Ouch. What's up with her? She seems even more intense than usual. If that's possible. There's a vibe in the house. I didn't even hear your Mom yelling today." Marcy sort of knew things but hadn't quite tapped into her powers the way I had.

I grabbed the cards and started shuffling them. I was afraid to pick one myself.

"Well, you know it's the anniversary of Jeevan's death. It's been eight years and no one wants to talk about it. We were supposed to have a nice family dinner but Dad went out and got Chinese food and he started eating it on his own."

"Well, I'm sorry Sar, but your family's not great at talking anyway."

"It's not about that. It's about respect."

"Yeah, there's respect and then there's letting go. I mean, I didn't want to say this but I think it's a little weird that you moved into his room." Marcy could feel her emotions superficially; they were on top of her skin like bits of sand and she could shake them off when she wanted to. I admired and resented her for that.

"You know, if you don't like it, why the hell are you here all the time?"

"Because *you're* stuck here. That's why."

Marcy lit another cigarette, and this time I took it from her and sucked so hard I thought my head would explode. Marcy was right. I was trapped in my dead brother's room.

MAYA NEVER DID GET MARRIED that following summer. I don't really know what happened except that he called it off unexpectedly, possibly for someone else. Mom was distraught about her reputation in the community. "I told you we shouldn't have let them go out so much together. Everyone probably saw them. They went to the mall together all the time. They never should have done that. What will people say?" Although she wouldn't talk about it, Maya was devastated. She retreated into herself and spent most of her time at work or in her room with a bag of chips, slowly putting back on all the weight she lost.

I started grade twelve that fall. I was more determined than ever to never end up like my deadbeat sister. All Marcy and I talked about was plotting our big escape after high school and moving to a big city. That was the one commonality we shared; we both wanted to get away from the stench of staleness that consumed our families and the rest of this town.

I sadly marvelled at how every day could be the same and that life could assume such a definitive pattern. Every morning Marcy picked me up at eight and we would traipse through the meadow towards school: cold polluted air stinging our eyes, dry weeds crunching under our feet, with the occasional encounter of fresh gooey shit. At school, we'd stand at our lockers with our rather bland little circle of friends and wait for homeroom. We melded into the crevices of the school in a way I found offensive; all of us wearing bulky, brand name sweatshirts, matching slouch socks, and scrunchies around our wrists. We avoided the nerds and snuck envious looks at the popular girls with their fake orange tans and tight, coloured jeans. There was one little group of Indian girls who congregated together and talked about other Indian boys. They weren't nerdy *per se*, but they were separate. One time one of them invited me to a Diwali party at her house and I pretended I didn't understand what it was. I didn't want to be compartmentalized with *them*. People weren't really mean to them, but they were still silently shunned and always picked last for sports teams. To be accepted you had to align yourself to a cool, white person or you had to be really good at sports.

I was at least loosely welcomed. I would go to my classes half-heartedly, believing the day could easily be condensed into two hours. My theory that the left part of my brain had been extracted at birth was always confirmed by my suffering grades in most academic subjects. I simply couldn't focus and very little interested me. When we had to cover the Canadian government and Confederation, I wondered why we had to bother. Why couldn't we just move on to British history where things were more exciting? Then we could learn about royal affairs, brothels, consumption and other interesting diseases. I thought – no I *knew* – that I was above all this and destined for something more. I had an arrogance that was backed up by mere intuitive musings. I would forget that I had brown skin and that my ties with England were connected more to submission than entitlement.

At night, I would sit by the window with warm milk and honey and look out at the moon. I would think of Jeevan and how he told me I could fly. One time I packed my bag and almost left without Marcy. I felt I would find him – that there was a spell preventing him from coming into the town's borders because he had broken rules. Perhaps he was just outside the city limits, somewhere in a forest, trapped in time waiting for me to find him. I pictured him staying the same age until I joined him and then we would search the world for meaning together. We would move to Vancouver because, at the very least, it was more progressive over there. The Chinese and Koreans were settling in with all their money and running the economy; people were taking their anger out on them. There was less stigma attached to being Indian over there. Indians simply existed among the labourers and middle-class – they minded their own business. Here, we were still Indian before anything else and that stifled me. I waited.

THE SECOND SEMESTER finally brought the change I was looking for; that something more that marked graduation year for me. It was the day I met Jesse James, the new drama teacher. Jesse James really was his name and he insisted on being called by his first name. Jesse was special and beautiful in a way that superseded any sense of time or place. Generations of women loved him: the sixty-year-old principal, teachers, and students. He was young, probably only a couple years out of college, but it was that Bon Jovi rock star quality about him that demanded a sort of respect. His long, wavy, brown hair was tied back in a messy ponytail and he somehow got away with wearing ripped jeans and a Kate Bush T-shirt to school. He was a self-contained unit with a force field around him that implied he didn't have time for frivolities, so people seemed to leave him alone.

He began each day with qigong for twenty minutes. "If you can't feel your *qi*, you might as well be dead," he would say. "If you can't connect with yourself, you can't connect with anyone else, including your audience." Jesse dismissed the drama curriculum and did his own thing. "Yes, Stanislavsky is good, but it's so much simpler than that. It's so easy to shape-shift into whoever you want to be when you have the right tools." To be honest, I can't remember what we did that semester – weird, dark, spiritual stuff around rites of passage and rebirth – rituals that he said were from First Nations tribes. In retrospect, I'm sure he was making it all up.

In spring, the culmination of all my dreams came true. Jesse announced he was finally doing a school play. "Listen folks, I decided I'm not doing something touchy-feely. No *Grease* production happening here. I have written my own modern play based on Henry VIII." He looked at everyone with eager anticipation, but they all just looked at each other. They clearly didn't get it – how dark and twisty and intense it would be – Henry with all of his women: sex, death, and betrayal. These idiots didn't deserve to be here. I loved Jesse more than anyone else. My depth of understanding him proved that. We were both visionaries having to ingratiate ourselves to the mediocrities of everyday life and those around us. "Look, I've already given you all parts so you can check it out on the noticeboard on your way out."

I knew exactly who I wanted to be. I could see it then – the tight corset, my heaving bosom spilling out at the top – okay, maybe I didn't have a heaving bosom, but I would make it work. I pushed past everyone and ran to the board to search for my name. Catherine of Aragon. *Catherine of Aragon? Boring, sexually deprived Catherine of Aragon?* Apart from having to play the most boring role ever, I felt hurt and betrayed that Jesse could do this to me and that he couldn't see what I was capable of. I looked down the list to see who was playing my dream character – the most one-dimensional slut of all time, Melanie Taylor – who wasn't even there. She was probably getting off with someone in the bushes behind the school.

No one else had an issue with the roles they were given. They ambivalently filtered out of the room because they didn't actually know anything about King Henry VIII. I went over to Jesse's desk and stood meekly in front of it, not sure what I was going to say. He was wiping dry mud off his shoe with a paper towel that he dipped in a cup of water occasionally. He didn't take notice of me for at least a couple of minutes.

"Mr. James?"

He finally looked up.

"Sara, how long have you been standing there? And call me Jesse, please. You should know that by now."

I decided not to acknowledge the irony of his irritation. He never got my name right.

"Jesse, I don't understand why you would cast me as Catherine." The voice that came out of my throat was like a tiny air bubble, hollow, and ready to pop any second. "I don't feel it suits me."

He put his other foot up on his desk and started wiping it. "Is that right? And why do you not think it suits you?"

"Because Catherine is a flat, boring character," I said.

He looked at me with amusement. "I think you'll find, Sara, that no one is boring or flat. You just gotta dig deeper." He was patronizing me. "With that said, who *do* you think suits you?"

"Anne Boleyn." I said it with an even voice.

"Anne Boleyn?" He laughed hysterically. "Alright, Sara. I'll give you two minutes to explain to me why you think you should be Anne Boleyn." He smoothed his hair, leaned back in his chair, crossed his arms, and put both feet on his desk. He was only dimly present and participating because it was break time, and he didn't have to plan lessons so there was nothing better to do.

My forehead dripped with perspiration. I decided to go for it. Screw it. I was in grade twelve and I needed this. I went into a rant about what I knew of Anne Boleyn; how she wasn't just a sexual temptress but she was a clever woman with a spirit that represented female strength and power.

He observed me with mocking sympathy. "Do you think you embody her, Sara?" he said.

I was confused by the question. "I think I understand her."

"That's not enough. If you want to be something you need to embody it. I hardly notice you around the school or even in this class. You walk around in your black turtleneck sweaters and I can hardly see you behind all that hair and your big glasses that cover your face. If you want to be a successful actress, self-consciousness is not something you can afford. If you want to be a sexy, confident, female character, then show me that. *Be* that."

"How?"

He put his feet down and leaned forward. "You need to figure that out. If you can't, there's no point. I'll tell you what. I will give you two weeks to show me your 'inner Anne' in lessons. Then for your midterm project, I want you to show me something special. The project is a five-minute presentation. Any type of performance that represents who you are. You need to pull out all the stops for that. Wow me. If you can do that, I'll give you the part. Deal?"

He put his hand out for me to shake and I took it. His hand was coarse, cold, and chalky. I felt a pulse of electricity run through me. This is what I'd been waiting for – this feeling – whatever it was.

That night I took the tarot deck out of my drawer and shuffled furiously.

Marcy observed me curiously. "What are you so freaked out about?" She had never seen me with this sense of immediacy before.

"Quiet, Marcy. I need a sign."

I closed my eyes and took a deep breath as I pulled out a card.

"Oh, that's freaky."

Marcy grabbed the card and ran her fingers over the image. It was the Death card, which depicted a skeleton riding a horse. Surrounding it were dead and dying people from all classes, including kings, bishops, and commoners. The skeleton carried a black banner emblazoned with a white flower.

I grabbed the card back. "No, Marcy, you don't get it. This is the most misunderstood and fabulous card in the deck. It's the transformation card. It's about letting go of the past and rebirth."

I bolted off the bed and ran to my dresser drawer.

"What are you doing?" said Marcy.

After rummaging around, I found what I was looking for, a small red leather wallet with a ladybug on it. I opened it and mounds of cash came spilling out. There was money from babysitting, from relatives that came to visit, and the odd twenty I snuck out of Maya's wallet.

Marcy was shocked. "What is that?"

It was meant to be my ticket out of town one day, but I thought, *What the hell.* "I need to go shopping."

With Marcy's help, I spent spring break at the mall redoing my wardrobe. I traded the loose, bulky greys and blacks for slim fitting, bright coloured tops and tight, red, blue, and purple jeans.

"Wow, you have a hot figure." Marcy was pleased and surprised. "You know that Anne Boleyn got beheaded, right?"

I spent hours practicing putting contact lenses in my eyes and I pinned my bangs back so they were out of my face. I straightened my hair so that it gave me a sharp, severe look. Marcy had just got a job at Sears, so her older college friend Rae-Anne taught me how to do my eyes at the make-up counter. I had big lashes and surrounded them with thick dark liner and mascara so they popped out of my head. My eyes were dark and deep.

"You look like a demon," said Marcy, "but in a good way."

"I know." And I did know, and it felt great. Jesse was right. Here I'd been waiting for this big moment to arrive when really, I just needed to do something.

Everyone had an opinion. Mom thought my clothes were too tight and commented that she didn't see other Indian girls dressed that way. *Good*, I thought.

Even Dad arose from his slumber one evening and looked up from his paper to take a good hard stare at me. "You look nice, Sarika. You look like Jeevan. I never noticed that before."

I stood in the bathroom, the night before spring break ended, thinking about this. I was living out Jeevan's life, the one he didn't get to live. He died at sixteen and I was carrying out his legacy in some way. It was crucial I did it with some sort of honour. Maybe he was watching somewhere from the moon, grinning mischievously while he smoked a joint.

Maya came in and stood next to me. "What are you doing? What is all this?"

I wanted to shake her and say that her judgements of me had become redundant the moment she decided to check out of herself and give in to carbs when her life didn't turn out the way she wanted. I fundamentally disrespected her for this reason alone – that she gave up on herself so willingly. I stared at her bulging tummy that hung over her jeans, at her hair swept back in a messy ponytail. I used to be insecure about how dark I was compared to her – Mom always reminded me of this – that technically she was the prettier one. But she was a bigger ghost than Jeevan, traipsing around the house with a bag of chips or escaping into recorded daytime soaps when she wasn't working at that boring dental office. I would not sit around my parents' house waiting to go to the Sikh temple on Sundays, waiting for the proverbial Mr. Indian Right with the perfect education, portfolio, and skin tone to come to steal my soul, only to become a washed-out spinster with no identity. I met her gaze in the mirror – her beautiful lifeless hazel eyes – a swamp of misery.

"What are *you* doing?" I said.

On Monday, I wore a low-cut red top to highlight my new padded bra, tight black jeans, and shiny, high-heeled, black leather boots. The boys told me how fabulous I looked, and the fake orange tan bitches looked at me enviously, wondering how I had transformed in such a short space of time. Marcy walked by my side with a look on her face that said *I told you so* – as if I'd been an incomplete painting she'd been working on for years that finally made sense. I could have carved out years in that state – feeding off of desire and jealousy in all of its glory. I was addicted to it already.

I purposely went to drama class ten minutes late to make a bit of an entrance. Jesse had everyone in a circle doing deep breathing exercises in lotus position when he saw me. He did a double take and the breath went out of him.

I didn't know a lot about the secrets of sexual power then, but I remembered randomly reading once about Shakti, the Hindu goddess of divine feminine creative power. She said female power was hidden in the womb, that primordial force that created life, and once that energy was awakened and harnessed, you could manifest anything. Maybe I'd finally tapped into that. I was definitely doing something. For the rest of the class and for the rest of the week, I waited for him to say something, but he didn't. I caught him looking at me all the time though.

Marcy gave me tips on how to walk, "Keep your shoulders back, your spine straight, and your face level."

Finally, on Friday at the end of class, he stopped me on the way out. "Sara, you ready for your midterm presentation?" I could feel his eyes graze over me and rest on my breasts, then back to my face, and he smiled.

"Yup." I turned and walked swiftly out the door, shutting it firmly behind. Marcy taught me that one. *Never look back, that's how you get 'em.*

The inspiration for my midterm presentation came from an unlikely source. Marcy and I were sitting on the living room floor trying to come up with an idea.

Why don't you sing a Mariah Carey song?" said Marcy.

"No, that's so lame. She's so phoney and commercial. I need to think of something unique that shows I'm a strong woman who knows how to redefine herself."

"How about Jennifer Beals from *Flashdance*?" Maya piped in from the corner of the room.

"What?" I said.

Maya took a generous bite of her toast, slathered in butter and homemade raspberry jam, while she continued watching *Young and the Restless*. "You know, from that eighties film. She was a tough miner who stripped for extra cash, and then she did that amazing dance in leg warmers and got into dance school. It's all about reinvention."

Marcy and I looked at each other, stunned. "You know, that's not a bad idea," said Marcy.

Sometimes I thought Maya was just a projection of the screen in front of her, that she didn't live in real life, and when the television was turned off she might disappear altogether. But I had to say, it sure filled her with a surplus of useless information that sometimes came in handy.

The day of the presentation I decided to go first to make a huge entrance. I wore a bulky, black sari to represent the shedding of the old me who was no longer bogged down by my oppressive heritage, and I set my cassette tape to "What a Feeling" while I prepared to strip for the entire class. Underneath the thick material, I was wearing a see-through, off the shoulder, grey top with a bright red bra, black leggings and grey leg-warmers. I danced around seductively while I stripped off the sari, eventually wrapping it around Jesse. Sequins fell off the cheap material onto the floor. Sparkles landed in Jesse's hair and all over the room. I bent my body in unspeakable postures and shimmied like it was the last dance of my life. I made everyone stand up and dance with me, just like a real eighties video, though most were hesitant and only moved their legs around a little. No one really knew how to respond, Jesse included. I didn't realize the full gravity of my performance until after the song was over, and I looked around exhilarated. Everyone gave each other bemused looks and no one clapped.

"Okay," said Jesse. "Well, Sara . . . that was a very interesting and unique interpretation of yourself. Who's next?"

Lucy Reimer went next. She read a poem from *Chicken Soup for the Soul*. Then Chantal went up and played "Pachelbel's Cannon" on a keyboard, inspired by her grandmother. As each person went up with their subdued performances, my face grew hotter and I sunk further into myself. I wanted to throw up. I had just humiliated myself in front of my entire class because I thought I was channelling some ancient Indian goddess. At the end of class Bryan Morris threw a dime at me. "Thanks for the show, Sar." Everyone laughed. I'd had a crush on him since I was in grade five. I was mortified.

I turned to run out before Jesse could see the wet mascara coming down my face, but he grabbed my arm. "Good job, young lady."

I looked up at him to see if he was mocking me, but his eyes were bright and intense. "I thought you might be upset. Just stay for a minute."

I watched his hand on my arm as he stood in front of me. It was still cold like the other day. I was aware of the clanging of the door as it shut behind the last student who left the room.

"It was stupid," I said. "I can't believe I did that. And everyone else was normal."

He reached up and touched my face with his hand. "You don't need to be embarrassed, Sara." Jesse's breath was full of licorice and cinnamon. "You took a chance and did something outrageous. You don't want to be normal." I felt that pulse of electricity again as he wiped away my tears with his finger. He tucked loose strands of my half-grown bangs behind my ears. This was inappropriate. I knew that.

He inched closer and kept my gaze with a question in his eyes. What was he doing? It was break time and I could hear the cafeteria lady counting change as everyone fought to get in line to buy muffins.

I felt a rush of exhilaration under the fluorescent lights. I had never been touched like that before. It was a new feeling. But I felt in control because even as a teenage girl I could see him for what he was – not a rock star – but just a perverted young man who manipulated women to feed his starving ego. He spoke about the synchronicity of things more than he ever thought about them. Still, he was handsome. His eyes were gleaming and he looked full of purpose like he did when he led us in meditation. I watched, exultant, as he caressed my face and leaned in even closer and slowly put his other hand on my waist.

"Sara." He whispered it in my ear and all of a sudden this needed to be my name. He kissed my cheek lightly, and I closed my eyes and then he kissed my neck and pressed my body into his, and I physically felt for the first time, so directly, the potency of my power if I used it correctly. The moment held itself. I observed it and was in awe of how okay it was. This was clearly what I needed.

The bell went off and I could hear the scuttle of people make their way to the door. And just like that Jesse had pushed me away and was already behind his desk again, smoothing his hair and taking a sip of tea.

I stood, paralyzed, not knowing what to do. "I guess I should go."

He smiled at me – a salacious smile – reflecting what was complicit between us. "I guess you should." As I walked away he asked, "Sara, you gonna be a Bollywood star one day?"

"No," I said, turning just enough to look him in the eye. "Just a star. Oh, and by the way, my name is Sarika."

Jesse did give me the part of Anne Boleyn in the end. We never talked about what happened that day and oddly there was no real awkwardness about it. Life resumed. I did a superb performance of Anne and the white boys looked at me with desire rather than mere acceptance. I celebrated what I had done: I had carved out a new possibility for Indian girls; we could be hot too. Everyone seemed to graciously buy into my new identity and so I eased into it like my new padded bra.

That summer I lost my virginity to Bryan, in the back of a filthy white truck at a bush party in the middle of nowhere. The stars were dim and pale in the sky, and I counted them while he was on top of me to numb the mild pain. The moon was nowhere in sight. Pearl Jam's "Better Man" played somewhere in the background while kids laughed and threw beer bottles into the fire pit. I didn't particularly like Bryan anymore, but I was glad to participate in this act. I was grateful even to watch his skinny, pallid face groan in ecstasy and raw innocence. Elsewhere, I knew Jesse might be scrubbing his boots with careful precision, probably not thinking of kissing me and what it felt like. But still, I let myself be inhabited by what he gave me. I couldn't stop thinking about it. I felt it was the start of something beautiful.

# MAYA

2002


THE LAKE BUZZED AND HUMMED. Its inhabitants danced and crawled around the uncertainty of unwanted guests. The park was packed with families eating KFC and sandwiches. Little white kids ran around in their halter tops and shorts playing soccer or Frisbee; their golden legs glistened in the height of the afternoon sun.

My hand drifted down to touch my own leg as if to make sure it was covered with loose cotton. I remembered the first time I shaved my legs and how silky smooth they were, and how I bought a pair of jean shorts to celebrate. My legs were nice back then – before I got fat – pin shaped and rounded in just the right places. When I went out the door to get on my bike, Dad had stopped me dead in my tracks. "Where the hell do you think you're going in *those*?" Apparently, openly displaying my legs might affect my marriage prospects. I was fourteen. The irony was that clubs in Mumbai were heaving with bare skin and tight-fitting clothes. In these small Canadian towns, Indians had no concept of the passage of time. Time had stopped the moment they stepped into a mall to buy sensible closed-toed shoes at Zellers.

At that moment, Dad was walking around the little lake and Sarika kept disappearing behind a tree for a smoke. She couldn't handle these strange contrived gatherings. Mom was at work. There were other Indians from the neighbourhood too. About twenty of us. Most of the men were also doing laps around the lake, wearing pants and full sleeved shirts in the sweltering heat. They stunk of sweat and onions but heaven forbid they offend us with their bare skin. A couple of them were excitedly showing each other iPods they had just bought but didn't know how to use, boasting and complaining about them at the same time. I awkwardly sat in a circle with some of the women on the grass, working hard to remain poised as they handed out samosas and rotis filled with spicy chickpea curry. They were covering their bodies with blankets and hats so they wouldn't tan, something Mom always stressed about. *Your fair skin is the one good thing you have. Put some lotion on.*

I could feel people looking at us, and rightfully so. We looked ridiculous. I was certain these Indian picnics were the same all across Canada. Immigrants scattered around parks with deflated soccer balls and nostalgic stories as they tried to turn the lake into their makeshift village from home. In their minds, they replaced maple trees with rice fields. There was always a better *there* than *here*. The past was always better than the present; the future would hopefully be better than the present.

My eyes squinted at the hot blaring sun as I sipped warm Coke from a warm plastic cup. Forget about bringing coolers or springing for some nice refrigerated Coke at the corner store right before the picnic. Nope. That could cost too much money. It had to be on sale. A dollar for a big two-litre bottle, probably bought three months ago, and past the expiry date. I would have brought ice, but I could hear Mom's voice yelling in my head. *Why would you pay money for frozen chunks of water that have been put into a plastic bag?*

But this picnic was no different than any other picnic. I only remember it because it was such an unusually hot day for Labour Day weekend and because my cousin was visiting us from Vancouver. Nina (Navpreet, but no one was allowed to call her that) was a twenty-seven-year-old podiatrist who called herself a doctor, and her husband, Ashok, was a chiropractor. She brought along her dreadful in-laws who lived with them in a three-story mansion. I don't know why they bothered to come all the way to Prince George for a road trip when they were loaded and could easily go on a resort holiday. But rich Indians were often like that. They would rather go on a cheap family road trip to drink chai all day and boast of their material success.

Nina's mother-in-law was telling the circle about the epic family wedding two summers before. "And I cried so much at the wedding, at how beautiful Nina was in her reception dress. . . ."

I closed my eyes and let the breeze hit my face. I started plucking blades of grass one by one. We were *there*. We were all at that wedding. That woman did *not* cry. As someone who was not much of a crier myself, I could verify this. She had looked at Nina with sheer dismay because *that* woman was taking her son away. I remembered that. I was standing behind her when she whispered in some old biddy's ear how Nina's neckline was too low for the reception outfit she chose, and how she should have picked an old Hindi song for the first dance instead of Madonna's "Crazy For You." And then she went on to complain how they were dancing too close for her liking.

But this conversation maybe isn't important enough for me to remember either. I only remember it because Nina was pregnant. I remember what Nina was wearing too. A pixie, white, cotton top with bits of red embroidery along the edges – the type of stitch that could be considered ethnic – perfect for such an occasion. The cotton clung to her pert little boobs and her rounded beach ball belly. It was one of those bellies that you knew was going to disappear as soon as she gave birth.

"So, when is it your turn, Maya?" Nina rubbed her belly and looked at mine.

"Huh?" I winced as a single spicy chickpea burned into the tip of my tongue. I took another sip of warm Coke and let it fizzle and burn even deeper. I focused on that burn. It was better than Nina, her belly, and her stupid question. I was thirty-five years old. It was the question everyone always asked me, or if they didn't, it lurked over my head like a thick smoggy cloud. She looked at me knowingly, friendly even, certain of her unspoken power in this circle. She represented an optimistic future for every woman there: complete submission disguised by material power and independence. She was an educated woman who knew when to recede into the background and let her husband organize mortgage payments and family holidays. It was better than what most of these women had. It was better than what they could ever hope for.

"Are you asking if I'm pregnant?" I leaned in and grabbed a cold samosa from some Tupperware. "No. Just a little fat." One of the ladies laughed a little nervously and everyone else just looked at me. I could play this game. I rubbed my tummy a little. It was an unfortunate tummy. I had a pear-shaped body with a big ass and a tummy that jutted out. It wasn't like other people who just kind of filled out everywhere. It was a tummy that implied eating too many carbs ambivalently.

Nina tried changing the subject. "It's almost the anniversary of 9/11. Isn't that horrible?"

"It is horrible," I replied. "And lots of other people are dying every day in other parts of the world. That's horrible too. And girls in India are being trafficked right now as we speak."

Everyone got quiet. I did care, but I knew that Nina didn't. I couldn't handle the idea of someone using a dreadful event as small talk because they had nothing else to say.

Nina tried again. "And Lady Diana, too. It was just the anniversary of her death."

"And Mother Theresa," I said, "But no one remembers her. She died five days later, you know. She did the real grunt work, but everyone cried over Lady Di who just pranced around in her pretty clothes." This time I had really killed the conversation and everyone just ate and stared at the grass.

The silence broke with a booming voice just behind me. "Why are you ladies so quiet over here?" I looked up, and there, casting a welcoming shadow over me, was my husband, Sunny. His name was

Sunhil, but everyone called him Sunny – probably because of his sunny disposition. Underneath the olive undertones, his rounded face was slightly red and puffy from running. He was sporting a loose Elton John concert T-shirt and old navy-blue sports shorts that were ripped on the bottom left side. I liked Elton John but begrudged Sunny's lack of awareness that the T-shirt made him look outdated and a bit square. His hair was neither curly nor wavy. His stomach was neither flat nor protruding. I often thought he was offensive merely because nothing about him was distinct or certain. But then, at other times, this was what I loved. This was what made me safe.

Sunny grabbed the samosa out of my hand and put the whole thing in his mouth, looking around curiously at everyone. "Ladies, anyone wanna rub suntan lotion on my back?" The ladies giggled and smiled and gestured for Sunny to have some food. I cringed. I never found his jokes funny but most Indian women did.

"We were just asking your wife when you were going to have a baby." Nina did that frequently when she spoke to Sunny, saying *your wife* because she knew it might annoy me.

"Oh, we're trying. Don't worry." Sunny kept munching on his food, completely unaware. "We'll catch up to you." Everyone looked over at me in surprise. I wanted to punch Sunny in the face.

"Oh Maya, aren't you the quiet one." Nina looked like she had won whatever invisible battle she was playing with me. "How long have you been trying?" I was very close to pointing out that she wasn't a real doctor because I couldn't think of anything else to say.

Nina's mother-in-law piped in. "It's okay. Maya's a late bloomer. She got married late and she can have babies late. She just needs to do it now. She can go to those Chinese people. You know, those people that stick needles in you and make you drink weird tea? Nina's friend tried that and it worked. She's old too."

I imagined Nina's mom on an acupuncture table with needles sticking out of her square chin and neck to cure her of her reckless abandon with words. I grabbed a piece of apple to demonstrate my dedication to my good health and got up. "I think I'll go for a walk around the lake." I smiled inanely at everyone – poised, I thought – as I left the circle.

"I'll go with you." Sunny could tell I was not impressed.

"Oh, you should stay and visit with us, Sunny. Have more food." Nina looked up at Sunny in a syrupy way. She was shameless. Even with her big self-righteous belly of innocence, she would flirt with anything that walked upright. Earlier that day, I swear she had been flirting with the pimply faced ice cream boy so she could get one for free. The other ladies chimed in for Sunny to stay and started opening Tupperware containers of food.

"Yes dear, eat some more. You're looking gaunt," Nina's mom said. I started walking towards the lake so fast that I was almost running. I looked at the ducks and felt like waddling away with them from the dangerous humans. He could stay with them and eat and flirt. They preferred him anyway – even my own family.

Everyone loved Sunny: men, women, children, and old people. He was agreeable. Anytime anyone suggested anything he just said, "Sounds good." Someone would ask, "Sunny, can you help me move furniture?" or "Sunny, can you lend me a hundred bucks?" His response was always the same: "Sounds good." His good-natured innocence darkened my cynical nature rather than balancing it out.

His response seemed to be enough for people. I think this might be how we got married. We had met at Nina's engagement party and someone suggested we go out on a date because we were both single. He said, "Sounds good." I told him to move out of his parents' place to buy a small house. He said, "Sounds good." Within three months he had moved.

We dated for four months and then one day we were sitting in Boston Pizza and I said, "Maybe we should get married." He paused to look over at a bunch of teenagers throwing straws at each other at the next table. Then he grabbed my hand and smiled. "Sounds good." We ordered milkshakes to celebrate and started planning the wedding right then and there.

When people asked him about our story, he would romanticize the whole thing, saying, "My girl proposed to me spontaneously on a Monday night." I knew what everyone was thinking: *How did Maya get such a catch?* They thought I was lucky to get someone like him at my age.

Sunny sidled up next to me just as I was finishing my first lap. I knew he would. "Hey. You look kinda mad."

I tried to think of a way to not lose my temper so I munched on my apple for a moment. "Why did you say that? Why did you tell those people we're trying? What were you thinking? No one needs to know our business. Especially those idiots."

"I'm sorry, Maya. I wasn't thinking. It didn't seem like a big deal. They're family." Sunny looked at the lake for answers. He often did this when I confronted him. He chose a specific visual point and hoped something would miraculously come to him.

"That puts a lot of pressure on me." My voice was a little high. "That's a general rule that every husband should know. You don't publicly announce to people you're trying to get pregnant." A girl and her mother wearing matching pink Britney Spears T-shirts scurried by us looking alarmed.

"Okay, I'm sorry." Sunny slowed down his pace and grabbed my hand. "Maya, the thing is . . . the thing is we never talk about it."

I was sharp with him. "What's to talk about?" Why did I have to be so sharp?

"This. Us trying. I think we need to get some help, don't you?" Sunny stroked my hand and wouldn't look at me. "I know you weren't into it before, but it's been over a year now, and you bite my head off every time I bring it up." He was terrified of me. I hated that but I used it.

"There's nothing to talk about. I'm not paying for what should be a natural expression of my body."

"Dammit, Maya." He dropped my hand and grabbed a strand of his hair with his thumb and forefinger and started twisting it. It was this weird thing he did when he was frustrated. Usually, he did it when he was talking to his overbearing mother on the phone. "Is this the religious stuff? Is that what this is? Is there something in the Bible that says you can't get IVF or even make a doctor's appointment?"

"Screw you." I turned around and started walking the other way. I wasn't used to him fighting his corner or taking a stand. I paused and checked myself. I didn't want to be like this. I wanted to be kinder, more honest. But I couldn't. So I kept walking.

He didn't call after me. I walked through the gravel path and onto the grass. Pebbles crept into my shoes, and I let them dig into my feet. It felt good – just like a spicy chickpea. It was something I could feel. I kept on walking through the trees and past more and more families of three, four, or five. There were babies and children galore, all laughing and playing, with smears of ice cream all over their faces.

I walked until there was nowhere else to walk, and I ended up in the parking lot. I found my maroon Pontiac and sat on the back of it. I could still hear kids, but they were far enough in the distance that I could tune them out. With my eyes closed, I lifted up my skirt a bit and let the sun kiss my legs.

"Are you done having your little tantrum?"

I opened my eyes to find my sister blowing cigarette smoke in my face. I coughed and swatted the cigarette away from me. "Well?"

I didn't know what to say. Sarika knew I was prone to passive-aggressive tantrums. She was my opposite. She wore her emotions on her fitted leather sleeve. Everyone knew how she felt all the time, and she did it with a charm and a flair that strengthened her position. Always.

"I'm fine. I'm getting some alone time. All these kids are noisy and I'm getting burnt."

Beads of sweat formed under my bangs. Sarika never sweated. She looked like a brand new sharpened pencil: lean, sharp, and polished. She wore tight figure-hugging jeans and a tank top. Her hair glistened with its perfectly straight layers that curved into her face. Her skin shimmered in the light, and her makeup was flawless and didn't drip like mine.

She examined me, as she always did, in a way that made me dissolve into myself.

"Nina said she could smell smoke on me, if that makes you feel better. And they all asked me when I'm gonna get married." It didn't make me feel better. With Sarika it was different. They still thought there was hope for her because she was twenty-four, skinny, and beautiful. Plus, her amused ambivalence just made me angry at her. She would cope by checking out, hiding behind trees, or leaving town when things got difficult. "So, are you okay or what?"

"I don't need for you to check on me. It's all good." I wanted her to leave. Her concern only highlighted my own indifference to myself. When we were younger, she was resentful towards me for neglecting her, and I could cope with that. When we got older, it seemed like every time I saw her, she tried to reach out to fix me. I felt like her niceness was directly correlated to my waistline. The fatter I got, the nicer she was.

"My flight's not for a couple of days. I've been texting you about the spa day and you haven't replied."

"I don't really use my cell phone." This was true. I had finally started using email years after everyone else but was overwhelmed by being held accountable to words that couldn't be deleted. And then everyone pestered me about using a cell phone. I didn't like being that available. I felt like technology was closing in on my safe little world by forcing its way into every private space in my life – my purse, my computer – always asking me questions. "I don't think I'm going to have time. Sorry."

"Doing what? Trying to get pregnant?" I looked back at her blankly. "That was mean. Sorry."

Sarika pulled out another cigarette and leaned back against the car. She looked satisfied as she took a big drag, and her shoulders relaxed. I felt the same when I ate a Snickers bar.

"You should come see me. You know you can come stay anytime." She paused. "You really look like you could use some time out of here."

"What are you saying? I look like crap?" I stared her down, and she flinched a bit and looked away. It was the only power I ever had over her. A leftover from our childhood. I knew it was pathetic.

"God, Maya. You're so defensive. I'm just trying to...I don't know, figure you out or something." She started going back to her high school self – the self-important one – that I knew was beneath the surface. "Are you happy?"

"I don't need you to figure me out. Who are you to swan into town and ask me if I'm happy?"

"Swan into town?" She looked at me piously in the way Jeevan used to. I could see him in her. Sometimes she channelled him without even realizing. "So, you're mad I left?"

She wanted me to fight with her. I wasn't going to cave.

"No, I'm not mad. I'm just . . . tired. Not feeling well today. Look, it was nice to see you." I leaned in and gave her a loose hug. "See you at Christmas." I went to the side of the car and opened the door and got in. Who the hell was she to diminish my home – my life?

"That's it?" She looked unsatisfied. She wanted me to admit that I had made the wrong choices to justify her right ones.

I smiled again. "That's it."

I started backing out without looking to see where Sarika was. She was somewhere to the right of me, in the periphery, standing like a misplaced peg or ornament. I began driving out of the parking lot onto the road. I could still hear screaming and shouting.

Thoughts piled up in my head one after another. I didn't fit in at that picnic. I fought with my husband. I fought with my sister. I never spoke to my dad. I had stupid tantrums all the time – big ones, little ones, silent ones. I walked away all the time. To my left, there was a waterpark. Kids were dancing and jumping in the water fountains. Off to one side by herself, there was a little Indian girl in a red bathing suit splashing and flailing her arms around. The water cascaded down her bare, innocent limbs. She gleamed and glistened with liquid hope.

I flipped back and forth across the few radio stations we had on the way home. I finally found "Rocket Man" by Elton John and sang along foolishly while I thought of Sunny's shirt. I only listened to eighties music. I had missed the nineties completely and couldn't get a grasp of rap or dance music, or the harder stuff Sarika listened to. I felt like a misfit all the time, even when I was singing in the car.

When I got home, the house was empty. We lived on a quiet street lined with maple trees. I had the perfect front porch. It was white and it wrapped around the front half of the house. I loved my space. Who could afford a beautiful brick house like this somewhere else? Who did Sarika think she was? Coming here and acting like she knew anything about happiness? I opened the door, went straight into the kitchen, and grabbed a bag of red licorice on my way up to my room. I lay in bed and put my hands on my stomach – sore. I fell asleep like that.

I awoke some hours later to the sound of the door opening downstairs and Sunny trudging up the stairs. Even when he tried to be quiet he was loud – his feet heavy against the creaky wooden floors. I closed my eyes and pretended to be asleep as he came into the room. I often did this to avoid his awkward overtures for intimacy.

"Maya?" I could smell beer on his breath from across the room. I hated the smell of alcohol on his breath. It was gross. But he was religious in his nighttime rituals.

I listened while he went to the bathroom, brushed his teeth, and moisturized his face. He was the only man I knew who flossed his teeth every day. When he came into the room, he went straight to the window to make sure it was open a bit because he knew I needed a bit of a breeze. He was a good man.

He lay down next to me on his back. I listened while his breathing slowed and within minutes he was asleep. I always envied that he could do this and opened my eyes to look at him. I often watched him in his sleep. I knew I was being creepy but I couldn't help it. I had insomnia. There he was, his limbs all awry, in a pose that revealed his unabashed trust in the world and the universal forces that governed his life.

He had not been my first choice. He had to live with the chronic disappointment of that. We never discussed it, but he knew that the man I had wanted to marry left me for some white waitress at a pub, and then shortly after married an Indian nurse who ticked all the right boxes. I didn't know why he had left me but I felt I had sabotaged it in some way. He was gorgeous and funny and I had blown it somehow. Although it was set up by family, oddly our dates had been romantic, and I couldn't believe my luck at the time.

Sunny's past was pretty textbook. He graduated from high school, travelled in Europe for three months, and then realized there was no place like home. He got a job at the mill and hung out with his buddies all the time at the country bar downtown. He possibly messed around with girls for fun but no one anyone would speak of. Then he waited for his family to suggest someone because that was the right thing to do. The only reason I got him was because his mom got cancer, and this delayed his search for a while, so it was okay for him to go for an older girl. In fact, he was a saint for sacrificing his twenties to look after his mother.

When I was younger, I never understood how nebulous love could be; you could love so deeply but so imprecisely at the same time. My love for Sunny was deep and uncertain like the cool, invisible under-currents of an autumn day. Sometimes the force of it overwhelmed me – like when I looked at him and remarked at his innocent beauty, the way a mother did for her most beloved child. I felt proud and happy for him in a distant way. I could support his ambitions because he deserved that, because he was a good salt of the earth man, and because he deserved to live out his dreams of having an ordinary life. Other times the air was too still, and I saw him for what he was: an obedient Indian man who settled for a mediocre life because he didn't have the capacity to question what might be possible. His parents taught him having enough was enough. Why couldn't he see that he settled for a chubby woman in a small town? Where were his dreams? Perhaps if I knew he had any I could respect him more.

When Prime Minister Pierre Trudeau allowed the Sikhs to come to Canada in droves in the seventies, perhaps their dreams were distorted and idealistic, but at least they had clear intentions. They worked hard, acquired homes, and made enough money to send back to family; they fulfilled their purpose. No one could question their motives. They were paving better lives for the future. They did what they came to do and it meant something. But what were we doing? We were told to continue on watered down traditions, but based on what vision? To acquire more houses? To make more money to send to our families back home? What family? What was home?

And of course, we were expected to have babies – to *want* babies – so they could look after us when we were old. But the future wasn't that predictable anymore. Not all Indian kids here were necessarily living with their in-laws anymore. So what was the point of having kids anyway? Sunny accepted that I wouldn't live with his parents, but it was a sore point between us. Who was going to look after *my* Mom and Dad? Clearly, not Jeevan.

I had thought these very things earlier that morning when I was lying on the table at a clinic. I was riddled with guilt and relief all at once. But I couldn't manage it. Not at that moment. I couldn't be a mother, pretending more than I already was. Yet, I had no reason not to be one either. I didn't have dreams or prospects. The worst part of it all was that there was nothing else for me to do.

I lied all the time. I lied to myself even about why I remembered that particular day. It wasn't Nina, the stupid picnic, or even the abortion itself. It was the image of my pale legs in stirrups that hadn't seen enough sun. That's what I really remembered. It was the little girl in the red bathing suit in the waterpark with her bare golden arms and legs – full of possibility – who looked like she had things she wanted to do.

# SARIKA

2006

THE FLATS on my street were all pale yellow, each with green or blue doors. It was charming and unremarkable at the same time. There was garbage everywhere and rusted pipes sticking out in places that seemed to make the street look tired rather than quaint. The houses looked like they were from a faded photograph – like the street could use a good power washing. But people didn't do that here. There were no hoses or people hanging around outside. People scurried quickly inside when they got to their homes, pausing only to fumble for their keys.

My bedroom window overlooked a pub that was run by Italians, who I'm sure were using it as a front for something else. They owned the street. They were the only ones who stood outside smoking cigarettes and playing their music. Sometimes they offered me pasta in a slightly aggressive manner as a sort of forced compliance to overlook anything that seemed suspicious.

When I was younger I watched *Notting Hill* every three months (even though I hated Julia Roberts) and decided one day I would live that dream. I would move to London and fall in love with some self-deprecating British shop owner and become an actress. But instead of living in Notting Hill, I lived in a dodgy part of South West London with three flatmates. And instead of being a West End actress, I was teaching drama at an inner-city high school, where an average day entailed walking through spit and blood and removing used condoms gripping the staff toilet doors.

But when I walked out my battered green door and the wind hit my face, I knew I was alive. That sounds like a cliché but it was true. Here, people wore scarves of all different patterns and colours. People didn't mince their words and meant what they said. Trust wasn't earned easily, but when it happened it was real. Here, Indian women smoked and hooked up with strangers without anyone noticing. I could embrace my aura of strangeness and I was considered an "exotic Asian woman" rather than an unmarried Indian girl with a questionable reputation.

Perhaps I was idealizing by pushing away the smell of the pulp mill and replacing it for the stench of another less certain form of pollution. But London filled my soul. The city didn't apologize for itself. The limestone and tar were tempered with the smells of strange cooking and the sounds of various languages. I silently congratulated myself all the time for simply being here. I would smoke in my open doorway and watch puffs of clouds disappear into the night, happy for their freedom to dissipate into a hazy skyline. I wish I could take what I had learned and send it back home in a sealed envelope: There was more to life than reasonable mortgage rates and owning space full of emptiness.

"Your boyfriend is here." My flatmate Phil came and stood next to me in his wet towel and together we watched my colleague Patrick get out of his Mercedes with perfectly coifed hair. I didn't particularly find him attractive, but he found himself attractive, drove a nice car, and was willing to drive me to this party.

"Definitely not my boyfriend."

"Good. His hair looks like a mop soaked with honey. He looks like a wanker."

Phil always commented on the men that showed up at my door, giving them a rating out of ten based on their shoes and hair.

"Takes one to know one." I grabbed my purse and headed towards the door.

"Has he been tested? He looks like Jack Nicholson. Why does he have that creepy smile?" Phil followed me to the door.

"Go put some clothes on before your Mum comes over. You're taking her out, remember?" I gave him a kiss on the cheek.

"That's the worst thing you've ever said to me."

"Gotta go." I slammed the door behind me and Patrick opened the passenger door for me without saying a word. He was smooth, but I met some of his women and saw their faces before and after dating him. They looked dull and worn out when he was done with them – like fused out lightbulbs. I did just enough to get rides to parties.

Patrick navigated the streets like a true Londoner, swerving here and there, and not flinching when a car missed him by a centimetre. He turned on some Latin music and started drumming his fingers against the steering wheel. "Do you like salsa?"

I rolled my eyes. "Is that a chat-up line? No. Men take up salsa as a sorry excuse to grope women. It's so pathetic."

"Alright, fine. Someone's got tight knickers on. What do you like then? Ballroom?"

"No, actually. Swing."

"Swing? Oh, honey, I thought we were talking about dance, but if you want, we can find some nice bird to join us later." He winked at me. Phil was right. He did have a creepy smile like Jack Nicholson.

"Very funny. Swing is classy and romantic. That music came to life when F. Scott Fitzgerald and Hemingway were writing the good stuff. It's soulful and beautiful and –"

Patrick turned up the music and was drumming his fingers even harder. The music turned into some horrible Bob Marley dance remix. I opened the window and lit a cigarette. "No smoking in the car." He looked at me and smiled. I turned down the music and returned the smile, puffing smoke in his face. He laughed. "Ah, Sarika. The poet, the dreamer, the romantic. I thought you were an actress?"

"I am."

"So, how's that going then?"

"I'm auditioning lots and just got myself an agent actually. Glad you care."

"Where did you train?"

"Back home."

I didn't really want to answer his question because I told everyone different things about my training. The truth was that I had taken a smattering of acting courses but never really completed an official program. My parents agreed to pay for my teaching degree in Vancouver so I took the safe route, thinking it would at least be my ticket out.

"Canadian acting school? Blimey. What are you gonna do? Bollywood swing dancing movies?"

"I don't have the energy to engage in this conversation."

I looked out the window at clusters of people walking out of a theatre and imagined them coming out from my show. *She's from Canada. She's so exotic looking*, they'd say. There'd be musings about what shaped my obvious presence as a strong feminist, what my political beliefs were, and how Indira Gandhi influenced me. I wasn't a narcissist like Patrick. I just wanted to be heard.

When we arrived at the club I felt like I'd just been transported to a seventies orgy. The backdrop was red walls with wide, leather, U-shaped sofas that looked like beds adorned with shiny, sequined cushions. There were mini Buddha statues everywhere and a wafting scent of incense mingled with beer. A braless woman in her fifties was dancing by herself on a mini dance floor. Her nipples popped out under her sheer, lavender top. Most people were sitting on the floor, smoking and checking each other out. I spotted my friend Bonnie sitting in a corner on a cushion, wearing a long, flowy, mustard-coloured dress. The orange flower in her hair glowed against the orange lanterns that hung from the ceiling. She was surrounded by men and bottles of champagne. She greeted me as if she hadn't seen me in years. "Sary! You gorgeous girl."

She handed me a glass of champagne and pulled me down to sit next to her, knocking over her own glass. She was already drunk. "Did he try anything in the car?" She laughed at my look of disdain. "Never mind. Look at all the men here. Come on lady, go talk to them."

"It's only nine. I need several glasses of these before I can even think of anything like that." This wasn't my usual scene – a party for PE teachers. I looked around to survey the crowd. It *was* mostly men and lots of them. I was both overwhelmed and underwhelmed at the same time. Some of them were attractive. Most of them were uninteresting. They were looking for beer on tap, confused that Bonnie had organized this party at this strange bohemian club instead of a sports bar.

Bonnie watched me as I gazed around. "Aren't we lucky? Look at us, people from all over the world, sitting here in a London club. You from Canada, me from South Africa, Gabriel over there from Brazil. . . Where else does this happen?"

Bonnie had a childlike enthusiasm that only waned slightly when she was really tired from dancing too much. She was the only one of her family to scrounge enough money together to leave and get an education. She already owned two flats and did it all herself. When she got off the plane at Heathrow for the first time and went on the Tube, a woman came up to her and said, "My goodness, your hair. It's so gorgeous." Bonnie cried afterwards because a white person thought she was beautiful without having to straighten her big curly hair. She said it wasn't that she was blind to the cruelty and injustice of life; she just chose to see it how it should be.

"You're right, we're lucky." I meant it and held a moment of gratitude, drowning out the music in my head. I was only twenty-eight years old and had already done so much. I thought of Maya sitting on her couch eating apple pie and watching *Family Feud* with Sunny. I had visions of Mom cutting out coupons while she slow-cooked the kilo of onions she bought on sale, the smell permeating her clothes and the outdated paisley sofa covers. Even though my story wasn't as poignant as Bonnie's, it was still a story.

I took a big sip of champagne and winced. It wasn't real champagne, of course. Bonnie laughed. "English sparkling wine, darling. So, you never told me. Where's that Aussie bloke you were seeing? The architect? The smart guy who was sending you photos of his work."

"Good question. Where is he? He probably went back to Oz, who knows."

"Okay, so why don't you know?"

Bonnie was a straight up gal. The other day she confronted her husband and told him he needed to go out without her at least one Saturday a month to prove he still had some fire. She didn't understand why my romantic life was so full of complications.

"Oh Bonnie, it wasn't serious. Remember, you told me I should have fun. And remember that talk you gave me about fun leading to good skin and good sleep?"

"Yeah, but you said you liked him, right? I thought you were going to Italy with him." She looked perplexed. She would never understand.

I handed her a glass of sparkling wine and grabbed one for myself. "Honey, right now I'm worried about keeping my nice skin and having a good time." I clinked my glass against hers to push the questions aside. I was good at doing this. I downed it like cough medicine – my mother taught me not to waste. I remembered her washing mould off tomatoes and putting them in our sandwiches.

I needed to get away from my friend for a moment. I wasn't sure why. "I'm gonna go to the bar and have a real drink. This is kind of gross, right?"

"Gin and tonic please."

I straightened my back as I started walking to the bar, my black heels crunching over some broken glass. I was trying to improve my posture these days. You never know when a good-looking chiropractor might show up. My gaze fell on a man standing on his own, his elbow perched against the bar as he casually sipped from his girlish cocktail. He didn't hide behind a phone or look like he was waiting for someone. He just stood there holding his position. He had brown shoulder length hair, and he was wearing a fedora and a green scarf that might have looked silly on another man, but his confidence made him pull it off. He caught me looking and returned my gaze squarely. His eyes were a beautiful brown colour, creamy and sharp. His whole being seemed familiar to me.

"Hey." He smiled at me.

I felt awkward all of a sudden. I was usually confident and full of myself. "Hey." I ordered drinks as I stood next to him and stared straight ahead at all the different kinds of gin. I could feel him looking at me without even trying to be discreet.

When my drinks came he said, "You like gin? You know what they say about people that like gin. That's heavy shit." He had an American accent and a lazy smile that I couldn't read.

"My friend likes gin. Look, I'm not interested, okay." I didn't know why I said that. I was annoyed he thought it was okay to stare, but attracted to him at the same time.

He started laughing. "Wow, defensive much? I'm not interested either." He held up his hand. He had a wedding ring on. "My wife's right over there." He pointed to a gorgeous willowy blonde woman about three feet away who was also wearing a fedora. She was standing with a small group of people in a circle. She looked over at him and smiled. "But I did want to tell you that you have a price tag sticking out of your shirt." He pointed to my underarm.

I looked down and sure enough there it was: $29.99. That's how much I was worth. It wasn't even in British pounds because I bought it back home on sale. I grabbed it and started pulling it off. I could feel myself going red.

"Hey, don't pull it," said Fedora Man. "You're gonna wreck it."

I pulled it anyway and the thread tore just slightly. "Great. That's great."

He started laughing at me and my face was so warm I wanted to throw my drink in his face. "Not funny."

"It is pretty funny though." He had a sparkle in his eyes that I wanted to pinpoint and connect to something I couldn't quite place. "Come on, admit it."

I smiled back and took a breath. I liked to see myself as a raucous girl, confident in my ability to laugh at myself and to star in my own comedy. But I couldn't quite do it. "Okay, it's funny."

"Can I say something?"

"You didn't ask before. What's holding you back now?"

"You're an attractive girl, but you have issues. I'm not sure you know you have issues. But you do have issues." His eyes weren't mocking. He smiled again, this time more compassionately like I was a small child. He walked away and put his arm around his wife. I looked at his hand on her waist. He kissed her cheek and I felt a pang of some sort of longing.

I went back feeling flustered, sipping furiously through the dull ache of whatever embarrassment had just occurred.

"Yo, Bonnie!" I held up her drink to join me on the cushions, far out of sight from Fedora Man and his pretty fedora wife.

Bonnie beckoned me towards the dance floor. She started dancing by herself. Her hair shook and shone and she reminded me of a full-feathered eagle soaring around the room with her arms outstretched. I loved the freedom she gave herself. I always thought I was like her, but I wasn't sure anymore. I felt like I was constantly living out different versions of myself. I fluctuated between modern cynicism and unreasonable wishes. I wanted to possess and control the stage in my own love story – the one where I was tamed by the most likely hero one could imagine and whisked off the stage at the end while I wore a flamenco dress covered in red feathers. It was okay that everyone who watched knew the couple would settle into a mundane life after the show, and they were happy for them.

I remarked on these fantasies when I taught some of the Gypsy girls at my school. They couldn't read or write but were plopped into a school setting for a short period of time. By the age of sixteen, their lives revolved around cooking and cleaning their already spotless caravans. On their wedding day, they wore enough crinoline under their tacky fuchsia dresses to hide several small children as they prepared for the next phase of life – getting pregnant. I was secretly jealous of their acquiescence and their ability to shamelessly ignore the different versions of feminism that have been played out over time. Sometimes people called me a gypsy, which ironically implied free-dom. I would agree with them, secretly fantasizing over the decorative teapot I might have in a caravan that never actually went anywhere. I craved stillness.

The other version of me wanted to trek into the wilderness with all the other strong bitches and chant in the forest with some strange goddess name like Aurora or Luna. I wanted to scream and name my desires out loud like they were holy scriptures, incited by a deeper part of me that was all-knowing. Truthfully, my desires were so conflicted that they felt like a curse. My lovers reflected that: some of them coarse, some of them clinging and wanting, and some of them scared of their own splintered male identities.

I decided to chat with some of the other guys at the party. Bonnie was right. I needed to take advantage of this smorgasbord of men from all over the world. I could've been back home at some Indian gathering where my parents introduced me to a potential suitor called Ramdeep. We would sit in silence through each tick of the grandfather clock as Maya passed out chai to everyone. The potential mother-in-law would glare at my black eyeliner, which coated my upper lids completely, and she would plot how to take that red lipstick off me permanently. The suitor himself would be trying to catch a glimpse of my cleavage while he wondered what my bra size was, if I would iron his shirts, and if I was a virgin – all equally important. After he proposed, I would pass out the wedding invites while friends gazed at the name on the card, smirking in sympathy.

I flitted around the room to see who was open. There was an artist, Marcello, who talked incessantly about capturing the personal-ities of birds through watercolour. I stared at his forehead, which had a scar that looked like a broken wing. I refrained from pointing it out, realizing I was drunk enough to say the wrong thing. Then I consoled a shy young guy who had just moved from Cornwall. He was nervous, new to London and its unforgiving attitude to awkwardness. He was too young for me, and I was already feeling too old for idle chit-chat. There were other men too, some of them noticing me, but I slid onto a lonely coach and visualized a much older version of myself hitting on young men because I still felt twenty-two inside. I imagined myself becoming the braless lady I'd seen earlier but less dignified, with coffee stained teeth and made up stories about plays I'd been in.

Patrick came and sat next to me, his red cheeks flushed and ripe. "You're doing well, Miss."

"What do you mean, I'm doing well?" I took the drink from his hand and knocked it back.

"You know, chatting up all the lads. That's a quick recovery. Heard your Aussie bloke left the building. I could have called that one." It seemed like Patrick's smile was getting bigger by the moment and his lips were getting fuller. His teeth sparkled under the orange lights.

"I don't really know why you seem to think I need your opinion. But it was a casual thing anyway, and it just fizzled out. You know, fizzled. Isn't that a thing guys say?"

"Right, is that why you were passing around all those pics of the two of you having some cheesy picnic at Green Park?"

"You're an asshole."

"Yep. And I'm also honest. You should take a beat from me. You could learn something. At least I know what I want." Patrick was looking down at my legs. "Nice hold-up stockings. Damn, I like hold-up stockings." My skirt was riding up. I quickly pulled it down. "I see you took off the sales tag you had hanging off your shirt."

"You saw that?"

Patrick threw his head back and roared with laughter. "I couldn't help it. I had to see if you got any offers."

I wanted to laugh too, but I couldn't. It was too much. "You're just mad because you're never the one I go home with."

"No, I'm amused that you won't admit that you want to." Patrick took back his pint glass and handed me a glass of the cheap wine. "But that's okay. Turn on some Nina Simone, girl. You'll be fine."

He got up and started chasing after some woman on the dance floor. I felt annoyed. But by what? That I forgot to remove a sales tag? That I couldn't will myself to be amused by my blaring inadequacies? Instead, I was skulking between bits of broken glass around the dance floor, avoiding the fedora man at all cost.

I grabbed more wine with the determination to push through. This was about me. This was about not letting people get under my skin and not being so easily dismantled in the face of criticism. After three more glasses of wine and two double gins, everything seemed clearer. Sometimes life was like that. Sometimes melatonin kept you awake and caffeine put you to sleep.

I decided to hit the dance floor. I went up to Marcello and asked him to show me some moves. He grabbed me and swung me around. "Let me show you how dancing is really done." We danced for a while and the floor cleared. People formed a circle to watch and started clapping. I was the star of the show. I was the bird.

Marcello eventually pushed me into the arms of the Cornwall boy. He looked flustered but people were still cheering me on. What was his name? "Mark? It's okay...you're doing fine. Just swing me around."

"It's Peter, actually. Look, I think you need to look down." He looked shy and sheepish.

"No, honey, dancing is about eye to eye contact. Look at me." He needed encouragement.

"No, I mean your stocking – it fell down."

Sure enough, Peter was right. My left stocking had fallen down. I stopped to pull it up but it wouldn't really stick. "It's okay," I said. "Spin me around." So I spun. Lights were like hands grasping at me, beckoning to keep me still as they flickered and glowed into multiples of threes and fours. Peter backed away from me a bit. I could spin on my own.

The people in the circle were looking at me. Were they looking at me? Things were spinning. Images were blurred. I tried making out faces which seemed to blur and merge into one another. Some people were laughing. At me? I don't know. I caught Patrick's face in the crowd. No, not his face. His smile. His stupid big smile which was animated, cartoonish, and exaggerated. I envisioned white paint on his face. He was the Joker and I was Catwoman, trying to hide and have adventures at the same time. But the Joker knew who I was. His teeth gleamed in the darkness. I kept spinning. It reminded me of that merry-go-round Maya used to put me on. She would spin me and spin me and I couldn't stop. I was hanging on for dear life. A hand reached out to grab me and pulled me out. It was Bonnie.

"Time to go." She grabbed my hand and pulled me out of a side door. I threw up in a bin and felt the gin burn up my chest. Things were blurry. Quick and stilted. There was a car. Bonnie put me in the backseat. Who was driving? Harry, Bonnie's husband. He tore down the street. Then he grabbed her hand. They were in love.

They drove me home. Bonnie got me inside and I managed to climb up the stairs. I could hear faint murmuring from Phil's bedroom. I sat on the edge of the bed and put my head between my knees. I closed my eyes. I was still spinning, and I couldn't stop. It was getting lighter outside. It was late. Or early.

"Oh, Birdie." I heard a voice. It was faint. "Birdie."

It was outside of me and maybe in me at the same time. I looked up. It was Jeevan. He was sitting in a swivel chair against the wall by my dressing table. He was tracing letters on the wall, his name I think. I saw him sometimes when I took certain substances, but occasionally it happened early in the morning while I was in a lucid state.

"What were you thinking, spinning like that? I taught you how to spin. Slowly. Gently." He was wearing what he always wore, his red hoodie with ripped jeans. He started spinning a bit in the chair. "Like this," he said. "Gently."

"You always show up too late."

"But I was there. I was with you tonight." He smiled at me, and I knew I couldn't get up to hug him, or he would disappear. I knew there might be the possibility that I was crazy and hallucinating, but I didn't care. Of course, I knew shrinks would say that this was part of the trauma I hadn't healed yet; that his sudden disappearance didn't allow me to process his loss so that was why I was conjuring him up. But I had a different theory. He was clearly a ghost. I had gone to a shaman who told me that we were strongly connected, and he was still with me. I only told Bonnie about this theory. She was skeptical. So was I.

"You're becoming a bit unhinged, Birdie. You know that, right?" His eyes were soft and piercing at the same time. The fedora man's eyes were just like this. Jeevan had been with me all night in his own twisted way, putting me in my place by channelling himself through hip men. When I looked at him I was reminded of what I was lacking. He was regal, smooth, – at ease.

"I'm not unhinged. I'm just a girl in a big city having a night out on the town."

Jeevan's eyes popped out of his head in a very still way. "Are you happy, Birdie?"

"Oh, for God's sake. You told me to leave, remember? So I left."

"Do you like your life here? Do you like what you're doing?" Jeevan leaned forward like he was trying to penetrate my soul.

"Jeevan, this is all a bit of a cliché. You, coming here, telling me to sort my shit out. Go help someone who actually needs it – like Maya. I'm actually well aware that you're not even here right now."

"Do you remember the last time I saw you? Or should I say, you saw me?"

"No." But I did remember.

"It was in the hospital. Two months ago." Jeevan's voice softened. "You were on morphine."

I closed my eyes and leaned back against the bed. I didn't want to see him anymore. I didn't want to think about hospitals or Jeevan. But I could still hear his voice.

"You've always wanted kids. Birdie, that's big stuff, you know."

"Get lost, Jeevan." I tore off my stockings and threw them at the wall. Jeevan disappeared. I ripped off the bed covers and stripped down to my underwear. Outside the morning was beckoning. A garbage truck emptied the green bins outside my house until they were bare. The past removed itself this way, periodically and noisily until there was only silence. It was a good system. Efficient. The crows lingered, picking up any remaining scraps, listlessly watching as a new day began.

# MAYA

2008

I LIKED to stack my dishes perfectly, row by row. The smell of lemon mixed with chemical comforted me, and I lathered them with care, placing each of them carefully on the dish rack as if they were children being tucked into bed. Then I'd Windex my stove and new marble countertops until they gleamed in every direction. I tilted my head every which way just to make sure there weren't any spots. I finished by sweeping and mopping the floors and then dusting the furniture, even the plants. Sunny said this was all a little much, but this was my ritual every day. This is what consoled me through the days, the seasons, and the years. It was good to take pride in one's home. It implied will, control, and seamlessness to one's life.

I don't know how I became like this, or if I was always like this and my habits grew, but I got a little panicky when Sunny left a crumb on the kitchen counter. I thought I might implode. I would punish him by not buying bread for a week and telling him to eat oatmeal. It was sticky, less likely to get away from you or wander off across the floor.

After dinner, I would grab a Dr. Pepper out of the fridge, open the pantry, and choose my escape for the night. Everything in there was organized row by row: candy bars, Wagon Wheels and various chips. I liked the classic flavours of ketchup and sour cream and onion. I wasn't into these flavours Sarika brought back from England – roasted lamb and all that weird crap. If I wanted lamb, I would just go out and buy a leg of lamb.

I would then sink into the couch, turn on the TV, and watch *Entertainment Tonight* right at 7:00 p.m. I liked watching stories of all those skinny, vacuous morons getting cheated on and ending up in rehab. Lately, I was obsessed with how Madonna was trying to hold on to her youth by wearing leotards. At least my life was consistent. Sunny used to join me sometimes, but he was always too nice about celebrities, and I was too accusing of him finding them attractive.

We would have dinner together. He got a stellar meal every night. I had all these recipe books and then there was so much on the internet. Potatoes were roasted in goose fat on a Tuesday night to accompany some sort of roasted meat with fairly outstanding gravy to go with it. Wednesday was curry night – that week it was butter chicken. There was always dessert, but sometimes he wouldn't eat it. His loss.

We talked a little at dinner, mostly about the dinner itself, or movies. I liked to complain about Kelsey, the receptionist at work who drove a Mercedes and had long, fake red nails that clicked awkwardly against the keys when she typed. Her greasy husband brought flowers for her randomly. I was certain he was cheating on her, but Sunny said I was too cynical. Occasionally, I'd ask Sunny about his work and he'd just say "good" because he knew I didn't really want to know more. To be honest, I didn't really know what he did at that pulp mill. People would ask, "What does he do?" I thought, *Well, I don't really know what he does. He works at the pulp mill like my dad did, and he makes decent money and I clean teeth, so who cares?* Sometimes Sunny would go to the movies by himself. I told him that was weird and creepy. What if he sat behind some teenage girls that thought he was perving on them? But he said it helped him decompress.

We were like a quintessential fifties couple. We knew our places and got on with our days. What more was there to life than living out the seasons with immediacy and precision? My goals were simple:

remembering to take out the garbage, seasoning food properly, and being on time for work. So much of my life had been complicated by the past, or by some glorified unattainable future.

We never spoke anymore about having a baby. It had been a few years since the abortion, which I obviously never told him about. I genuinely tried to get pregnant after that. I saw the doctor, followed my cycles, ate all the right foods, and let him touch me when it was necessary. I tried to be a good person for him, whatever that meant. After some time, it seemed like it was too late to undo the past. I had messed up badly, and all I could really do then was cook, keep the house clean, and try to be as nice as I could be within the confines of what I was capable of. We went on like this for quite some time, and it was okay – until Sunny started to change everything.

It happened in such progressive stages I didn't even realize what was happening. First, he started going to the gym instead of going to the movies. I didn't even notice that he was getting leaner and more muscular until he got out of the shower one day. "You have abs," I noted in surprise.

"I made this friend at the gym. Actually, he used to be a personal trainer, and he's showing me how to work out." Brody was his name. What a stupid name. Brody was from Vancouver and had just transferred here. He was a doctor. They needed doctors, and I'm sure they begged him to come. He had that arrogance about him, that entitled demand for respect because he was a professional from the city. A big fish in a small pond.

Brody was single and into going out for a beer or two every night of the week. Sunny started going with him. "He's lonely," Sunny said when I commented on his dwindling presence at my evening television routines. After a couple of months, Brody insisted we meet. I don't think Sunny was actually into it. I sensed he would get embarrassed when Brody finally saw me, and that up until then he had been coasting along – projecting a distorted image of who he'd like to be. "You wanna join us at the pub?"

The idea of sipping beer with meatheads in a room with sticky floors did not appeal to me. "He can come here for dinner."

"Sure, but he doesn't eat really heavy food. Keep it light."

Sunny had never told me how to cook before.

Brody was exactly how I imagined him to be – buffed up and plastic looking – and he loved talking. He talked about medicine, politics, his travels, and more. He didn't even notice that I wasn't listening or that I left the room several times. He only asked me questions that could be redirected back to himself. "Did you buy that teapot from Thailand? One time I went to Thailand . . ." and so on. Sunny gazed at him with an admiration I had never seen before. I was jealous and fascinated at the same time.

At one point, I went outside for a really long time to take out the garbage. When I came back, he was describing neuroplasticity. He said we could unlearn our childhood history of low expectations, so we could reconfigure the neural pathways in our brains to want and desire more. I was certain he had read some article in a medical journal and therefore thought he was a brain specialist.

"We just need to explore new ways of being and then we can make better choices." Brody looked at Sunny and then looked at me. He gazed at my oversized orange sweatshirt that made me look like a big M&M. I'm sure he was indirectly referring to Sunny's choice in me. Ironically, I would have loved for Sunny to make this friend a long time ago, but it was about a decade too late.

Then he started talking about driving Sunny to Vancouver for therapy to help him "heal" his past. I was somewhat alarmed by his ideas, and I didn't trust people who didn't eat my food. He kept talking while spreading bits of apple pie around his plate like a child. I had worked hard on that crust and made it from scratch. I imagined he talked his way out of everything and no one could be bothered to challenge him.

"Don't like your pie, Brody?" I wanted to display my disinterest in his musings. I realized then that I was similar to my mother; I didn't like many people.

"Uh, yeah. It's delicious. I'm just really full though. I'm not used to having a full roast dinner on a Tuesday night. It was good though. The biscuits and gravy were good." He smiled at Sunny but he wouldn't really look at me, so I stared at his dyed blonde tips. They were spiky and shone brighter than my countertops. Nothing should shine brighter than those.

"Anyway, I should make a move." He got up and the table jerked, causing a bit of pie crust to fly off the plate onto the floor. "But Sunny, you should do this road trip with me to check out a few therapy sessions with my uncle, who's actually a specialist in this stuff."

"What about healing *my* childhood? Am I invited?"

He laughed awkwardly, possibly terrified at the prospect of me sitting in the front seat of his car with a bag of gummy bears. "Thanks for dinner, Maya." He bolted out the door quickly before I could say anything else.

Sunny grabbed a cloth to clean Brody's crumbs off the floor. "I think I might go."

"What?" I watched through the window as Brody got in the car and looked at himself in the rear-view mirror to smooth out a few of his tips.

"I think I might go to Vancouver with him. I'm due for some time off, and you don't want to go anywhere anyway. And I have stuff I could figure out." He looked like a little boy scrubbing the floor, asking for my permission but not looking me in the eye.

"What stuff do you have to figure out?" I was intrigued by what he might come up with after all these years of being a passenger in the backseat of his own life.

"I think I have stuff with my parents. You know they were traditional parents who expected things of us, but then didn't give us much back. I don't know. . . . I just think it might be interesting."

"And you're coming up with this now?" I sat down at the table and sliced myself another generous piece of pie. This was better than *Entertainment Tonight*, observing this new idea flourish into Sunny having a midlife crisis and actually having a meltdown. I pictured

Sunny and Brody holding hands in a group circle, crying into mugs of cold coffee, and having all sorts of coloured wires and neon probes taped to their heads.

"Yeah, I'm coming up with this now." He looked at my pie and looked back at me, as I shoved a bite into my mouth. He had been doing this a little bit lately – watching me eat. Maybe even judging. "So . . . okay, I'm gonna book it."

"Okay, fine." I smiled at him. I must have known on some level that I was losing him. It was obvious to me that Sunny had been talking to Brody about our problems. I don't know why I had thought so little of his capacity to question his happiness. I felt deceived even though all the signs were there.

He left for Vancouver with Brody in August. I watched him get into Brody's car, noticing his hair was gelled up like Brody's and that his T-shirt was plain black and slim fitting. He said he'd be back in ten days or so and that they wanted a few extra days to explore Vancouver Island.

I took that time to do some things for myself – like go to the grocery store. I didn't need to cook much while he was gone. I bought pre-made ribs, creamy mashed potatoes that just needed to be heated up, along with bags of cheese puffs because Sunny wouldn't be around to watch me lick my orange fingers. I stocked up on chocolate bars, cookies, and pastries from my favourite bakery. My work wasn't used to me taking time off, so they believed me when I said I was really ill. After going through all of my eighties movies, I indulged in several different daytime soaps. Why did Hope from *Days of Our Lives* look the same after all these years?

I went to see Mom and Dad a couple of days before Sunny was meant to come back. It was a painful obligation, but I had to do it since my sister had run off to a foreign country. It was Mom's fake birthday since she didn't know her real one and had to make one up when she immigrated to Canada. I brought her a strawberry cheese-cake. "How old are you, Mom?" I cut up the cake in generous pieces.

"I don't know." She was kinda like me, sitting there watching her stupid Indian soaps and wearing a turmeric-stained Roots sweatshirt that was one of my hand-me-downs. "Maya, what's wrong with you?" This was always the question Mom posed to me when I walked through the front door. "You look like you haven't combed your hair."

"My hair is like yours, Mom. Frizzy."

She looked at me for a moment and then went and poured me some chai. She handed me the cup and sat down. Normally, she had verbal diarrhea but this time she chose her words carefully. "Maya, you're so . . . fat. You've become so fat. I didn't want to say anything."

"You always tell me I'm fat. What are you talking about?"

"No, this is too much. You are really fat. You look terrible. No wonder you can't get pregnant. No good for you. That wedding a couple of weeks ago, everyone was looking at you in that bright pink sari. You just looked so fat. Your face looks fat. Me and your dad are worried about you." It was true that I should have worn a Punjabi suit that night instead of the sari. It was far too tight and people were staring at my overhang when I dropped my purse and bent over to pick it up.

Dad was rewiring a broken radio. He looked up at me sympathetically. "Maya, we love you. Please don't take offence, but you need to think about your health. It's no good." He looked like the radio: a bit dated, out of place, and in need of rewiring himself because he wasn't sure how to conduct himself properly in this new day and age.

"Okay." What could I say? I was fat. And not in that lovely shapely way that suited some women just fine. I was obese and unhealthy looking. I had bad skin and puffy eyes. I wasn't going to appease him or make him feel better the way Sarika did.

"How's Sunny?" my dad asked.

He always knew when something was up.

"He's fine."

I never told them he went away.

There were long silences after that with Mom and Dad both

engaged in the soap. Indian soaps were very dramatic. Lots of close-up screenshots of the villain or evil mother-in-law and lots of dramatic music. They had given up too; that was their final plea. I took a bag of frozen samosas from the freezer and left.

Sunny called me the next day to tell me that he'd be staying for a couple of weeks longer, and that therapy was helping him. "What did you tell work?" I asked.

There was a long pause at the other end of the phone. "I took a leave of absence."

"Did you do that before you left or just now?" I asked him accusingly.

"Well, I left with an open-ended return date."

I had never accused Sunny of lying before. I never had to. One time he called me from work because a colleague was flirting with him, and he didn't know what to do. He wanted to come home because he was scared she would ask him to have an affair. I laughed my head off for days. This was the first time I had sensed distance; this questioning of his life circumstances. It was the one thing I had always wished for – but at that moment I wanted to erase. I wished Brody had never infiltrated our lives or Sunny's neural pathways.

"Well, we can't really afford for you to be away," I said. That was weak.

"We have tons of money, and I haven't taken time off in years, and you know it." There was another pause and crackling on the phone. I could hear sprinklers go off outside and a baby crying in the distance. Leaves fell from the tree out front – an early fall.

"Okay then," I said.

"Okay. Goodbye."

The phone went dead.

I ruminated over what he was actually processing other than his pathetic marriage. Was he discussing his childhood? He had never really complained about it. His sister married a perfect Indian doctor, and his father moved with her to New York, which was highly unusual for an Indian family. He should have been living with his son, but his dad never liked me. Sunny never said much about it all, but maybe this upset him.

He was gone for over a month. When he came back, I pretended nothing had changed, even though everything had. There was a wall. He traded in all his weird T-shirts for plain white, black, or grey ones. He was harder and more certain. He didn't tell me a lot about the therapy or what he had done over there. I was only told "a surprising amount of stuff had surfaced," and he and Brody had done a lot of sightseeing. I knew it was over when he wouldn't eat the fettuccine Alfredo I cooked for him. "It's too rich, Maya. The food you cook is too rich." For me, rejecting my food was more personal than rejecting my body; it was all I had left to define me.

It ended on a weeknight in the most undramatic fashion. There was nothing thrown – no tears or revelations. We were watching the news together. The stock market had crashed three days before in a big way. There were interviews of frenzied business people in suits scurrying around the streets of New York like displaced mice. Sunny shook his head. "Wow, I can't believe it. This is shocking. This is gonna affect millions of jobs, you know. This is bad."

"Well, it won't affect us here in big old Prince George. I'm sure your boss at the mill isn't too bothered."

I changed the channel and settled into *Entertainment Tonight* with a packet of licorice and a Dr. Pepper. He looked bothered that I didn't care more about the economy and stared at me while I looked at the screen.

"No gym tonight?"

"No, not tonight."

I offered him a piece of licorice out of politeness.

"Maya, I'm leaving you." There it was.

"Okay."

"Okay? Is that all you have to say?"

"Is that all *you* have to say?" I looked at him. I could see the hardness in his eyes. Did I put it there? Did Brody put it there?

"We can't live like this."

"Like what?"

"Like we're just existing."

That was not the type of sentence Sunny would come up with on his own. "Is that what Brody told you? That we're just 'existing'?"

"Are you happy, Maya? With me? Because you don't look like it."

"Why? Because I'm so fat?"

I saw a look on Sunny's face that I'd been seeing for months. The expression I didn't want to see. Pity. "Did you cheat on me, Sunny? While you were away?"

He didn't get offended. "No, but I thought about it."

"Get out then," I said it in an even voice.

"What?" He looked surprised.

"What the hell did you think I was going to say? I'm happy for you?"

"No, but I thought we'd at least talk about it – like how we haven't been close for months – years to be honest. You don't seem to care about anything anymore. You don't even look like you care right now as I'm saying this to you."

"Do you want me to fight for you, Sunny?"

"No, but I want you to fight for yourself at least. I want you to get some help for the things you don't talk about – like why you're like this."

All of a sudden, I left the room. I mean, I was there physically, but I left. I was outside on the back porch looking at leaves falling off the tree. I was good at leaving. I did this when I used to sleep with Sunny, which was over a year ago. It was a skill to leave, to vacate your body, and to go the other side of the room or outside. I would imagine I was Ariel in the *Little Mermaid* swimming around with dolphins, skinny, and graceful. Every thrust was just a wave pushing me forward. In my imaginary world, I was light, buoyant, and unburdened by the heaviness of my flesh.

"I assume you're going to stay with Brody, so feel free to get your stuff whenever you feel like it when I'm at work."

He hesitated. He wanted to say more but there was nothing else to say. I turned up the volume on the TV and took a sip of my Dr. Pepper. I imagined him in clubs with Brody, wearing matching T-shirts and gazing at svelte, city girls who wore those heels with the little bows on them. I could picture him shy and uncertain when he noticed one of them smiling at him. Revelations would hit him: he was an attractive man, he'd been alone for years, and he'd been limiting himself. I could see it happening all in one moment; the way the light hits a prism and it sparkles in every direction.

He left quietly, taking a duffle bag full of clothes. He stood at the door for a moment, hesitant – like he was waiting for permission from me. He was wearing one of his old Rod Stewart T-shirts. I liked that he was wearing it – that he was leaving my life just as he had come into it – looking displaced, inappropriate, and in the wrong place. Then he left. I felt a solidness when he went out the door that made me complete somehow – more certain of what I had become. I breathed a sigh of relief. I could let go.

I spent a few days feeling a new kind of peace. I didn't have to pretend anymore. I didn't tell anyone about the breakup. I went to work, continued to cook elaborate meals for myself, and went promptly to bed at nine every night. I did get a little freaked out at night sometimes; it was the time I felt my aloneness the most. It was different than when Sunny had just gone for a month. I paced around the house a few times before I went to bed just to make sure no one was there. I thought about strange things while I paced: like how destabilizing it must have been for my mother to not know the day she came to be in this world; and then how she had to lie about her journey on this earth in such a deep way by having a fake birthday and celebrating it. I wondered if that had fragmented her identity in some way and set the tone for the rest of her life.

I went to a Catholic church one Tuesday afternoon. I tried a couple of different ones, and to be honest, as a Sikh I didn't know much about the differences between Catholic, Protestant and all the other denominations. I just liked the big statues in the Catholic ones. But I didn't like Sundays. The rush of loud whiny children being dragged in and old women smelling like rose perfume made me cringe and think God was ambiguous. It was the silence of the church coupled with the echo of clanging doors that made me connect. I gazed at Jesus on his cross, mounted on the wall directly in front of me, but I wouldn't look him directly in the eye. He was too ostentatious with his blood dripping everywhere. There was a Mary statue in the corner which I thought was supposed to be centre stage. She glistened in the dark on her own, marginalized like the other women I knew – like Baby in *Dirty Dancing*. I laughed out loud that I was comparing Mary to Baby. It was that inappropriate laugh that caught people off guard sometimes. It caught me off guard too.

I was wearing Jeevan's socks. They were bright orange and had blue planets on them. I kept a few of his socks and wore them when no one was around, which was quite a lot lately. What would he think of all this? What would he say to me? It wouldn't be as overt as everyone else. It wouldn't be "Lose weight, Maya" or "Fight for him, Maya." It would be something else. It would be "What do you want, Maya? *What do you want?*" I would clutch my cross and turn my back on his silly question. At that moment, he was in an urn adorned with elephants and peacocks in my parents' closet. They had turned a corner of their closet into a shrine with pictures of the Sikh gurus, Jesus, Buddha, and Jeevan. I had told them to scatter his ashes in their garden, but they avoided the subject. I felt like he was trapped in there; I wanted to free him. He deserved to be outside where he felt the most comfortable. That seemed like a practical place for him to be.

Our last summer together, Jeevan and I were shucking peas from the garden. "Stop eating them all," I said to him.

"Oh Maya, always the overachiever, even when it comes to shucking peas." His face looked ashen and grey.

"You're drinking too much. You look like shit."

"Uncle G is coming over tomorrow. Is that what these peas are for?" Jeevan looked at me with those eyes that made his words expand and fill up the whole room.

"I don't know." I looked at the peas – how green they were. There were eight in one pod.

"Uncle G is kind of an asshole, isn't he?" The pod was veiny, smooth, and hard. It encased the peas nicely, keeping them safe. "Maya?" I wouldn't look at him. "He grabbed me one time."

"What?" My peas flew out of the pod and onto the table.

"We were playing football outside and he tackled me and threw me to the ground. And he grabbed me...down there. He pinned me down."

I started picking up the peas one by one. Jeevan continued. "I mean, it was a couple of years ago, and it was so fast. And I just pushed his hand away and got out from under him. It was okay. I was okay, but it kind of messed me up, you know? He was weird other times too. I didn't tell anyone."

I looked at Jeevan and stared him down like I used to. "Well, I wouldn't make too much of it. He was just messing around. You think too much and then dramatize a perfectly ordinary event."

"Right. Of course." His pale brown eyes shone against his grey face. I felt frozen and numb, swallowed by both his pain and my hollow rejection of it. I called his pain an ordinary event. I saved all the peas instead. I remember picking them all up and placing them carefully back in the pod.

There I was in the church. It too was a perfectly ordinary event. My husband had left me while the stock market had crashed. That made me a modern woman, which I suppose was slightly more extraordinary. I might become a divorcee. How exciting for me, the prospect of having that story. People would feel sorry for me, bringing me casseroles and cakes.

Jeevan did what Jesus did. He put himself on a cross, bled himself out, and got revenge on all of us. He became some deity that we couldn't confront. He chickened out of playing out this story. I felt angry as I left and made my way home. It was raining. Actually, it was pelting down. I stood under an awning and waited. I had walked over in some mild attempt to be physically active.

A yellow taxi pulled up and the driver unrolled the window. "You want a ride, lady? This won't be slowing down anytime soon." He was a harmless looking little Italian man wearing a red baseball cap. He reminded me of Dad.

I had never taken a taxi before. It wasn't the kind of thing Indians did or were allowed to do. Indians talked about people who paid for public transit. It was the strangest thing. It implied a wildness or some sort of indiscretion. One time, Dad's friend saw Sarika get on a bus with Marcy to go to the mall, and the whole town talked about it.

"Why not?" I said, feeling rebellious. I didn't know if I should get in the front or the back. I opted for the back.

"You come from church right now? Some event?" I could tell he was curious because sometimes people thought I was Greek or Iranian with my light skin and eyes.

"No," I said, "Just praying for new beginnings." The truth was that I meant to pray, but I didn't. I couldn't. I chatted about the weather like a normal person – like someone who had taken many taxis in her life. During the short ride home, he told me about missing Sicily, and I lied and told him I had been there once many years ago with my family on a big European holiday.

"Really? Most people don't make it to Sicily when they go to Italy the first time."

I told him my family were world travellers and explorers and that my dad had lived in Italy for three years before he got married. He looked surprised. "You single?"

"Yes, I am." He was quiet as we pulled up in the driveway, processing this idea of this Indian family jet-setting their way through Europe. I decided to give him a big tip of five dollars. I thought this was quite generous for a seven-dollar journey. "Thank you," I said and tried to smile more warmly and generously than I usually did.

He smiled warmly back at me and then said, "Can I say something to you, young lady, with love?"

"Sure," I said certain this elevated version of myself was about to be rewarded with fresh insight.

"You're a beautiful woman. You have a beautiful face, beautiful eyes." He paused, compassion in his voice. "You're just too fat."

That might have been the moment I decided. That was it. I would lose the weight.

# SARIKA

2008

I DIDN'T GO HOME out of guilt. I went because I wanted to. Because it grounded me and reminded me why I left in the first place. I needed the details of that life – those familiar curtains and old lamps from the seventies to source my identity.

The evolution of Christmas in our family astounded me in a peculiar way. Our large, plastic Christmas tree took over the living room and blocked the window out completely. It was garnished with long rectangular wrapped boxes underneath it. These were all cheap chocolates, all the same, that were either given to my parents or would be given to their friends. My parents confused what came from whom as no one labelled any of them. One time they received a box they had just given to someone else a few days before. We knew it was the same one because there was a little blue mark on the corner that shouldn't have been there. This same box was then saved until the following year and regifted to someone else (hopefully someone different). On the rare occasion that we actually opened one of these boxes, the chocolates were often stale, hard, and discoloured.

There were several social gatherings in the Indian community around the holidays. Everyone went over to each other's houses during the week of Christmas leading up to New Year's Day. Years ago, they would just make Indian food. Then they started making a turkey to accompany it. There were various curries and rice and then a dried-out, chewy turkey with a knife sticking out of it that someone had the courage to roast. One time it was served with raspberry jam as the cook didn't know any better. The next year someone added starchy mashed potatoes and stuffing with loads of cumin and garam masala. Eventually Maya took over Christmas Day and told everyone she would provide the "Christian" food.

The social interactions, sadly, were exactly the same – stale and hard to swallow. Mom refused to go to most of them and said she had lived her whole life talking to people she didn't like. She had nothing to left say. Dad missed his friends and invited them over on New Year's Day, knowing I would be roped into being the subservient daughter.

I passed around the plate of Indian sweets to the men. I hated Indian sweets. "Sarika," said one of the men as he stared at my bare legs, "How old are you now?"

"Thirty," I replied reluctantly. "How old are you?"

"Thirty? Time to come back to Canada and settle down. Or have you found an Englishman? And why would you want to live there anyway? Houses are much too small." He continued to gaze at my legs as he took a bright, rectangular, orange sweet off the plate. A few crumbs gathered in his greying moustache as he bit into it. He shifted his gaze off my legs to my boobs. "She really is getting older. She's much darker than Maya, huh?"

"Oh, she's stubborn," said Dad. "She won't let us set her up. Anyway, she'll be fine. Her astrology chart says that her stars are clearing in three months." Everyone laughed. "I got detailed charts done for the girls in India a few months ago. They're quite accurate, actually."

The men proceeded to tease my father for subscribing to such nonsense. He agreed they were probably right. I was irritated by how small he looked in the corner of the room, sitting with his shoulders hunched in his big leather armchair. He would change his opinions constantly to adjust to any situation, abandoning his lofty ideas for the unimaginative ones held by his peers.

I gathered the empty teacups onto a bright silver tray and put a sweet in my mouth without tasting it. Then I went to the bathroom with my purse. I took out one of my little mini bottles of vodka and downed it. It was my new thing. It didn't really smell if you followed it up with a strong mint. It wasn't too many calories if you shot it straight. It was four o'clock. This was reasonable to get me through the more challenging situations. I knew it wasn't right, but that was okay.

My mom was in the kitchen frying samosas with a look of contempt on her face. There was flour all down her old turmeric-stained shirt and caked all over her flushed face. Her frizzy hair was tied back loosely, cascading over a thin scarf around her neck that she used to wipe the sweat off her forehead. I silently joined my mother, trying to avoid the spurts of oil flying up at my face. I could see pieces of myself in her features. Same long, straight nose, almond-shaped eyes, sharp chin. I liked to think my own face exuded less anger and hardness – more possibility. At least I hoped it did.

She caught me looking at her and gave me a quick once over. My little denim skirt met her eyes with a look of disapproval. I suppose I wore it on purpose, and then resented all of them for judging me. "Go get the extra bowls from the dining room."

I wasn't going to mess with her. All instructions would be followed promptly and efficiently. I imagined my mother disappearing into the haze of burning oil and running into a meadow somewhere, escaping her role as a dutiful wife and leaving me to take her place as a means of revenge. Not just towards her husband, but towards her daughter for never being there, or for being there at that moment in low-cut denim.

Dad walked in with an empty bowl. "Do we have any more nuts? Is dinner ready soon?"

"You've asked three times already." Mom's face was clenched like a baby's fist. She hated alcohol. Though quite often I slipped her a pear vodka with lemonade, and she pretended to not know there was booze in it. "Why don't *you* come and stand here and start frying? I've been on my feet all day. And how much have you had to drink?"

He ignored her and looked at me. "Sarika, get more peanuts. Make sure you bring the spicy ones this time." He handed me the bowl and walked out. He became something else when he was around his friends. I wanted to go into the living room and tell his friends the truth – that it was all a horrible front – that normally Dad made dhal and did dishes all the time.

I could feel a headache coming on. My limbs felt heavy and so did the empty bowl. I looked around and wanted to wipe everything clean with some Windex, starting from the Las Vegas key ring holder next to the Temples in India calendar – then the family-size bottle of ketchup next to the fake pink carnations on the table. The house was cluttered with a blend of odd, displaced objects used to fill empty spaces and imply abundance.

I opened the pantry and found an alarming array of strange snacks: stale cookies, coloured marshmallows and Indian mixed nuts. I filled the bowl with trail mix that had Smarties and raisins in it. I liked the idea of watching them eat Smarties and stain their tongues purple and green.

Loud drunken laughter came from the living room as I went into the hallway. I dreaded going in there and having that letch stare at my legs again so I tried pulling down my skirt. I hoped Dad hadn't exceeded his two-drink limit. He was a bit of a lightweight when he drank, slurring words and bumping into things. But as I stood in the doorway, I could see he was too busy topping up everyone else's drinks – typical solid square glasses filled with scotch on ice. There they sat, three Indian men, pretending they were back home sitting in forty-degree heat on a work break discussing the value of a rupee.

In actuality, they were discussing the fake fireplace Dad had installed – the real signs of success for male Indian immigrants to Canada – discussions of property value, square footage, multiple mortgages and investments, and brick versus stucco. I had an urge to confront them and tell them they were babbling and slurring about things that didn't matter. They had sold out by walking away from their heritage, their ancestors, and fields rich with texture. And not for something better, but for fake fireplaces and ugly plastic blinds that kept the sun out.

The moustache man was playing with the strap of his ugly gold watch. It was a fake Rolex. His belly burst out of the buttons of his ugly beige shirt. The other man carelessly dribbled his drink down his shirt and onto the carpet as he took a sip. He earned the title Tissue Eater due to an incident when we were growing up when he was so drunk he mistakenly grabbed a tissue and shoved it into his mouth instead of eating the huge mound of chicken he had heaped on his plate. This infuriated Mom to no end, who considered meat a vulgar indulgence and hated being forced to cook it. When we laughed, Mom threatened to shove his chicken in our mouths to shut us up. She later rinsed the chicken with water and made Dad eat it.

But as a woman, the amusement was gone. I had abandoned my mother, who endured lunches where wives didn't exist, while I pursued frivolous dreams that weren't coming true. Why couldn't my father just join the community centre, play card games, and go swimming? I looked at the hideous, framed family photo above the fireplace that had been taken in the eighties at a portrait studio. Mom looked uncomfortable in her sari. I remember she wanted to wear a pants suit because she didn't like wearing Indian clothes in public. Dad proudly put his hands on his son's shoulder, while the rest of us smiled to mask the despair of pretending to know who we were. Jeevan would've been about twelve at the time. He looked like he wanted to leap out of the photo any second, whip off his itchy, collared shirt and escape out the door.

Suddenly I didn't want to be seen in my denim skirt, and I felt hot and claustrophobic as I stood at the door and burped vodka into my sleeve. I craved the raw streets of London again that seemed more familiar to me than this room. I was halted by my father's booming voice behind me. This was a voice he only adopted around these men that always seemed unfamiliar. "Sarika, go get us a bowl of ice."

I turned and looked at him – at all three of them – clinking their scotch glasses together, and at that moment the purpose of my existence came hurtling at me in a flurry of rolling pins, freshly ground coriander, and generations of repressed rage. The words went flying out of my mouth and smacked each of them in the face with a loud thud. "Go get it yourself."

Silence. The tissue eater giggled nervously. The other man looked bewildered as if he was waiting for someone to translate. Dad stopped mid-pour and caught my eye. I felt like a magician's assistant that refused to play along with the big final trick. If only I'd allowed myself to be sawed in half instead of showing the whole audience it wasn't real. I turned around and marched away, imagining myself in the meadow with my mom, knowing what I had done.

IT WAS STRANGE BEING HOME. Everything seemed distorted or out of place, and not just because I was kinda drunk all the time. It was some larger sense of not being sure what was what. The town had sort of turned into a city over the years, and I hadn't noticed. It expanded outwards with a university and big ugly houses and strip malls everywhere. The demographics had changed with even more Indians in the area.

Also, there was hardly any snow on the ground this year. This disturbed me the most. "It makes life easier. Who needs snow?" said Maya.

"But you love snow. What's wrong with you?"

"I can run to the gym now."

Maya was different. She had lost so much weight that she was unrecognizable. She hardly touched any of the fancy food she made on Christmas and soaked in all the compliments on her weight loss. I was happy for her. I guess she was happy too – except that along with the weight, she had disappeared too. It was like her essence had left her when she shed the pounds because there wasn't enough space for it. She had an overly animated smile and her eyes were vacant.

She was also becoming the better sister in everyone's eyes because she was skinnier and married, whereas I was just skinny and getting older. Apparently, the family decided to just tell everyone, including me, that Sunny worked out of town. I said to my parents, "You, don't actually believe that, do you? What is he really doing?"

To which Mom replied, "And where is *your* husband?"

Maya wouldn't tell me about how she lost the weight or what happened with Sunny. Instead she kept telling me about her personal trainer who looked like Jackie Chan. She refused to insult me overtly anymore, but there was an undertone of biting sarcasm. She complimented my blonde streaks by telling me it was bold of me to try something that didn't necessarily suit my dark skin tone. Part of me wondered how she didn't see what was happening to me – that I was unravelling a bit. I thought of telling her I spoke to Jeevan sometimes just to get the stupid grin off her face.

I knew it was strange to sleep in Jeevan's old room even though I was freaked out by his ghostly presence in my life. I thought about the way he used to move so organically in the space around him, and I know I tried to move like him too. The problem was that there was no one to swing me around anymore and remind me that I was a bird. There was no one to move me. Oddly, he never appeared when I was actually in his room. I would lie in his bed staring at the fake stars on his ceiling.

"Jeevan?" His name hung in the air like a low buzz. He had become a stranger.

I wasn't sure if anyone knew him the way I did. The spirit of him was alive in me. I could feel it but only distantly. I tried to catch the feeling or chase it, but it was always behind me a little. I felt like this when I auditioned. I couldn't place the feeling I was looking for, but the yearning for it was so visceral.

It reminded me of this one memory of Dad when I was a teenager. He was digging in our dead garden, but he kept pushing the shovel in further and further and overturning the soil in frustration. He couldn't seem to get in deep enough to find what he was looking for. He wore oversized hiking boots and a plaid shirt, and he looked like a seasoned Canadian lumberjack from the north who, spanning generations here, was coached by his forefathers on how to tend this particular soil. I remember thinking he looked a little silly. He didn't need the hiking boots for this little plot, but he was like that – always compensating – never really being sure how to be, how to look, how to act.

"Dad, what are you looking for?" I had asked.

"Good soil," he said.

"It's the same soil all the way through. You've never changed it."

Gardening was actually Mom's thing, but she gave up on it when Jeevan died. I had thought he might have been looking for Jeevan or Mom's green thumb, or the part of himself he had lost in the overgrown weeds. Eventually he gave up and laid the red shovel on its side next to the garden as if it too had died.

Following the ice incident, he didn't speak to me for a week. I forced him to go out for coffee with me. I was annoyed. I was leaving soon and we'd wasted all this time. And yes, I embarrassed him, but where the hell had he been all these years? After Jeevan died, he buried himself at work or the temple, or in digging around for things he couldn't find.

"Here, take this." He shoved a ten-dollar bill in my hand and unfolded the newspaper in front of him.

"Seriously Dad, I can afford to buy you a coffee."

"No, take it."

I watched him while I stood in the line-up. He looked smaller. He was older – more aware of his fragility. Sometimes I imagined my father as a young boy in India; his bare feet burning against the dry crackling earth beneath him as he made his way to school in forty-degree weather. I could see the same creamy, light brown eyes, long torso, and thin long legs. He washed the same white T-shirt every day. His father had done the best he could, but with a family of seven, shoes were a luxury. Then I tried to imagine him as a young man in the army during the war between India and Pakistan. It was only much later that I found out this information. I asked him why he'd never told me before. He said it never occurred to him.

I wondered if he felt as displaced as I did, with his Seattle Mariners baseball cap covering up his journey, covering up his past. I imagined the colour of his turban – something majestic – maybe royal blue.

"Dad," I said, "Tell me what you're reading."

"I was reading your horoscope."

"What does it say?"

"Well," he said, "It says that love is on the horizon, but you should let your parents pick someone for you."

"Very funny."

"These horoscopes aren't as good as the ones we get from India."

"I bet."

Dad was like me. He went through phases with these things – palm reading, tea leaf readings, astrology. He said he didn't believe in them but actively sought them out, and when a prediction finally came true he would announce, "I knew it!"

He folded the paper. "I'm just kidding, I'm not worried about you. Your fate is up to the universe." He rubbed his eyes and looked down at the table.

"Are you okay, Dad?"

"I'm not sleeping very well," he said. "I keep having these dreams lately. I don't know what they mean. I'm a young boy in India, only twelve, and I'm late for an important exam. I just can't seem to get there. I keep getting distracted. Either I get the time wrong or a rickshaw driver hits me. And then I wake up sweating. I was never late for an exam in my life, so why these dreams? It's like I forgot something."

I felt a painful burst of tenderness for him. I wanted to tell him I understood the importance of metaphor and dreams. "I'm sorry Dad, about the ice."

He looked at me for a moment as if he were making a decision. "You don't know how your mother shouts at me. She drives me crazy.

I make her a cup of chai, there's not enough milk in it or I put too many cloves. 'You left the pot to soak, why didn't you wash it right away?' she says. I like my tea with less milk and more spice, but I make it her way."

I didn't know what to say. "Dad, you need to get out more. Do things on your own."

"It's too late. This started when I was born – I never did things my way. I wanted to divorce your mother."

*Divorce.* This was not a word that had possibility or meaning in their world. It was contained somewhere on its own in an empty white room that had no space to exist in my parents' house or my father's mind. I could feel the walls of my parents' house crumbling, the imposing fake fireplace remaining on its own. "But Dad, you would never get a divorce."

"No. I wouldn't," he said. He picked up his half-full coffee cup and swished it around like a vortex, trying to capture and sort through all the words he had just said to make sense of it all for himself. "And that's okay. That's my life and maybe my destiny. And you have yours. Although our hands are the same, the lines are different. All parents grieve for not knowing where the lines on their children's hands will take them. You left, and I don't know you, and it's okay." He placed the cup on the table and stared down for a moment as if he were looking for answers in my stark red nail polish. I felt inadequate for the smoothness of my fingers, for not having laboured or suffered more. "Grace comes from accepting nothing is ever yours. This was my karma in this life – to learn that."

And what could I possibly say? I imagined him sweating and toiling every night in the exam hall, waking up in a panic when he realized reality was much worse. He was an old man surrounded by plastic and synthetic materials. I should've apologized for my mysterious self-indulgence while he grasped at some sort of dignity. *I'm sorry your only son is dead, that I'm kinda drunk right now, and that your remaining children are empty shells who left you here with this fake fireplace.*

*How dare I strip you of your last morsel of pride by refusing to get a bowl of ice?*

I looked down at his hands that spoke of a love too ravenous for words. These hands had given up personal history to build houses and dreams in the snow. They were coarse with years of labour, full of liver spots and wisdom. The lines on his hands were etched with marks and scars that couldn't be distinguished from the ones he'd been given.

"Dad, you're not drinking your coffee."

"It's too bitter."

"Can we go home and can I make you a nice cup of tea?"

"Yes, and put lots of cloves," he said.

I didn't drink for the rest of my stay. I lay awake at night, sober for the first time in a long time, and stared at my hands under the glow of the lava lamp. I imagined Mom running through a meadow wearing a loose flowing dress, and Dad in some community centre teaching astrology to all his friends. I pondered over the burden of both having choices and not having them, and wondered if it was an unrealistic pursuit for any of us to ever to feel whole.

# MAYA

2008

I DECIDED I NEEDED THERAPY. I decided this in a very logical way, not even because I was fat or because I lost Sunny, but mostly because I was so tired of cleaning all the time. I knew there was something wrong with that. I was getting sick of myself as it was getting worse, chasing myself all the time with cleaning products. Before, I could blame it on Sunny and say how messy he was. But after he left, I knew I had a problem. I got upset at myself when I left prints on a door handle. It's really hard to not touch anything – ever. I stopped eating toast because I couldn't cope with the marks I left on the toaster. When I did clean it, I was taken aback by the distorted image of myself reflected back at me – fatter and even more misshapen than I really was. I felt conflicted about all the clean surfaces in my house, wanting them to be immaculate but being afraid to see myself in them. It was strange because my own self-care was so uneven. My hair was clean but dishevelled. My clothes were washed but outdated.

My doctor looked relieved that I was finally going. "You know, this might go hand in hand with you losing weight. I can recommend someone, but I sense you would take to a therapist better if you found one on your own."

It was true. I was stubborn. It took me a while, but I overheard a patient in the office talk about his therapist. His wife had died seven years ago but he looked happy, except that he had dry mouth and kept getting cavities. I told him my husband lost his mom to cancer and needed to see someone. "I have a lovely psychologist. She looks like Sally Field."

I booked an appointment right away. I was so into Sally Field. She was kind and nurturing, and I loved *Forrest Gump*. It made me cry every time. I hoped she wore floral.

She didn't wear floral. She wore a black pants suit, pearls, and black high heels. She sort of resembled Sally Field. I could see it in her chin and her nose. But she had this obvious determination to keep her eyes level with mine throughout the session. There was a way some people resolutely tried not to look at my fat which created an awkwardness and distance between us immediately. I'm sure if she looked down, she would have noticed the little round turmeric stain on my white cashmere scarf. One time I was on my way out and I decided to give the dhal a stir, and it splattered up onto my scarf. It was a beautiful, soft, flowy scarf that Sunny had bought me for my birthday, and it was such a small stain. That day I wore it with a solid black shirt, which I thought was a good purchase, but when I sat down, the buttons stretched and mounds of flesh popped out between them. Also, my skin had never really seen the sun so it was remarkably pale against the black fabric.

Sally Field asked me how she could help me, kind of like a shoe salesperson. What could I say? I looked around the office. There was a painting of a beach on the wall with a sailboat in the distance, a filing cabinet, and a beige leather couch which looked unused. I imagined myself in the painting: alone on the beach, skinny, and in a polka dot bikini. I almost inappropriately laughed out loud but then I remembered I wasn't doing stuff like that anymore.

"Um, I guess I'm here because my husband left me."

"When did he leave?" Sally sounded tired when she asked this. She was probably thinking if I was skinnier the session would have been more interesting.

"A few days ago."

"Do you know why he left?"

I wanted to ask her if that was a rhetorical question or if she was blind. I had promised not to get angry though, so I thought I'd be matter-of-fact. "Probably because I'm fat."

Sally shifted a little in her chair, but her eyes remained even as if she hadn't noticed. "Oh, is that the reason then?" From that point on I hated Sally Field and couldn't believe I had come to this stupid session. What was I expecting to get out of this? But I pushed on, so I could tell myself later that I had tried.

"Yes, probably. And I was angry all the time. And all I did was cook and clean. And actually, the reason I'm here is not just because he left, and I'm fat, but because instead of losing weight I just clean more." There. I got it all out.

After prodding through details of mine and Sunny's relationship, Sally Field launched into an explanation of what OCD was all about. How it had to do with trying to gain a sense of control over one's life, and how it would make sense that this would be magnified because he was gone. She gave me some pamphlets on OCD, told me she would help me regulate this, and asked me more questions. Was I on an anti-depressant? Had I told her everything? What would give me a sense of control rather than cleaning?

"Exercise. Make plans. Have a hobby." I gave her the answers she was looking for. She handed me a notepad and made me write out a plan of what steps I would take and when. I would go to the community centre and take a drawing class (I lied and told her I liked drawing). I would go to the gym and book a personal trainer. Did she honestly not think I knew how to make a list or plan?

When I stood up to leave, she offered a polished smile. My flesh wasn't bursting out of my buttons anymore so it was easier for her. "We are as powerful as the choices we make, Maya. When you leave here today you are going to make choices that will lead to change. You will become a powerful woman." I wanted to tell her she was not Oprah Winfrey. She was just a white woman, in a redneck Canadian town, who probably had a fairly boring middle-class upbringing and made more money than she knew what to do with. She probably went on tacky cruise ship holidays every year thinking she was cultured, with no regard to all the food they threw away or the poor immigrant staff who only got a day off every month. I bet she didn't know what cumin was, or turmeric for that matter. I bet she thought that stain on my scarf was orange juice.

"Next time we'll talk more about the OCD and how you can manage that. For now, I want you to do your homework."

"Sure." I walked out, knowing I was never going back.

A lot of things happened in those few months. Well, maybe not much happened, depending on how you looked at it. There was the man in the taxi that called me fat and the session with Sally Field. Then there was the news about Sunny. Apparently, he got a job in Vancouver. It was unclear to me what he did, but it was something about working on boats. I wasn't sure how he went from pulp mills to that. Brody was there too, of course. They had left together, probably with matching outfits and hair products. They were a better fit than Sunny and me. It made sense that he should leave, and it was easier for me to not have to see him around town.

Also, Kelsey had gotten a botched nose job. It was too flat. It looked like someone had tried to erase it and stopped halfway through. She didn't get flowers anymore, and she always had a pained look on her face. Her husband worked out of town increasingly. She was a different person – humbler. We had reached some common ground. She was skinny and lonely, and I was fat and lonely. Lonely was lonely. She was the one who ended up giving me the courage to go to the gym.

"I'll go with you the first day, you'll see. You'll love it. You can go to my personal trainer, Riley. He's lovely."

"Oh, I don't want a male personal trainer. I'll feel too awkward. And I'll be too embarrassed to let him assess my layers of fat. He'll watch me huff and puff while I roll around."

"No, honey, he's not like that." Kelsey called me "honey." I used to find it annoying but then I liked it. "He's gay."

"Oh, okay. But I want to go on a weekday when there's not many people, and I need a few days to find a gym outfit that will hold me together."

We went to the gym on a Wednesday at three o'clock. I had never been to a gym before, but I didn't want to tell her that. I was daunted by the machinery that jutted out in all different directions. I felt like I was in the way as Riley showed me around. I politely tried not to walk into things as he gracefully manoeuvred his way through, but I cut my thick ankle on some piece of metal bar. I didn't say anything as my ankle bled. I wasn't sure how people did this. There was a faint smell of sweat and chemicals, awful house music playing in the background, and lime green signs everywhere pointing at different things. It was worse than a club. At least at a club, I could have sugary drinks.

Riley Lee was Chinese and had the best skin I had ever seen. I wanted to ask him why his name was Riley. Kelsey had pretty much abandoned me as soon as we got there and was running on a treadmill in a baby pink sports bra that showed off her boobs. I started having those old feelings of disdain for her, but then I stopped, reminding myself that along with the weight I was trying to dissolve bitterness.

Riley did a bunch of things to me that I didn't really love, such as measuring various parts of my body and forcing me onto a weight scale. He didn't gaze at me with any looks of disgust, so I stepped into a familiar exercise routine for a few days. But then he asked me what I generally ate on a daily basis. I tried to be vague, but he told me it wasn't going to work if I wasn't honest. He made me keep a food diary, and I promised to go see a nutritionist.

I did try for a couple of weeks. I munched on carrots and celery, and I made spinach smoothies with berries. I came up with all sorts of marinades for chicken breast: tandoori chicken, southwest chicken, lemon chicken, garlic chicken, and tarragon chicken. I only lost five pounds in those two weeks which was good according to Riley.

"You need to lose the weight slowly for it to stick." Riley wrapped his little arms around me and gave me a squeeze. He was skinny and short, and it somehow made me feel fatter every time he tried to do it.

Also, the treadmill was so boring. I watched *The Young and the Restless* while I tried to jog but could not stop and gasp at appropriate moments when someone died or came back to life. I had to keep going. It was difficult being this engaged with life and having a purpose. Because I was trying to achieve something other than keeping floors clean, I wanted results immediately.

So, I bought diet pills from the shopping channel one night. I had just finished bingeing on a bag of bacon puffs when I came across this slim, happy couple selling quick results. "Five pounds a week," they promised. *Well, that was better*, I thought. Also, the couple looked really tanned and in love, and they looked like they went on holidays to tropical places. All of these things were implicitly promised to the customer when making the purchase.

I lost the weight a little too quickly, I suppose. I took diet pills, had heart palpitations, and ate lots of cabbage soup. I starved myself and ran on the treadmill until my muscles burned and my bones hurt. I had stretch marks, but I paid a ton of money for some cream from China that actually worked at fading them somewhat. My therapy was action. I cleaned all the cupboards out of junk food and replaced them with cans of diet pop.

Riley became suspicious after a few weeks. "I'm happy for you – that you lost weight – but it all seems a little quick. Are you doing something I don't know about?"

"No, not at all."

He was torn because he knew I was lying, but he thought I looked great. I had lost nineteen pounds in five weeks, and the big rolls were starting to reduce into molehills. They were firmer and smaller. After a month, my face looked different. I looked in the mirror and I was shocked to see it was actually forming an oval shape, and my eyes looked bigger. I didn't feel a lot different on the inside though. I mean I still recorded my soaps, and I suppose I still felt a bit dead inside. I tried to compensate for this by buying some plants and two goldfish in a bowl. I named them Dr. Jekyll and Mr. Hyde. I loved that book. It was one of the only books I had read in school, and I thought there were so many truths to it. We were all hiding grotesque, unintegrated aspects of ourselves, weren't we? We all had wildly inappropriate repressed fantasies and thoughts. The world was driven by and held together by suppression, cake, and diet pills.

I had started going to a Christian church every Sunday, and I wasn't sure why. They had tea and snacks afterwards, and I would sneak little bites. I believed in their cake more than I did in Jesus. I believed if I could figure out this relationship and build on it, I could solve an inherent problem I had with the rest of the world. I envied their worship; their display of unwavering trust when they sang the hymns with their hips swaying and their bodies pulsating – their eyes full of milky optimism. I still felt like a spectator. I was so willing to participate, yet so remarkably unable to. It was like that dream where you are trying to get somewhere, but your feet are firmly planted in the ground. On the way home, I would drive by the Sikh temple feeling guiltily disloyal to the sea of turbans outside and find myself craving Indian sweets. Guru Nanak lived there if I ever wanted to see him. He was patiently waiting for me to come back so he could tell me he was the more understated hero in my story.

After a couple of months, women at church commented on how great I was starting to look. "Maya, you look like a star!" said Brianna. She was super thin and always wore tight turtlenecks that made me anxious.

*No, I look just tolerable now,* I wanted to tell them all. Before, they put up with my fat *and* my Indian heritage. One of those factors was starting to dissolve, so they were elated. One time I brought samosas to a function, and they thought it was pierogis. Another time I brought dahl, and someone asked me if it was flavoured hummus. No one really touched it, but it was an unspoken suggestion that I was accepted on the basis that I did not allude to my Indian background too much.

Other than going to church, I filled my days with routine and discipline, and this seemed to get me through. I watched the pounds come off as the weeks went by. I commended myself on how self-sufficient I was and how impressively I was running a household on my own. I thought of my own mother – bewildered for years after she came from India – as she scuttled up to the cash register to pay for groceries, looking down the whole time, fumbling through her purse, trying to find the right bills. She examined nickels and dimes close to her face just to make sure. The first time I took her to the ATM she jolted a bit when the card came rushing back into her hand. "What will I do when your father passes?" she said. "I don't know how to use a credit card and where is all our gold?" She believed she'd be safe if she could hide the gold between her mattresses instead of a safe at the bank. I had some of it. Tacky gold bangles and necklaces that reminded me of the colour of apple juice.

Nights were more difficult. For the first time in my life, I thought about what safety meant for me. When I stopped cleaning and I turned off the television at eleven o'clock, there was the hum of the refrigerator, the odd car passing by, and nothing else. The absence of ghosts was sometimes worse than the presence of them. I thought about when I had gone to the supermarket with Sunny. We traipsed through the fluorescently lit aisles while I read my list and he grabbed the wrong items. I had planned, in great detail, the baby room: colour schemes, crib, rocking chair, and Winnie the Pooh wallpaper. It had been planned with the absence of longing. Back then, logic was an adequate replacement for desire. I wished for things the way one wishes for items on a grocery list because those things are needed in the house: toilet paper, butter, apples, and baby. It all belonged to the same list.

Sometimes I thought about Jeevan too, which aggravated me. I hated that I wished he could see this metamorphosis taking place in me. It would have been him who took me shopping, making me try on outrageous hats and scarves to accompany some garish outfit he picked out at a thrift store. He would have made me pose for his Polaroid camera and then posted them all over the fridge. Jeevan had always said I would end up being a cantankerous old woman and that it was his job to stop me. "Don't cry over spilt water," he'd say. There was the guilt too – of everything that I had done to him, to Sunny – to everyone. It was muted by the guttural sound of emptiness. I felt his absence – but not the way Sarika did; I felt the absence of myself as if I had only existed or had relevance because of him.

I won't say how much I weighed before the weight loss, but I will say that I lost sixty-four pounds within six months. In that time, I learned to love diet drinks, rice cakes, and grapefruit. Okay, I did not love the grapefruit.

Mom and Dad were both alarmed and pleased by the dramatic change. Dad asked if I had enough money, thinking I was starving to death. "Remember to eat – it's the most important thing – three meals a day. We didn't bring you from India so you could starve yourself. Here." He handed me an apple. "You look very beautiful, just like your sister."

"But don't eat too much either," Mom said. "You look way better." Then she paused. "Have you heard from Sunny?"

I had told them a big long story about how Sunny had to move because he got a way better job in Vancouver and that eventually, he would come back. I think on some level my parents knew; they just didn't want to admit it to themselves.

During that transition time, I didn't buy too many clothes. I wore oversized sweaters and leggings. But it was approaching spring, so I took myself on the shopping trip that Jeevan might have taken me on. Only, I didn't go to thrift stores. Instead, I drove to Vancouver by myself. I convinced myself I couldn't buy nice clothes in Prince George and that was why I needed to go.

While I was walking the streets of downtown, hands full of shopping bags from places I could never shop from before, I was looking for Sunny and his stupid sidekick Brody. I'm not sure it was even Sunny I wanted to shock, but rather Brody. I wanted to make his blonde tips wilt when he realized I was a size seven. I wanted to share my groundbreaking moment in Gap when I tried on a pencil skirt and a clingy white top, and I didn't have any overhang. The salesgirl said I looked like a model (though she was probably trying to sell me stuff). No one had ever called me a model. And I wanted them to see my new haircut; I got it cut in a short bob. I was hesitant but the hairdresser said, "This hair at the bottom screams years of old vibe. Don't you want to get rid of it?" Part of me was rebelling against all the Sikh women that weren't allowed to do it. It was a strict policy in traditional Sikhism to "cherish the gifts" God gave you by not cutting your hair. There were women out there with stubble and beards who adamantly clung to their devotion and endured the ridicule. I was eradicating my past by cutting the edges off. This is what white people did in such a polite way, wasn't it?

I felt like *Amelie* in that French film. Small, uncertain, but ready to be loved. I even felt on the verge of romantic as I tied the belt of my new trench coat and cinched it around my new waist. It was extraordinary having small arms that could fit in such small spaces. There was a power in this lightness – like I could hide and float away. Before I was just too heavy and visible. All of my inadequacies couldn't run away quick enough. This was how Sarika got through life: gliding through like a bird, flitting here and there, and being able to take what she wanted because her presence didn't seem like a hovering imposition.

I thought of her during this time too, but I didn't want to see her again. I saw her briefly at Christmas after I had lost most of the weight. She seemed unhinged – like she had been partying too much. And then she suspiciously grilled me about Sunny and how quickly I'd lost the weight as if *I* were the one who might be unstable. "You look great, but are you eating? You look pale. You shouldn't drink diet drinks." It annoyed me. Why couldn't she celebrate with me just once? When I asked her about the dark circles under her eyes, she shrugged and said, "Tired of London, tired of life."

Maybe I should have been a better big sister and inquired more. Maybe she was trying to be better too. But it seemed we couldn't hold that kind of space for each other. We never could. There was too much between us, and it seemed we were both too tired. We were like Mom's failed garden that was never going to make it, due to dry infertile soil. There were just too many weeds everywhere because it hadn't been tended to. Somewhere in that soil was the story of her doll I had thrown away, along with angry stares and stilted conversations. We were like my turmeric stained scarf – a sort of stain that couldn't be removed.

After three days of intense shopping and watching bad television in my hotel room, I got a bit bored. In the past, I might have gorged on room service or bought an array of snacks and eaten them in bed. I couldn't do that anymore. I tried on one of my outfits and looked in the mirror. It was a bright red V-neck top with a high-waisted, black skirt. Where would I wear this? I looked unrecognizable. For a moment, I got a bit anxious. Who was I? *Anyone I wanted to be,* I heard this voice in my head say. I put on some red lipstick Sarika had given me a long time ago and some boots (I wasn't ready for heels yet). My eyes were big and round like my siblings' eyes, and there was something new there – some sort of spark – or at least a possibility of one. I wouldn't look for Sunny. I would go somewhere else.

I walked through busy downtown streets and felt my body, my limbs, and my gait in this new self. I had never done this before – this much walking. Ever. In Prince George people just drove everywhere, and of course, I always wanted to hide. This new awareness sprung up that I was actually part of the world around me. When someone accidentally bumped into me, I wasn't afraid to smile. People, in general, acknowledged me in ways that implied I belonged to the circle that held normal problems and struggles – like mild disagreements with partners and speeding tickets; not dead brothers and specialty clothing for large people.

I walked for almost two hours noticing people noticing me. A boy on a scooter cut swiftly between me and an older man. I thought of the last time I interacted with a child. I had been struggling to get through a revolving door and he and his friends laughed because I could barely fit. "Sausage roll! Sausage roll can't get through the door!" I realized then that it was nice not to be noticed too.

I wasn't sure what to do. The shops were starting to close, and I wasn't about to go to a restaurant to eat. I ended up at English Bay right on the ocean. I walked right down and stood where the ocean touched the sand. The waves were black and furious but I didn't care. The air was crisp and bitter, and it moved right through me. I shuddered. Getting cold was a new thing for me. I didn't have layers of fat to cushion me anymore. It felt good to be alive. I closed my eyes and listened to the waves crash. I thought of the painting in Sally Field's office and what an idiot she was. I needed to go buy a polka dot bikini. It was always my dream to wear a bikini and run into the ocean. And then I realized something – I was free. I was free of Sunny, of the fat, of my parents, and of that small town. I could do anything I wanted. Maybe I would move here, rent an apartment, and go back to school. I could sell the house. But then I thought of my wrap-around porch, of the brick, of the way the snow glistened in the sun.

I opened my eyes and realized it was too much – all this thinking. I asked myself, *What am I going to do now? Right now.* I didn't need to stand there getting pneumonia in the freezing cold thinking my life away. I headed back up to the busy streets and down to Granville street where all the bars were. I would go have a drink somewhere by myself on a bar stool, kind of like they did in the movies. I could finally fit on a bar stool. I walked by bars that seemed more like clubs with house music oozing out of them. On a corner stood some guys smoking outside of an Irish pub. One of them threw a cigarette butt. It landed on my boot, causing ashes to dust all over it.

"Oh hey, sorry!" The guy had reddish-blonde hair, was tall, and lanky. He couldn't have been more than twenty-eight. His friends smiled.

I started to feel anxious. "It's okay." I was about to quicken my pace.

"Hey, wait! Can I buy you a drink?"

I looked at him and didn't respond, not sure what he meant.

"Is that a yes?" His smile revealed the slightest gap in his front teeth. His eyes were warm.

"Are you serious?"

He looked amused. "Or how about a cigarette?"

One of his friends nudged him and told him to leave me alone. "Dude, she's out of your league."

The boys weren't mocking me at all. They weren't about to throw me into the mud and call me "Paki" or "fattie" or anything else. It was the first time a white man had ever offered me a drink. I was forty-one years old and up until that moment I had seen the world as a menacing place.

"I can't actually. I'm late for something." I enunciated each word as if this might be the first and last time this ever happened to me. "But thank you very much."

I thought of my confusion when I had looked in the mirror earlier. The disjointed feeling of being separate from myself had turned into something good. I walked by a couple of busy bars and wasn't sure about myself. Maybe this outing had already been indulgent enough for me. Achievements had already been made. A white man, much younger than me, had offered to buy me a drink.

A dim red bulb hanging off an awning on a side street drew my attention. Jeevan used to have one just like it in his bedroom. I went over and peered in the window. There were people inside drinking martinis, and I could see there was a bar with stools and a crimson red wall behind it. This was the scene I was looking for.

I walked in and sat at one of the many empty red, cushioned stools. I had never been anywhere like this; Italian-style painted ceilings, luxurious red velvet cushioned booths, and Ella Fitzgerald playing in the background. There were only a few people scattered at tables here and there, looking like they were having covert meetings, possibly about who should die next or where the drugs were stashed.

The bartender looked like he belonged in one of the Gap ads I saw in the display window when I bought my skirt yesterday. He wore a black collared shirt and slim fitting jeans, and he had perfectly coifed brown hair and smooth porcelain-like skin. His eyes were really clear and blue like the ocean I saw in pictures of Hawaii. He was mixing a drink like he was in a science lab; he was very precisely measuring shots, burning an orange peel, and gracefully placing it on the edge of an evenly sugar-coated rim.

I watched him the way I used to watch Mom in the kitchen when I was really little before I started cooking myself. She used to make paneer. She gathered it in cheesecloth at just the right time so it didn't curdle and bunched it up real tight to make sure it was drained properly. Her lips pursed as she concentrated. This was different though – way more fun. This guy was agile. He knew what he was doing, as he darted back and forth to get different garnishes and effortlessly poured without spilling. He knew I was sitting there, but he ignored me for quite some time until he handed the drinks to the server, cleaned his workspace with a cloth, and then abruptly looked up at me.

"Hi, what can I get you?" His eyes were so piercing I almost fell off my stool.

I hadn't looked at a menu yet. I knew nothing about cocktails. But I wasn't going to be a nervous idiot like I had been outside earlier. "I'll have that greenish cocktail you just made."

"You mean the sour apple martini?"

"Yes, that one. And I'll have a bowl of olives too."

"Olives don't really go with that sweet drink." He was patronizing. He could tell I was a bit awkward.

"That's okay, I'll have them anyway." I didn't have a lot of tools for intimidation, so I gave him the stare I used to give to my siblings. It was all I had.

"Okay." He smiled after a few seconds – like I had passed the initiation, and proceeded to make my drink. He served it on a beautiful red cocktail napkin with frilly edges. "You know this drink is almost the colour of your eyes. That why you ordered it?"

I looked at his skin again. His arms were muscular and white, with blue veins sticking out everywhere.

"No, I was just overwhelmed and didn't know what to order. But I do like green apples."

Porcelain Man laughed and leaned in towards me. I could smell his cologne – sharp and sweet – different than Sunny's soapy smell. "What's your name?"

"Amelia," I said. The name rolled off my tongue easily. I imagined Jeevan on one shoulder and Sarika on the other, both of them urging me onwards with anticipation and jealousy at the raging sense of possibilities.

# SARIKA

2009

I'M sure I wasn't the only one who drank at school. There was the caretaker, who often went to the pub at lunch with the special needs teacher. They both came back reeking of smoke and wine. And of course, there was Ross, the American head of science. He was a functional drinker like me, only worse. His bourbon was stowed in the top right-hand drawer of his desk underneath some files. Everyone knew about it. He never went to the pub and avoided all social gatherings because he wanted to drink in private. At least I wasn't in that place yet.

I hated my job – *a lot*. There was no one interesting on staff apart from the PE teacher, who drove a Mini Cooper, and he was only interesting because apparently, he was distantly related to Emily Blunt. Everyone on staff represented what I was desperately trying to grow out of – mundaneness – submission to the mediocrity that I had tried to avoid my whole life. It was no different than walking to high school with Marcy. I stared up at the grey sky on the way to work and found it impossible to imagine, even on the days when the sun tried to break through, that I was living in a benevolent universe.

When I swiped my ID card to open the iron gates, I often wondered, *How have I been in school my whole life?* I had tried getting acting gigs for a little while but nothing came up. When I moved to England I thought brown people were given great roles. The first time I turned on the TV I was shocked to see a whole Indian family on *East-Enders* with proper storylines. It wasn't like back home where Indians were only scripted as taxi drivers or doctors. I was excited. I imagined playing a subversive character, an exotic working-class temptress who lured British men into cobblestone alleyways, away from their middle-class wives who grew up with horses and only ate thin sandwiches. But then I got busy working, and I couldn't keep calling in sick or faking appointments to go to auditions or see agents.

I had tried for a few open auditions in contemporary plays that I thought I might have a chance at. The competition was stiff; the scene there was saturated with desperate, out of work actors of all different ages who actually had impressive portfolios. Why didn't I choose New York? It didn't appeal to me. I wanted the romance of British history that I, as an Indo-Canadian, could never be part of – other than through colonization. Maya had said to me when I first moved there, "You realize you're moving to a country that dominated your people. *Both* sets of people. Do you see a pattern in your life?" She went on some tangent about how I always pursued elusive things.

I gave up my pursuit of acting when one agent told me that, although I was attractive, I still had too much of an "Asian" look.

"What the hell does that mean?" I asked on the verge of tears.

"It just means I can't cast you in certain roles because you don't fit. You don't fit as a stage person because you have an American accent, *and* your skin is a different colour. And unfortunately, the roles we need to fill are still largely white and British. I'm sorry. And you don't sing or dance."

We were sitting in a pub's beer garden when he told me the news. It had been raining and my cigarette was limp and the air smelled damp like stale laundry. He was nice enough to end the relationship in person, unlike previous agents who just sent an email.

"Oh okay, so it's okay that Angelina Jolie played an African woman in a movie? How about that?" I gave him several similar examples, and he shrugged. "Well, what roles do you have going right now? I'm not asking to play bloody Snow White, and I'm not asking to be in historical stuff."

"I got loads. For example, I need women to play Irish Catholic sisters at a funeral in a contemporary play." He paused and gave me a kind smile. "Maybe you'd have better luck back home?"

"What about TV? What about the Indian family in *EastEnders*?" I knew I sounded ridiculous, and I couldn't help it when a tear rolled down my cheek.

"*EastEnders*?" He looked at me like I was a bit nuts. "Yes, there is an Asian family on there, but they're a whole family, see what I mean?" He was chewing on a toothpick and threw it into the ashtray in front of him. "I think they fizzled out for a while, but now they're back." I stared at him blankly and couldn't speak, knowing I was being pathetic and desperate. "I don't know what you want me to say, but you can contact the people on that show and find out." He knew that wasn't really a possibility and obviously thought I was a complete idiot.

He knocked back the rest of his drink and stood up, looking like he couldn't wait to get out of there. I guess the *EastEnders* question was a bad call. "Look, when I write a play myself, I think of the characters in my head as being white. Not because I'm racist, but because I'm white and British myself, so that's what in my head. Don't take it personally. Do you speak the language of your heritage? Is it Hindi? Can you not get into the movies of your people? You're a pretty girl, but then again, you don't sing or dance." He looked down, ruminating to himself. "Right. Do you want me to grab you a drink before I go?"

I wondered if I should report his discrimination to someone, but then what? He was only saying what was true. "Yes, I'll have a double vodka on ice."

I drank vodka from water bottles, mixed with diet tonic or diet Sprite, at break and at lunch. My fantasies bordered on melodrama. I pulled myself into old cathedrals after school sometimes and prayed as if I were a spun-out witch from the 18th century; I hadn't evolved since high school. In my mind, I stepped in and out of characters to create a less bleak picture for myself than the one that I was in. I got my students to act out my fantasies. "Okay, kids. I want you to imagine you're a famous Hollywood actress. How does that look? How does it feel? How do you walk?"

"What is Hollywood, Miss?" one boy asked. He was thirteen years old and from Sudan.

I got tired of putting on school musicals that meant nothing to me. I would change the lines in some of the plays just to make them more amusing or provocative. When we did *Charlie and the Chocolate Factory,* I altered the lines to suggest Mike Teevee's mother was a bit of slut, who threw her kid in front of the TV while she had the repairmen over. Sometimes I would spend my free period in the toilet with my hand against the cold metal door in front of me, thinking about where I would go next. What story could I live in? I would settle for being in an anecdote if it meant change.

I felt bad about being such an ambivalent teacher. I knew I was a hypocrite, a horrible person really, for saying that my ultimate goal in life was to inspire others when I had the perfect platform to do it with those kids. They'd been disillusioned themselves; a majority of them coming from broken homes and experiencing marginalization far greater than anything I had ever experienced. Who was I to complain?

My guilt about the kids combined with my fear about being deported kept me in check ever so slightly. I was functional, at least until five o'clock at night, when I managed to go to the gym and get through supermarket queues. It was nice, in England, being able to buy bananas and vodka in the same place, and not having to go to a separate store. Back home you couldn't really hide your addictions in the same way when you went to the liquor store every day. The checkout person had to smile and pretend it was normal to see you so frequently. Here, you could just add a bottle of booze to your basket along with shampoo and vegetables and no one cared.

I spent my evenings drinking vodka or wine and listening to Nina Simone in my room. Sometimes I did cocaine on my big square mirror.

Phil would come in and tell me his filthy stories, and sometimes I would make up stories as I didn't have them anymore. I had grown tired of all that. I had done my share of online dating and was worn out from the pretense of it all – the politeness of men asking me what I did for a living and how many brothers and sisters I had. And me pretending to care – while all they really wanted was to get into my pants. Dating was a bit like going to the breakfast buffets Maya used to take me to; getting plates and plates of food until it all started to taste the same and you felt a bit sick at the end. The last time I'd gone on a date, the guy got teary-eyed because I looked like his dead ex-wife. Consoling him wasn't really an option after five drinks, so I gave him a tissue and hurried out.

I eventually got my own place. I needed solitude. I don't think I was depressed – not like my sister. I was listless and had lost some sort of hope. It was hope that had always sustained me through the deep-rooted, tragic sense of despair that was infused in my family. They affirmed life was a constant struggle, while some part of me had always believed you could create the life you wanted if you were a good person.

When Mom and Dad heard I had a new place, they decided to come over and stay with me for a few days on their way back from India. It made me laugh when they said they didn't want to ever go there again. They said it was because it was too far away. "But you want to go to Australia," I said.

"That's different," said Dad. The truth was that they were too Canadian now but didn't want to admit it. If it was over twenty degrees Celsius, Dad would complain and put on the air conditioning.

They couldn't handle too much heat and dirt, street food with bad oil, or packed trains and buses that rattled their bones because they shook so much. The beggars were insatiable, easily able to tell that my parents were westernized by their healthy bellies, round faces, and light skin. Instead of being able to celebrate their success stories, they had to feel guilty about what they had left behind.

When they got to my place, my mother narrated her whole experience with disappointment. "The stairs are too narrow. The kitchen is too small. How do you cook in here? Why is there so little water in the toilet? Why is it so hard to flush?" I tried answering her questions soberly but found myself going to the bathroom frequently to top up. I kept the vodka under the bathroom sink in a Windex bottle.

Dad fumbled with the remote for the small TV and asked why I had so few channels and why the windows weren't double glazed. "Get proper things," he said. "You're a professional, and you don't have proper things. Why is everything here so old?" He was upset with my mismatched dishes that came with the furnished flat and the old outdated sofas. "Buy your own place," he said. "You should at least have your own home with nice things." What he meant was if I didn't have a man, I should at least have the security of material things to display some sort of achievement.

"Then what, Dad?"

"Then I can go ahead and die. My job is done." He shoved his fingers in a hole in my bedroom wall. "Do you have any paint? Do you have any plaster?"

I wished I could explain myself in a way they could understand. But who had time for creative pursuits in India? I didn't expect them to get it, and at that time I wasn't sure I did either. I didn't understand why I was pursuing acting, why I had gone there, or what I was looking for.

"You're getting too old," Mom said. "You should be having kids. You need to think about that." I could see the fear in her eyes that I might end up like my barren sister. The death of an immigrant dream after everything they had done for us – barren children. No grandkids, no passing on the family name, and no extended family. *What was it all for?* my mother must have been thinking.

I couldn't tell her the truth – that I wasn't sure what my real dreams originally had been. My move to London had been about some sort of mystical romance being fulfilled, but I wasn't sure I was ready to face what that meant, whether it was having a family of my own or becoming an actress or both. One of my dreams had definitely died and I was trying to live off the embers of another. "I want to see the world, Mom. You don't get it."

I didn't get it either. I was a flake.

I took them out for Indian food. I was sweating under the pink lights of the restaurant as I looked at other people ordering beer and bottles of wine. I tried to order a scotch for Dad so I could get a drink, but he told me he wasn't drinking anymore and that he was focusing on his meditation practice. He got annoyed by the menu and threw it down.

"What is this vindaloo and rogan josh and tikka? I just want a spicy curry, please," he said to the waiter, "With onions and tomatoes. These are made up names by these English, Sarika. Do you understand that?"

"Yes Dad, I understand."

I understood they were angry that I had moved to a country they felt took more than it gave – that it was an unhealthy relationship for me – like England was a boyfriend that I had settled for just because I thought he was cool.

I took them to the British Museum thinking they would be impressed by all the Indian artifacts of paintings, sculptures, and manuscripts. But my mother was appalled. "Look at all the things they stole from us and now they put them here behind this glass case. Show-offs. No shame." The security guard looked startled at her comments, and I had to tell her to keep her voice down. She was right, I suppose. Here it all was on display for tourists all over the world to fawn over without any thought to how it got here in the first place. The East India Company officials had justified their actions by saying they took it all to learn about the customs and history of the people. As a somewhat educated woman, I failed to see the oppressiveness of the glass case and how insulting it was to someone like my mother. I naively pretended a place could overcome its history with charm and beauty. They had a system there of sweeping things under the carpet by encasing them in shiny glass. Maybe that's why I liked it so much there and wanted to hide behind it. My parents didn't realize that they were doing it too, by connecting to their roots through a TV screen with bad Indian soaps that depicted elaborate mansions in Mumbai.

They left England disappointed and this perpetuated my feeling of emptiness. I was so sure of what I would show them there, but I was unsure of what any of it meant to me anymore. The clarity of my convictions had become diluted by the reality of just having to live out every day.

I wasn't sure if I sought love anymore either. I had grown to settle for pleasure. Love created victims and implosions. Pleasure created only a need for more of the same. For a while, I thought I had been curtailing my ability to be the best version of myself by drinking. Now I wasn't sure about that either. Maybe there wasn't much else.

I started reading *Twilight* novels as my way of replacing hope with fantasy. Of course, I couldn't tell anyone about this. I read some dumb article that attributed the success of the series to the economic crash of 2008. It claimed that there was a historical correlation between economic crisis and the success of fantasy fiction and films. Apparently, vampire related things always did well when the economy was poor. It sounded preposterous.

Yet as I sat there eating dry popcorn and thinking of Bella and Edward flying through the wilderness together and justifying the eating of innocent animals, I thought maybe there was something to it. There they were with their ivory skin, timeless in their love. There wasn't that pervasive sense of fear of what might happen after. They were invincible to death and poverty and the constraints of time, so in the end, the dream could continue for the reader without fear or vulnerability.

*Twilight* mothers all over the world had gatherings and parties while their husbands watched porn or went to the pub. Afterwards they would get cheap home facials and stare in the mirror at the newly formed wrinkles on their faces and their sagging breasts. They would brush aside the raw feelings that were just under the surface – that men didn't look at them on the street anymore. They ignored when their husbands, who loved them dearly, gazed at the waitress who was perky, sweet, and still untainted by motherhood, age, and loss.

But for me, it was okay reading these books. I wasn't a mother, or a wife, and I still looked great. There was something powerful about self-imposed isolation that gave me a sense of place. I could rely on being somewhere else in my stillness. I could etch and pave out different realities for myself right there in that room through characters I could judge and adore. I could experience the fragility of hope through them and be okay.

I went to the pub most Fridays with my staff because it was a change from drinking at home alone and Fridays were the most socially appropriate night to get blind drunk.

We went to the same pub every week called Temperance. It sort of smelled like urine and bleach all the time, but the drinks were cheap. Teachers in England were a funny breed. They were all pent up from yelling and freaking out all day at the kids – their bodies all boxy and tense, their voices strained – veins pulsating through their temples. But at three o'clock on a Friday, all bets were off. They got changed into jeans and were at the pub by 3:45 p.m. You could see the bodily shifts within an hour – shoulders would sag, eyes would soften, bodies would open. It's funny how people begin to trust each other after a couple of drinks – how there is a readiness to embrace the other's flaws and see the good. Sometimes I wished I wouldn't drink so I could just observe this transformation.

One Friday in November, I thought I'd just head straight home and listen to some Guns and Roses, maybe watch the "November Rain" video, and drink some really good red wine. I had a half a gram of coke leftover from the previous weekend, but I thought better of it. I needed to pretend to myself I was on the brink of being normal.

I sat sandwiched between the boring history teacher and the even more boring English teacher. They both went on about aspirational teaching (as opposed to inspirational teaching) and how important it was to set long-term targets. I wanted to stab both of them with a fork.

Instead I stared at the young couple at the next table. The girl wore purple stockings and a purple beret and the guy had on an oversized green blazer that he probably bought at a thrift shop. He had his hand on her knee, and he kept kissing her every few minutes in between his jokes and stories. Although she was listening to what he was saying and laughing, her eyes were busy darting around the room. His eyes were completely transfixed on her. They couldn't have been more than twenty. I envied her and the way he leaned into her. She didn't have to do anything to sustain his adoration. They looked like theatre students or something, by the way they were dressed, and the way they were speaking about matters of the world as if they understood hardship. Of course, I knew nothing about them and was making huge assumptions about their happiness in an effort to mask my projections of envy. But still, there was something about their youth – that naïve innocence where dreams were not skittish shadows in the night – where they still had sparkle and shape. I wanted to walk over and tell her she was taking this moment for granted, that there may be a handful more like this, but soon she would become complacent or jaded – or worse – irrelevant. I wanted to tell her that as you got older, time was one big freight train that kept gathering all your shit and had speed too, and it could topple you over unexpectedly if you didn't pay attention. There was nothing worthwhile about being stoic. I was only in my thirties, and I was feeling all of this already. Where would I go from here?

The pub itself was cavernous and cold and had high vaulted ceilings. It used to be a cathedral. I went to the bar and waited my turn for my drink. It took ages to get a drink, even if there were twenty staff members working or if it was midday and no one was there. There was an extensive cocktail menu but no one knew how to make any of the cocktails.

"I'll have a mojito," I said to the mousy girl behind the bar.

"Sure. Is it okay if it doesn't have any mint?" She had a wooden demeanor, like she'd been working there too long and it was too late to leave – a bit like me.

"Are you serious?" I laughed. She didn't say anything. "Well what's in it then?"

She looked at me like I was wasting her time. "Lime, soda . . . rum."

"I wouldn't do that if I were you." A voice came from the right of me. It was a wiry man in a suit wearing a pungent aftershave, probably a city worker on his way home. He had blonde hair and a bit of an outdated boy band hairdo. "I would stick to something quite basic if you know what I mean." He winked. His eyes were a bit crinkly and nice – a reddish brown. He looked quite a bit older than me but handsome. I was taken with him instantly. I felt the proverbial gut flutter. I hadn't felt that in a long time, maybe years.

"You buying?"

"Sure, but not that." He had a really smooth deep voice like the kind that should be on the radio or doing voiceovers.

"I'll have a gin and tonic."

"Great make that two." He didn't take his eyes off me while he said it.

The lady at the bar looked thoroughly unimpressed by our rather unimaginative flirtation. "Single or double?"

"Definitely double," he said.

I looked back over at the young couple, who were now joined by friends. They laughed fearlessly and looked like an ad for something promising. "My name is Sarika." I stretched out my hand to this man, who looked at me with anticipation, in the way the boy in the blazer looked at the girl in the beret.

"I'm Tom."

He held my hand for a moment, and I knew then, that there was a little bit of story left in me after all. It was a feeling.

# MAYA

2009

IT WAS QUITE easy the way the lies came out of my mouth, but they weren't really lies. I really was Amelia, or at least I felt like her. She was the new me. Maya wasn't even such a bad sounding name – that was the funny part. There were far worse Indian names out there with "deep" or "inder" hanging off the end. I guess it was about wanting to be the French girl in that movie without being too obvious, and a desire to forge a new identity. I wondered if Mom ever felt like that about her fake birthday.

I went to the martini bar three nights in a row and flirted with the Porcelain Man, Steven. I had no expectations. In fact, I was terrified by his presence – really, by the mere idea of him. However, because I was in a new city, and there was a bar between us, with me on one side and him on the other, it seemed okay. I wanted to know what it was like to flirt with someone so I could assess what was supposed to happen in these situations. When he made a joke was I always supposed to laugh, or should I tell him he was full of himself? It was nice to sort of be on dates without the pressure. I had time to observe him and monitor myself while he served other customers. I never got to do this with Sunny because there was never any nervousness. That was the consequence of both of us settling for someone and neither one of us wanting to admit it to ourselves.

Steven would bring me a bowl of olives as soon as I was seated. It didn't matter where in the room I was or how busy he was. He understood the power of attention to detail. Eye contact, meaningful looks across the room, and his hand on my arm while we spoke. He was profound, articulate, and graceful. He was basically the opposite of me. He told me he had a dancing background too, and he was in the Nutcracker every year. I tried to be regal and not slouch while I sat on the bar stool.

On the third night, he knew I was leaving to go back to Prince George in the morning, so he asked me to go for a walk after his shift. He held my hand, and we walked for hours through cute little streets in the West End. We looked at old heritage homes of all different colours – reds, yellows and blues – Lego colours. We didn't have anything like this back home.

The streets were filled with cherry blossoms that curved and formed archways. There had been a windstorm the day before so everything was covered in pink: the streets, the cars, the branches and the balconies. The way it was so bright, even at two in the morning, it reminded me of snow. "You're lucky," said Steven, "That you grew up with snow. It's so beautiful. It's so dull and grey here. It just rains all the time."

In the short time I knew him, I sensed Steven had a chip on his shoulder. Maybe really good-looking people were simply allowed to be like this. He complained a lot. "I'm thirty-six, you know." He said this like it was a major confession, so I lied about my age too and told him I was thirty-four. "But I'm training to be a physiotherapist. I only work there to earn a bit of extra cash."

"There's nothing wrong with working there."

"Sure, of course. Actually, I'm an artist too. I paint."

"Great." It seemed like he was trying to make a big impression on me. If only he knew all I could think about was his white hand over my beige one. The contrast was so striking to me, and I was so taken by it. That, and the fairy-tale pink leaves and rainbow houses. I couldn't be bothered worrying about what he did for a living.

"You're quiet. What are you thinking about?" he asked.

"Oh, just how I have to drive back tomorrow."

"You need to come back. It's so amazing meeting you. We have a connection. Do you feel it?" He said this with urgency and I wanted to laugh.

I wasn't sure what the feeling was, but I liked it. And when he kissed me there on that magical street, I felt like all the months of treadmills and rice cakes had paid off. This was more than I could ever hope for.

I drove to back to see him a month later and told work it was a family emergency to do with my sister. Kelsey hooked me up to stay in her sister's apartment that overlooked the beach. "It's okay. She's gone for six months of the year. Enjoy. Just don't get anything on her Italian furniture. I'm so proud of you." She handed me the keys and winked. She had already moved on herself with a dentist she met at a conference.

It was easy an eight-hour drive. The roads were clear. Spots of snow pervaded the landscape, and the mountains looked blue from a distance. Spring looked clean when you felt romantic, but I could still feel the struggle for things to come to life. I was happy probably for the first time in my life. I still had my old Pontiac that had a tape deck and turned on one of my old mixtapes that had eighties love songs on it.

I stopped along the way and ate my homemade salad as I sat on the hood of the car. I thought about the times we used to go on family road trips and stopped at Dairy Queen for a treat after eating spicy potatoes and roti for lunch with warm soda. I remember more snow being on the mountains back then and thinking it was beautiful. Jeevan would talk about how one day he'd go skiing like white people, and he wondered what the view would be like from up there. "I wonder what it's like to breathe up there?" he said. He often started sentences with, "I wonder . . ." and it would drive Mom and Dad crazy as they just wanted peace in the car.

"I wonder if you should shut up?" I said once.

"Maya," he said, "It's wonder that sparks imagination. It's wonder that created telephones and electricity."

"What are you going to create then?" said Dad from the driver's seat.

"Some sort of pill to get this family to cheer up," he said. Sarika was little then and she was the only one who laughed hysterically at his jokes.

I had a beautiful moment then, there on the winding roads surrounded by the jaded landscape. The wind was cold, but it opened up my lungs. I was somehow grateful for the memories, for the looming mountains, for what my family had given me. They had pushed me in ways I never considered. Each one of them had brought me here.

I played it cool by telling Steven I had to come into town for a wedding. I didn't want to freak him out even though he'd been texting me almost daily. We met every day and had fun dates around the city. We walked through Stanley Park and went to cute food markets. We went on long hikes, rented bikes, and rode around the city in the freezing cold. I hated that last part but pretended to like it. He took me to offbeat cinemas and made me watch a lot of foreign films. He seemed like the kind of guy Sarika would go for. Maybe this was the kind of man she dated.

At night, if he was working, I'd sit in his bar with a book and pretend to read. But really, I would just stare at him while he flirted with everyone so he could get more tips. It was harder seeing him in that context than being alone with him because it highlighted my insecurities. Why was he spending all this time with me when he could have anyone? He often caught me staring at him. "Here, can you please water the tables?" He handed me a jug. The staff didn't quite know what to make of me. I couldn't tell what they thought of us.

"How much do you know about him?" one server asked. I could hear the curiosity in her voice.

"What should I know? Are there other girls that come sit at the bar and wait for him?" Maybe I was making a fool of myself.

The girl laughed. "A lot of girls like him, but he's never let one hang around like this. Well, see what happens I guess. No one can really figure him out." He seemed well-liked, but I could sense his intentional distance from everyone. Maybe I was on a reality show right now that Sarika had orchestrated. This was the sort of thing she might do to get back at me for becoming thin. I looked around the room for cameras.

I wasn't sure what Steven was so interested in, as he didn't seem to know much about me and did most of the talking. He told me how beautiful I was and took me shopping to buy matching hats and scarves. "You need to accentuate what you have."

He loved food, all different kinds, which was one thing we shared. He loved spices and talked about what herbs went with which meat. He said he was disgusted with himself that he liked meat but said he couldn't help it. Unfortunately, he had a gluten intolerance (though I wondered if he was making this up) and said he couldn't eat cooked tomatoes. There was something about how they changed chemically when they were cooked. So, he wasn't really into Indian food which initially stressed me out a bit.

We went on lots of sushi dates. I wanted to tell him Indians didn't eat raw fish and that I hated sushi, but I didn't and ate it anyway. Sometimes I had to go to the bathroom and throw up, as I wasn't used to eating that much rice. In fact, I had to throw up a lot, as the man loved eating and my body just wasn't used to all that food. I had to be careful. Throwing up is something I never thought I'd resort to, but I promised myself I'd only reserve it for special circumstances. One night a woman at a French restaurant could hear me as she was washing her hands. She gave me a sympathetic look when I came out. "You don't need to be doing that," she said.

I smiled back at her and tried to telepathically convey everything I had done to get me to this singular moment: on a date, in a restaurant, with this man. "I have the flu."

"One day you can come over, and I'll show you my art and cook for you," Steven said to me towards the end of the week. It was strange, but we only met in his bar or went out. He never invited me to his place. "I live in Point Grey. It's a bit far away."

I looked on a map. "It's not that far." But he didn't press and neither did I.

I stared at his hands a lot when he touched me. His veins were so different from Indian ones, so pronounced that they popped out of his skin. His muscular body glowed in every light. When he walked me to the apartment every night, he didn't expect to be invited in. "I like that you respect yourself. I'm happy to wait," he said as he kissed my cheek. He made the decision for me, it seemed. Oddly, he was in no rush. I wasn't sure if he knew that I was nervous about it.

When he finally stayed over, it was my idea. It was my last night in town. He cooked a meal for me first – of risotto with peas, pancetta, and truffle oil. He made love the way he made a meal – with detail, precision, and effort; he really put himself into the presentation. Then he detached and curled up into his corner of the bed. I was surprised at how ordinary it was. I expected to feel more because the otherness of him was such a contrast to Sunny in every way, but the anticipation of it was more intoxicating to me than the actual event. The cherry blossoms, films, and restaurants were more of a revelation. His fascination with me was the mystery I wanted to uncover the most.

"Be my girlfriend," he said the next morning. I laughed at how juvenile it sounded – that I was the object of his passion.

"Don't laugh. I'm serious. Let's make this long-distance thing work."

I stared at his white body – at his chest which had not a single hair on it. I felt that strangeness again, that otherness that made me feel like a young girl. Indians were so hairy – both the men and the women.

"Do you wax your chest?"

"Yes."

He was annoyed and got up.

"I'm sorry," I said. "This is just such a surprise – all of this – it's so fast. Why do you like me, Steven?"

"What's not to like? Please don't tell me you're one of those people that has issues with themselves. Please, Amelia. Life is too short for that." He enunciated my fake, ridiculous name, and I wondered why I didn't choose something ordinary – like Jennifer or Melanie. He was pleading with me to be normal and to keep up the mask.

So, I did. I came to Vancouver once a month to see him for long weekends. There was never any suggestion of him coming to see me. Neither of us brought it up. I shared only parts of my life about home. I couldn't tell him I was a dental hygienist as that seemed too boring. So I told him I was studying psychology, but I was working as a receptionist at a dental office.

"How dull. You must be so bored. You must have to see snivelling, whiny kids who come kicking and screaming and beg for treats." Steven thought kids were vile. He said didn't have time for them and didn't understand why people procreated. "It's just so selfish and self-indulgent. 'Look at me, I've made a mini-version of myself, so I can right all the wrongs of my own childhood, when really I'm just going to screw up another human.'"

I agreed, saying it was overindulgent and the world was overpopulated anyway. "I like how you get things. I like that you're not idealistic and you're real about the world." Somehow, he seemed to understand me fundamentally, even though I lied about my personal history. We shared the same views, only his views were darker and slightly elitist, which allowed me to feel important, but also softer and nicer in comparison to him.

"I bet you were cute when you were little," he said. "I bet you were a rebellious teenager who snuck out all the time to join rallies and protests." I didn't tell him that there were very few protests that I knew of when I was a kid in Prince George, and that I was too busy making dhal and roti for my parents to do any of that. He knew I was

Indian, but he didn't seem to know much about what that might mean
for me. "You're only half Indian, right?"

"No, full."

"Really? You're just so fair, and your eyes . . ."

"My parents are from the north. It happens." I was annoyed and
flattered by his assumptions. I liked the picture he painted of me of
being some outlandish hippie when I had given him no reason to
think so, yet I marvelled at his audacity to construct me the way he
wished. He was a strange man – imposing an identity onto me and
presuming I would just take it on – just like that. I still wasn't sure
why he had chosen me. I think I was like a project to him. "It's
amazing to paint, to know you can create whatever you want when
you have a blank canvas." I think he might have been more control-
ling than me.

I loved to see him once a month, but at the same time I found it
exhausting. Everyone in Vancouver was so skinny and had perfect
teeth, and never before had I seen people so joyful about running. I
wanted to gag when I watched them doing laps around the seawall.
When I went home, I ate grapefruit and rice cakes and caught up on
televisions shows that he would have been mortified to know I was
watching. He had no clue the effort I was making to maintain this
persona that I didn't completely understand.

Spring became a glorious summer in Vancouver, and it was the
cliché setting for the unfolding of a new romance. The blossoms transitioned quickly into lush maple trees. There were the scents and
colours of various flowers that filled the city. Steven and I often just
walked around the city holding hands, with the smell of hot dog
vendors, barbecues, and food trucks in the air, grabbing bits of food
here and there. Or we would sit on a log on the beach and just watch
the tide go in and out. He didn't feel the same need to talk anymore to
fill in the empty gaps.

"You don't need a lot of conversation, do you?" he asked.

"No, I don't." I mostly didn't want to talk much because I couldn't
always remember what lies I had told him and didn't want to contra-

dict myself. I had never thought this relationship would go on for so long or that it *would* turn into a relationship. Aside from concealing my real name, I also hadn't told him I was married – a huge secret that was looming over my head. I kept waiting for him to end it and move on to someone else, but he didn't. After four months, in August, he suggested I meet his parents.

"But I haven't even been to your apartment."

"Is my apartment really that important to you? I didn't realize this was such a thing."

"Well, I just think it's weird I've never seen it." It might have been one of the first times I was honest about something I felt.

"Do you not trust me?"

I thought about his question for a moment. Until he had just mentioned meeting his parents, maybe there was a part of me that thought he was married or something. But then it didn't add up because he spent so much time with me when I was in town. But it was possible. There were stories of men having completely double lives with two different women.

"Yes, I guess I do. But you know I can't use the apartment anymore. Kelsey's sister is coming back to stay there for a while." Kelsey's sister had generously let me use her apartment the whole summer, saying it was good to have someone keep an eye on it.

"Well that's fine. I haven't had you over because I have a room-mate, okay? And he's kind of weird and never goes out, and I need the rent. My place is very dorm-like. It's kind of embarrassing. So there. That's the truth. Happy?"

He literally pointed his chin up and turned away slightly when he was annoyed at me, which made me want to laugh. There were so many things I wanted to laugh at all the time, but the guy took himself so seriously. He was angry because he was such a snob but his standards of how he should live exceeded his reality. He saw this as a huge shortcoming. I realized he was doing his fair share of hiding too.

"You should know I would never care about any of that." As soon as I said it I thought, *Should he know that?* What did either of us really know about me anyway? He knew I valued order and cleanliness the way he did. He had OCD like me. "Amelia, you're moulting. Pick up your hair." He would say this to me if a single hair fell off my head. He also folded things very precisely and was even worse than me when it came to dust and smudges.

"Are you really ready for me to meet your parents?" I asked.

I thought about him meeting *my* parents. I thought about Steven politely taking a bite out of an Indian sweet or stale cookie while Dad talked over the television, which was always on high volume at their house. He watched the news and weather forecast every hour no matter who was over. I thought of Steven looking at the fake flowers and outdated lamps that still had plastic or price tags on them, and me having to explain to my parents that Steven had a gluten intolerance. Dad would pass him a samosa and say, *Don't worry, it's potato. Don't be shy.*

"I don't see this ending soon, do you?" he said. "I can see a life with you." I pushed all those images out of my mind when he said that and realized, right then and there, that although I had changed externally, I had a lot more work to do to fully embrace this new reality for myself. I couldn't quite fathom it, but I knew there was no turning back. I had to see where this would go.

Steven's parents lived on Vancouver Island, in Victoria. They had a quaint little house overlooking the sea. He wouldn't tell me much about them before the visit.

"There's not much to tell. My dad is a butcher and my mom's a lawyer," he said while we were on the ferry over.

"Oh, interesting."

"What? Why's that interesting?" He sounded defensive. It was interesting for many reasons, none of which I could constructively communicate to him in a way that he would consider appropriate. "I don't think what people do for a living is important," he continued. Though it seemed important to him to tell me about his physiotherapy training, but I didn't bring this up. I didn't want him to get all moody.

Victoria was cute with its English-looking parliament buildings and its small urban scene close to the harbour. We took a taxi to their house. "Why can't they just pick us up?" It still confounded me that white people wasted all this money on taxis when they didn't need to. I thought back to that day I took one – the day that changed my life.

"They didn't feel like it."

"Oh. That would never happen in my family. Everyone would come pick us up, maybe cousins too."

He looked a bit alarmed by this idea but was fixated more on our visit with his family. "I hope you like them."

"Don't you mean you hope they like me?"

"They'll love you." He was tapping his foot furiously next me and his whole leg was vibrating. What was he so nervous about? What kind of weirdos were they?

"They might not like me. I can be pretty unlikable, actually. Seriously."

He didn't laugh. Were these people going to kill me? Were they rednecks? Maybe they were racist? I could see the headlines: "Indian dental hygienist disappears after significant weight loss." I laughed a little and then remembered I wasn't supposed to do that anymore.

When we got to their house I was surprised that – on the surface – the house was no different than the one I grew up in. It had faded siding that needed updating and lush green hedges. He took me straight through to the backyard. There were flower pots everywhere. And there was an herb garden with rows that were so concise and evenly spaced as opposed to Mom's old, overgrown plot made with a grow-as-much-as-you-can philosophy.

A tall, burly man with rubber boots and a grey beard came out of the shed that was detached from the house. "My boy!" Steven's dad was like a big bear. His hands were dirty, and he grabbed Steven and hugged him hard without worrying about Steven's pristine white shirt. His presence was completely different from Steven's – big and loose – in a way that surprised me. Then another man came out. He too had a beard, only his was brown and he was much younger.

"Amelia, this is my dad, William, and my brother, Lucas."

"Your brother?" I shook their hands, shocked by the revelations that were unfolding. I somehow didn't know there was a brother, and wasn't sure how that information escaped me.

"Nice. Glad he told you about me. Call me Luke." I was taken aback by these men. Both had the same dazzling blue eyes, only theirs had a bit more sparkle and ease to them. Their skin was tanned and glowing from the sun. Their faces were red and spotted and spoke of the earthiness spilling out of them. I couldn't believe the contrast. "Dad got your shirt all dirty."

Steven tried to look in good humour, but he was tense as he tried to dust off his shirt. "Where's Mom?"

"Folding linens for you." Luke punched Steven on the shoulder. Steven flinched and gave him a deathly stare that beat any of the ones I gave my family. "We don't use cloth napkins unless Steve comes around. If it's just us, we use paper towel." He winked at me and I laughed. I liked him.

When I finally met Steven's mother it all made more sense. She was in the kitchen preparing a platter of cheese. The platter was as elegantly put together as she was. She wore a cream coloured dress that clung to her perfect figure. She might have been a size four. Her face was porcelain-like just like his. She had a pointy nose and chin and blue eyes that weren't quite as soft as her husband's.

"Hello Amelia, welcome. My name is Claire." She kissed both of my cheeks and looked me up and down approvingly, but not in a condescending way. She almost seemed nervous herself.

She led me through to the living room and asked me what I would like to drink, offering me wine or tea or coffee. It was then that I realized, as "white" as I had tried to become in my own house by cooking roast dinners and refusing to put up pictures of Sikh gurus, I was quite sheltered and didn't really know the ways and manners of a white family. The bookshelves, filled with travel books and photos of the family camping and fishing, were a striking contrast to the barrenness of my house that had nothing but two shiny vases on the shelf.

Steven's family was delightful. I would have liked to vilify his mother, at the very least, but I couldn't. She was refined but seemingly enchanted with her husband's down to earth nature. She was a privileged woman who knew who she was. She didn't need to flaunt her success as a lawyer. If we were at an Indian gathering, that would have been the highlight of the conversation. "How much money do you make?" someone would ask.

I expected them to ask me questions in reference to my background, like whether or not I was from a mixed-race family, or if I was vegetarian. But they didn't – maybe because of my fake name. They asked me if I liked to travel and what my hobbies were. I wanted to tell them my hobbies included counting calories and watching *General Hospital*, but instead I told them I wanted to be a psychologist and that I was interested in the human condition. "I know I have at least three personality disorders that I can think of." I laughed awkwardly, and everyone laughed with me, thinking I was joking.

I could tell that they all really loved Steven but there was a concern in the air about how withheld he was. "You gotta get this guy to loosen up," said Luke. He was a mechanic and drove a motorcycle. "Do you want to go for a ride?" he asked at dinner.

I looked at Steven, who arched his back up and continued eating, and I could tell the answer needed to be no. I wasn't sure what Steven's problem was. From what I could see, his family didn't have the same middle class hang ups that he did. His status driven behaviours seemed self-imposed and somewhat isolating.

They asked me questions about him as if I might let them in on his inner world, and I expressed my surprise at this. "I've only actually known him for a few months."

"Well, you must be having an impact on him," said his father. "You're the first woman he's brought home in many years." I looked over at Steven in shock as we sat outside sipping tea. He smiled at me, and his shoulders relaxed. A tension broke around the circle. So this was the secret. It was a big deal to be bringing someone home.

"Really?" I said.

"Really." He grabbed my hand, and I looked up at the sky while I

thought about Sarika's obsession with the moon. I wanted to share
with her that I believed in her fascination with its mysteries, maybe
for the first time.

In bed that night, I thought of everything I had learned about:
different cheeses, serving spoons, and wines that were strategically
paired with flavours. I had witnessed the simplicity of having fresh
grilled vegetables that weren't cooked to death with too many spices. I
had never eaten tender fish before. I wanted to learn how to knit or
crochet as I marvelled over the colourful, handmade blankets
adorning all the sofas in the house. I had been trying so hard to not be
Indian that I had missed the point completely all these years. My
house was empty.

"Your family's lovely, Steven. Why were you so tense around
them?" I thought of the way his father hugged Claire openly in front
of the boys. It had never occurred to me that I had missed that
growing up.

"You don't see everything. It's easy to glance at a snapshot of
someone's life and say that. There are dynamics you don't understand." I thought about the photo of Luke and his dad holding a big
fish together while Steven stood off in the distance. "Also, it was a big
deal bringing you home." He smiled at me again like he did before,
with that relief in his eyes.

I looked at him differently after that. For all his quirks and weird-
ness, he wanted me. "Steven, why do you not ask me more questions
about myself? Don't you want to know more about me? Aren't you
worried I might be a freak?" He never asked questions about my
upbringing, my parents, or my siblings. I had told him about my dead
brother early on. I blurted it out one day when I didn't know what
else to say. He listened but didn't ask about its impact or how it had
shaped me as a person.

"I already know you're a freak, I don't need all the details."

"Seriously, I think there are some things I need to tell you." I
wasn't sure where to begin. I thought of his family, their house, and
how I was already attached to it all. I thought of his hands and the

foreignness of his skin, which I was just getting accustomed to. I imagined him looking at a photo of me three years ago, and I wondered why he didn't notice my extra bits of loose, stretched out skin. Did he just ignore it?

"Okay," he said. "Tell me one thing right now. I'm really tired. Then we sleep." The floorboards creaked below and there was a whisper from the trees outside through the open window. They were telling me it didn't need to be about lies and reinvention, but rather a revised version of myself – no different than the trees and mountains changing shape across the seasons.

"Okay. My name's not Amelia."

# SARIKA

2009

I FELT a bit gutless in those early days of dating Tom. I was thirty-two and hadn't really had a proper boyfriend before. I didn't bother telling him that. Tom and I were good at skirting around issues. He told me he was taking a break from banking and was now a real estate agent, but I figured out he had lost his job during the crash and just couldn't find another one. When I suggested this, he didn't deny it and said, "Does it matter, in the here and now of things?"

I fell in love with him quickly. I wasn't sure if it was because he was passionate about me or if it was because he saw me the way I wanted him to – exotic, impetuous, and maybe even hopeful. He wanted me to explain what it was like being an "Asian" woman. I had to tell him I didn't really know what that meant. I was still getting over how British men objectified Indian women in a gratuitous way, that was equally as strange as Canadian men stereotyping me by assuming I'd get an arranged marriage. Back home there was still a sense I had to apologize for my heritage, but in London I was expected to flaunt it. He took me to the fanciest Indian restaurants to impress me. I didn't particularly want to go for Indian food, but still, I had never really been courted before.

Incidentally, Tom liked to drink too, though maybe not as much me. And he liked a bit of coke. We only saw each other two or three times a week, so it was fine. We got drunk together without him knowing about my issues. But there was the one time we got snowed in, and he couldn't really leave my place. None of the buses were running and the Tube was closed, so he decided to stay. I was getting a bit antsy by one o'clock in the afternoon and gingerly poured myself a vodka, hoping he wouldn't notice.

"Are you drinking again? Babe, we just had a big night that ended at three this morning. Jesus."

I laughed at him and jumped onto his lap and kissed him. "I think it's just because I'm a few years younger than you, and I can handle it."

There was a glimpse of concern on his face, but I knew how to distract him. It had only been a few months, but I knew him. I knew he hated onions even though he loved Indian food. I knew he came from a privileged background and resented that he relied on his inheritance. He didn't believe in his ability to make it in the world, and he wasn't really sure if he was ambitious.

"To be honest, I don't get how people say they would get bored if they won the lottery. I could easily sit and watch *Judge Judy* all day and be perfectly fine."

He would tell me about the rich wankers that would come for viewings in Hampstead Heath. They would complain that the kitchen was too small even though it was the size of his entire flat.

"So essentially these people are like your parents?"

"Yes."

I asked him if he liked his parents, or if it was just their money he was waiting for.

"I don't really miss my parents the way most people do." His parents lived in York, a drive a few hours north. "To be honest, I'm not sure I would miss them if they died. I know that sounds horrible. I mean they're alright."

I looked at him with surprise.

"You're judging me."

"I guess. But then I'm from a culture where parents are revered."

"So, I guess that's why you're here, in London, then?" I was about to get mad and then he winked and squeezed my waist. We could spend hours doing this to each other – bickering back and forth – and calling each other out on things.

I often questioned him about his past, and at first, he was cagey with me about his wildness and indiscretions. I knew he went to Oxford, and because he was clever, he had time to be a rebel and a playboy. I told him he didn't have to hide from me.

He'd often say to me, "You tell me a secret then."

"Okay." I took out a bag of pills and two little bags of coke. "I've had this in my purse for three days, and I didn't share it."

His eyes grew wide and I said, "Oh come on, it's a snow day." He laughed and passed me my big mirror.

I corrupted him. I'm not vain in saying that. Although he was into this stuff, he wasn't prone to doing it in the afternoon. It became a regular thing after that. He came over more frequently in the afternoon and instead of going out for dinner, we would get takeaway. We were more passionate when we did drugs, staying in bed for hours listening to Leonard Cohen.

"He's Canadian, you know," I said boastfully one day.

"You don't even like Canada, so who cares?" he said.

"Well, you don't like *anywhere*, do you?"

We could sense each other's inertia; we both knew the other was full of contradictions. He discussed how his father crushed his dreams to be an architect by telling him he lacked a creative spirit. I complained about white privilege – how marginalized Indian women had no platform to be creative. Together, we built each other up by romanticizing each other's broken dreams without any personal accountability. It was the perfect relationship. I taught him things about reincarnation, destiny, and the afterlife. We talked about being soulmates and what we could do long-term to make the world better. We'd run a B & B in some small village and donate ten percent of our income to charity. I'd run a free arts program to underprivileged teens.

Of course, the plans were always some distant time in the future. But that was the nature of romance and optimism, wasn't it?

One day he found my *Twilight* books. I kept them in a dresser drawer by my side of the bed. It wasn't a conscious decision to hide them. "What are *these*?"

"My students." I said.

"What, you mean your students gave them to you?"

I wasn't sure what to say. "No, my students are so into them, and I wanted to see what all the fuss was about." I could feel my face getting hot.

He laughed. "Bullshit." I felt exposed. "It's okay if you read trashy teen books. It's fine. Even though I fell for your façade – reading me Walt Whitman poems every night." I felt scared for a minute. Then he gave me a big smile and started tickling me and I pushed him away. "Come on, don't be like that." I backed away and he started chasing me around the room, trying to bite my neck. He tackled me to the floor and said, "Do vampires like snow?"

"Yes, they do." I wanted to stay mad at him but this was always his way of appeasing me, with humour and drugs, mixed with a bit of adoration.

I felt bad for getting him involved in my shenanigans but found him weak for being so susceptible. *He* was the catalyst that was supposed to change *my* life. He was supposed to make me a better person, or make me whole, or whatever the cliché was. But he was looking for the same things I was. I thought addiction came from wanting to numb pain. I wasn't sure if that was true. I thought maybe it was because people wanted to feel something.

"It's amazing," Tom said to me one day. "I feel better, and so much more connected to myself and to you when I do this."

That high lasted quite a while – at least six months – which was a record for me. We embellished on that with swinging sometimes; adding people to the mix. There was a girl called Suzie who came around a little too often, and I didn't like how it made me feel.

"Sorry honey, it'll stop," he said. And that was it, our first fight.

We then searched for the next high because coke and pills was getting boring. Our dealer, Pete, said he might have something more special. I heard people say if you take heroin on Friday you are hooked by Sunday. I saw what they meant.

"Not sure I want to do this, hun," Tom said. He was apprehensive. "I have a job in sales. I have to be on top of things. You do it, I'll watch."

Of course, that was never going to work in a relationship. "Look, vampires and humans can never be together. Ultimately the human becomes the vampire," I said.

"You are insane."

"You love it. You must be crazy too or you wouldn't have come here. Don't they say something like that in *Alice in Wonderland?*" He gave in that day because he was afraid of missing out, or that we'd disconnect. I knew I was playing on that a little. We floated that night, him and I under the stars. It was glorious. My body felt like sand. It was a clear night and we stood on the balcony holding hands. I started thinking about things. "Do these stars belong to us, Tom, or do we belong to them?"

"What, honey? Is that Nietzsche?"

"Is this your home, Tom, because you feel it? Or because you're English and it always gets to be yours?"

"What are you talking about?"

"I'm talking about home. Having a sense of place, or something."

"What does that have to do with the stars?"

"Everything."

"You're beautiful," he said.

It made me think he wasn't really all that intelligent when he responded that way. In fact, he never really had much to say about my meandering thoughts, and I wondered if I really was a narcissist and only loved him because he supported my goddess-like fantasy of myself.

I could see Jeevan in the corner of the room that night. I'd been mixing all sorts of pills, so who knows if it was him. "This is shoddy,

Sarika. You can do better than this," he said. "This guy is a dick, and he wears pinstriped suits. Seriously."

"Go back to the moon."

I had noted its absence tonight, and I was happy for it.

"What?" Tom looked alarmed.

"Sorry, I'm just speaking to my dead brother."

"You have a dead brother?"

I had never told him about Jeevan. I told him everything else about my family and what they were like. Somehow the story of Jeevan got redundant.

"Yes, I do, but let's not talk about that."

"I thought we talked about everything. I thought you said we knew each other. Isn't that the point?" He looked vulnerable, as if I were telling him his own brother had died.

My response was more pills and other things. Life was grand and small at the same time. My living room was a huge stage of six hundred square feet. I pulled out a tarot deck and made him pick a card. It was the Devil card. We both roared with laughter and rolled around on the floor.

He missed a big sale the next day because of me. One of his clients wanted to put an offer on a house and Tom was asleep at two o'clock in the afternoon. "God, Sarika, you fucked it up!"

"*You* fucked it up. I'm simply Eve with the apple."

I smiled at him and expected him to relent. But he walked over to me, grabbed my wrists, pulled them up towards him, and shook them. His grip was tight.

"Dammit, Sarika, it's not always funny. It's not a big joke. This is my life. This cost me a lot of money. Do you know that?"

"Ow! That hurts!" I tried pulling away but his grip was tight. "Let me go, you're hurting me!" His eyes went wide and he looked down as he let go. My wrists were red and marked by his fingers.

"Sorry, I'm sorry." He went to the window with his back to me. "You know, Sarika, it's just difficult. I have to make ends meet, put on a show for my family, be the successful schoolboy who left banking so he could make more money doing something else on his own. Not this middle-aged estate agent just making ends meet." I went to the window and put my arms around his waist. He turned around and looked at me, his eyes sunken and hollow – dull flames that had been poorly managed. Mirrors were difficult things; you wanted to wipe them clean hoping you'd see something different. "And then I have this life here with you. And I feel like myself, and we have a good time, but I get confused. We get out of hand sometimes, don't you think?" He looked like a young boy – like one of my students.

"That's who we are. That's what we love." I was too high still. "You're questioning it because you've been taught to judge it." I was on the moon, wherever it was. I didn't want to come down. "We're good people."

"Are we?" He stroked my cheek and put on his coat. "I have to go." He left and forgot to kiss me goodbye.

I poured myself a gin and tonic. I was coming down in a bad, jittery way. My dentist had asked if I had anxiety because I'd been grinding my teeth so much.

I thought about our conversation, but I was also thinking of *Oliver Twist* as I'd been practicing scenes from it with my students: "More please." More pills, more lines, more booze. I thought about how it jarred me, the way Tom grabbed me and shook me.

I took two sleeping pills just to level out my jitters and fell in and out of sleep. I dreamt about Maya in our house growing up. She was wearing an evangelical, black choir robe, and she was singing hymns. I was a little girl wearing a yellow dress, with big yellow clips in my hair. The yellow moon was hanging low above our house. It had no roof, and it matched my dress exactly. Jeevan was in the dream too, only he was floating around and went up to into the sky. He was silent in the dream but kept pointing at my dress. I looked down at the dress, but I didn't understand. Then all of a sudden, I was an adult. Jeevan kept pointing at my dress, but I didn't know what he was saying. When I looked down, I saw that it was stained with blood. I opened my mouth to speak, to ask him what he meant, but I couldn't for some reason.

I woke up sometime in the middle of the night. My mouth was dry and my jaw ached. I went to the window and the sky was empty and dark, punctuated by the occasional star. There were less stars than I thought.

I knew I was unwell. I knew that I had led Tom down a road that was shaky and uncertain for him and that it was wrong. But I felt like we could have something good if I would just stop ruining it. We could have a future together once I sorted myself out and figured out what I wanted to do with my life. *I'll try for more auditions*, I thought to myself. *That's probably what Jeevan meant.* I vowed to pour more energy into my work.

I went back to work with a new lease on life and decided I would cut back on the drugs to save my relationship. I even cut out drinking from Monday to Wednesday. It was difficult, but I did it. On other days, I would wait until after six o'clock at night. When I saw Tom, I apologized to him. "Let's be real now," I said. "I'm gonna be more real."

He was relieved. "I love you, Sarika. You'll have that home we talked about. I'm going to give that to you." His voice glided through my body and carried me home.

I threw all my energy into a *Wizard of Oz* production. It was my favourite movie growing up. My passion came out when I spoke to the kids about self-discovery and identity – things that mattered to me. I got rated outstanding on a lesson observation leading up to the show. There was hype and buzz around the school because of something I was doing. It felt good. We had the most elaborate set and the entire community came to watch it. I even starred in it myself as Aunty Em, and cast a couple of the other teachers to be in it.

By the time it was closing night, I was exhausted. It had been three months of non-stop rehearsals and seven nights of performing. I was thriving though. Everyone was proud with me, including Tom.

"I like this you. You're focused. And you look like you care about what you're doing."

He was doing well himself, as he'd made some big sale. He talked about how maybe we could leave London and he would design and build a house for us somewhere small. I imagined our wedding in a gazebo full of sunflowers and mason jars. Tom would make all our furniture, and I would learn how to make jam.

I was excited that he was coming that night. He would see the head teacher give a speech about me and hand me flowers while parents and teachers and other members of the community would stand and cheer. I sat at my desk just before it was time to sort out costumes and swiveled around a couple of times, feeling remarkably relaxed. I'd just had a bit of wine. Not much – just a glass to take the edge off.

My phone went off. It was an email from Marcy. I hadn't heard from Marcy for almost three years, and before that our contact was sporadic. I knew she had the same struggles as me. It was unspoken, but it was like we highlighted each other's shortcomings because of our shared history. I felt a flip in my stomach, as if I was hearing from my first love. I opened the email:

Hey Sarika,

How are you? I know we haven't been in touch but I wanted to share with you that I met someone. He's from William's Lake, but his parents are English. Isn't that weird? And I had a baby girl. I named her Venus in honour of all our witchy days together. I know this is all a shock. I'm still shocked. LOL! I think I didn't want to jinx it, but I'm so happy, Sarika. I can't wait for you to meet them both. When are you back? How's your glamorous life over there? I've attached a pic – check it out! We're getting married soon. We'll do it in the summer so you can come. Will keep you posted on dates!

Marcy

I opened the image and there they were. Marcy's long blonde hair shone through the photo, and so did her love for her man and child. It looked like the kind of photo that came with the frame when you bought it at the store. They were all blonde and had perfect teeth and skin. Marcy didn't look rough anymore. She looked great. Her baby had the most beautiful blue eyes that spoke of contentment, joy, and a good middle-class life full of stability, birthday parties, and two holidays a year in the sun. I closed the image and opened the bottom drawer of my desk. Under a stack of files was a small bottle of Jameson whisky I had confiscated off a student. I never drank any kind of whisky, mostly because it reminded me of Indian men, but I opened it and took a large swig and then chased it with some wine. I did this a couple more times before I had to go, convinced I couldn't feel anything.

Some of the kids looked at me funny when I was pinning their costumes, but I just tried to keep my mouth closed and sucked on a strong mint. Katherine, the art teacher, told me I looked a little nuts. "You don't need to be nervous anymore, the show is pretty much over for you."

"Yes, the show is pretty much over for me." I repeated the words back and stared right through her. I managed to get the kids ready and let the stage manager deal with the rest. I told her I had a headache and she needed to make sure everyone was cued to go on at the right times. I got through my Aunty Em bit in the first act and had loads of free time after that. The half-empty whisky bottle was in my purse, so I went to the toilet periodically to top myself up. It was strange. I normally felt a buzz or a high or something, but I just felt dense and heavy like I was too compact and I could burst any second.

The rest was a bit of a blur. I remember discovering the stage make-up and looking in the mirror, thinking it was unfair that I had to be frumpy and not dazzling like Glinda, the good witch. It seemed like a good idea to glam myself up with some glitter. I thought I was being subtle, but somehow, I had dumped quite a bit all over my neck, face, and hair. *I look like a shiny star next to the moon*, I thought to myself. *A star.*

I'm pretty sure I fell asleep in the toilet. Katherine nudged me awake and looked horrified. "What are you doing? It's your turn to go on. You missed your cue."

I remember being in the spotlight and knowing I was caked in gold glitter as I slurred through my lines. The crowd wasn't completely dark so some faces of shock and disbelief stuck out at me. I looked for Tom but couldn't see him. I wasn't sure if he was there but I was hoping he wasn't. I didn't get flowers afterwards, and the planned speech by the head teacher didn't happen. He pulled me aside afterwards and told to come to his office first thing in the morning.

I'm not certain I had even sobered up when I spoke to him the next morning because I didn't feel much shame at the time. I didn't feel anything when he told me to take some time off, get some help, and that we would speak about my career at the school in a few weeks. I might have been relieved, and I stopped to get wine on the way home. I was tired of performing.

My only real concern was Tom, who finally showed up at my door the next evening without any texts about why he didn't turn up at my show.

I opened the door in anticipation of the fight we were about to have. I would cry that he didn't come, and he would apologize. I straightened my shoulders and looked right through him. "Where the hell have you been?" I tried to channel Maya's sternness, but I had a feeling I was doing a poor job.

"Sarika, let me say something." He looked different. He wasn't looking at me properly. "I *need* to say something."

"Okay, come in." I grabbed his hand but he pulled away.

"It's over."

"What?"

"It's over." He motioned with his hands. "This. It has to be over."

"Why?" I could feel my voice shake. On some level, I was always waiting for this.

"Look at you. You're a mess. I can tell you're drunk right now. You need to get help. Surely you must know that after last night." I could see Tom looking carefully – at my pale greyish complexion and my messy hair – like he was seeing me for the first time.

"You were there?"

"I had to leave. I couldn't bear seeing you like that, stumbling around the stage, not making any sense. Why the hell were you covered in glitter?" He was yelling at me now. "Do you even have a job anymore?"

"Okay, I know I was a fool, but something happened earlier to set me off. I'll tell you about it. Just come in, please."

"Sarika, we are not good for each other. Don't you see that?"

"We're soulmates, don't *you* see that?" I didn't know what other platitudes I could offer him. That was probably the best one.

"She's having a baby."

"What?"

"She's having a baby, Sarika. I just found out a few days ago."

"Who?"

I saw the curtains go up again.

"You know who."

The show had to go on.

"I want you to say it."

"Sarika, come on, you know this is hard for me."

"You never say it." I pushed him further. "Say it!"

"My wife. My wife, Margo. Happy now?" He knew what this was for me. "Sarika, I'm sorry. I know –"

"Shut up! You don't know anything, you hypocrite. Telling me I'm a mess. Look at you, you deadbeat. You lie to everyone – to your tighty-whitie family and your wife – about who you really are and what you really want and that deadbeat job where you suck up to all these clients you hate. You told me that you never wanted your own children, that we could make this work, that it was soon. Always soon."

I'd never really displayed myself this way before – even to myself. He looked shocked.

"I didn't plan this."

"Sure, but it means you were with her. Just as much as you were with me, you were with her."

He couldn't reply. He was staring somewhere behind me. Probably at my living room which had tissues and bottles everywhere.

I lowered my voice and took a deep breath. "What about . . . our home. And everything else?"

He finally looked at me, and it was like he was remembering me before the glitter debacle. "I love you. But I'm not sure if I believe enough in the things we talked about. And I can't walk away from my life."

I had nothing else to say. "Go."

"Sarika."

"I think it's time for you to go."

"Sarika, prove me wrong. Make yourself better. Go after something – for real. I don't think much of myself, but I do of you. I believe in you."

The lights flooded the stage. The audience stood up, applauding his speech. I shut the door in his face.

# MAYA

2009

STEVEN TOOK my revelations fairly well that night at his parents' house, or at least he pretended to. He went to sleep saying he didn't believe me and then was quiet all the way home the next day, while I made him listen to things he didn't want to hear about my family and marriage. He understood the bit about me hiding my separation from Sunny, but he had a harder time with me lying about my name.

"Why would you lie about something so ridiculous?"

"I don't know," I said. "I just wanted to be someone else." I didn't tell him how fat I used to be. I figured I had a right to keep that a secret and that I wasn't betraying him too much. "And anyway, you really don't ask me anything about myself. I find it really strange."

"Well, I figure why waste time on people's pasts? We are who we are right now, in this moment. I figured you'd tell me what was relevant."

We were on the beach when he said this to me. I felt like I breathed for the first time in a long time – like I had been sucking in my belly to pose for photographs the way I used to. What he said liberated me, and I released a ball of guilt that had been sitting in my chest since the day we met. He had his arm around me, and I collapsed into him in a way I hadn't before. "This is good, what's between us," he said. "Truth doesn't need detail. Truth is simple. It's what we have here before us, right now, Maya." It felt good to hear him say my name. I closed my eyes and let go of it all, right then and there – Sunny, my parents, my need to pretend. I took a deep breath in and the air was fresh and cool. The waves collapsed against each other, and I could sense them washing into my new story, which was the acceptance of the old one. The ocean was finally mine.

"Let's go home and cook dinner," he said. Of course, home still meant Kelsey's sister's apartment. She would be back soon and we would have to stay at his place after this visit. I didn't want to push him so I waited until the following month to see what he would say.

"So, am I staying at your place?" I asked on the phone.

There was a pause on the other end but he said, "Of course." It was strange, but we didn't speak much between visits. He said he wasn't a phone person and wasn't into small talk. "I don't need to know about your day. That has no relevance or meaning."

I felt split. These two lives were happening simultaneously but completely separately. At home, I was mainly the former twisted version of myself, who didn't eat but still gave in to binge watching soaps and mopping the floors every day. Not speaking to him made me forget sometimes that things had changed, and I got a bit depressed until it was time to see him.

I was excited by this new step in our relationship though and intrigued by what his apartment might reveal about him. I imagined him apologizing for his roommate's wet socks being hung to dry on radiators and dishes lining the kitchen counter. Maybe there would be a faint musty man smell that I would have to deal with. I was prepared for having to cope with a bit of mess, and it was okay; this was an integral part of me becoming a well-adjusted person. He would be stressed out and vulnerable, and maybe I would have the upper hand for once.

The morning before I flew out, I got my nails done for the first time in celebration of that next step. They were aqua-blue like the sea. I avoided red. It reminded me of a new Indian bride. I was something else now – a confident city girl – with a white boyfriend who painted.

When I landed, Steven asked me to take a taxi. It was getting annoying spending all this money just to see him, but I let it go.

He didn't answer the door right away. There was the sound of fumbling footsteps and cupboards opening and closing. What was he doing? I had an image of him madly trying to shove body parts into the freezer. Frozen and hard bits would fall onto the floor – a leg here, an arm there. Maybe he was a serial killer and his family suspected it too.

He opened the door looking out of sorts, as if I were dropping by unexpectedly.

"Hi."

He looked down and checked himself to see if he was wearing a shirt. "Shit, sorry. Come in, let me grab your bags." He was wearing jeans and a hoodie that matched his blue eyes. I had never seen him so casual before.

I walked through the long hallway that led to the kitchen and living room. All the doors were shut. It was a creaky ground floor suite with hardwood. The kitchen was spotless and orderly with everything in place; a bit sterile like my house. It lacked the same warmth as his parents' place, but there were canvases and framed prints hung up everywhere. I guessed some of them were his. I dreaded having to comment on them. I didn't particularly care for abstract art. On the coffee table lay a silver tea set.

"Is that a real silver tea set?"

"Yes, it's my grandmother's." He looked annoyed that this was the thing I chose to point out. "And some of these paintings are mine." But what man had a silver tea set on their coffee table?

A door opened and I could hear rustling from the room nearest to us. "That's Kevin." As footsteps approached, I got excited by the anticipation of meeting the roommate. I imagined him to be thin and pasty from eating only cereal and playing video games all day in his room.

"Hello." Kevin walked in, came right over, and shook my hand.

"Pleasure to meet you." He had a thick accent, perfect teeth, and beautiful olive skin. He really looked me in the eyes in a way that was disarming but not creepy.

"Nice to meet you, too." I tried to hide my surprise. Kevin seemed lovely and normal.

"Kevin is from the Philippines. He's here for a couple of years to study engineering."

"Great! I've heard so little about you." Kevin didn't get my joke and smiled.

Steven looked irritated already. "Do you want a drink?"

"Tea?" I pointed to the tea set.

"Is that really what you want? I'm not making it in there."

"Fine, I'll just have water."

Kevin stared at me curiously and asked how I knew Steven.

"I met him at his bar."

"Oh."

It was a strange he didn't know. I tried making small talk but felt like Kevin was studying me, or studying Steven with me. It was like he wanted to make sure I was telling the truth. He got quiet and said he needed to go read, and that he'd be going into the suburbs to visit a friend for the weekend.

"His English isn't the greatest," Steven said as he smoothed out a table cloth that had little sunflowers and ladybugs on it. He had placemats too, red and yellow that matched the tablecloth.

I almost started laughing. "Steven, what is wrong with you?"

"What?"

"Your roommate seems alright, and this place is pretty nice. It's not dorm-like at all." I was trying to ask him something but I wasn't sure what. Why was he such a perfectionist? Why was he even more messed up than me?

He just smiled and said, "You hungry? Wanna go for dinner?"

We had a nice weekend together, going to local restaurants and watching movies. He was quiet and deliberate, as if my presence in his home made him feel scrutinized and drawn in. I caressed his forehead and kissed his cheek when I left, feeling somewhat motherly towards him. It was so hard for him to relax into life; even harder for him than it was for me. It was nice to nurture someone who had the same issues as me – but amplified. There was something therapeutic about this – like maybe if I could make him relax we'd both be okay.

I didn't see him for a couple of months after that. The timing just didn't work. I had to work a couple of extra weekends, and then he had a friend visiting him from San Francisco. "You could sound a little sadder – like actually you miss me. Or you could call me once in a while." I didn't want to sound needy because I knew he hated that, but he displayed an indifference that resembled mine towards Sunny.

"You know I miss you." He sighed on the phone as if he were a kid talking to a parent from a college dorm room. "You can come whenever you want."

"Well, how about I come for longer? I can take a week off."

He paused. "Sure. Actually, my parents have been asking about you too, so maybe they can come over and have lunch with us one weekend. Though I'll have to explain the name thing."

I felt a calmness flood over me. Everything was okay. He wanted his parents to see me again. I just needed to get used to the unconventional nature of our relationship. I knew I was a bit crazy. I needed time to be crazy on my own. Maybe God was finally giving me what I needed, but it didn't quite look how I expected.

His parents instilled confidence in me at our meeting, displaying excitement at my presence and making future plans. "You have to go boating with us when you come next," said Claire. Steven vacillated between being subdued or tense, often sulking when his father teased him.

"Did you see his tea set?" said his Dad. "And there's a sewing machine in his room you know. Get him to make you a blouse."

"That's a Singer sewing machine, actually. It's a decorative piece, Dad. I've told you this many times." Steven went a little red and stormed off, leaving us at a gelato shop with his ice cream in my hand. I couldn't eat two. Well, I could, but I was holding back.

"You shouldn't do that," Claire said to her husband. "You know he doesn't like to be teased." She turned to me. "He's a bit sensitive, isn't he?" I wasn't sure what to say.

"He's not just sensitive," said Bill. "He doesn't have a sense of humour. I'm just trying to get him to lighten up, Maya. He doesn't let us in, so then I end up poking at him to get any sort of reaction, which maybe isn't right. We just feel like we don't know him."

They both looked at me for answers. It affirmed to me what I already felt about parenting and what a thankless job it was. What was the point? I wanted to tell them to stop wasting their time and to go home and eat cheese in their lovely backyard. "Look, I really don't know why he's like that except maybe he feels different from you and Luke." I didn't know what else to say. They told me they had always celebrated the boys' differences. I watched the ice cream melt in my hand. It was maple walnut. I wanted to tell them I was the last person they should be asking for insight into anyone's psyche.

Steven's father found him and apologized. His parents left later that day, looking forlorn after pandering to Steven's quiet tantrum. It turned me off a bit, I have to admit. I wanted to tell him that in Indian families there were no "talks" where parents tried to connect with their children's feelings.

"You really are weird about your parents, especially your father. Why did you snap over a stupid sewing machine comment?"

"Because he always makes these little comments to suggest I'm not a real man like Luke. And my mother doesn't stand up for me. She just adores him. And don't tell me this is Freudian, that really pisses me off."

"I wasn't going to say that." Though I was thinking it. "Your Dad just winds you up because it's so easy. Stop being so sensitive."

"Really? That's rich coming from you." His eyes cut into me as he sat across from me at the kitchen table. He kept swiping his finger through the candle that flickered in front of him like he was testing himself to see if he was immune to pain.

"What does that mean?"

"You're the most sensitive person I know. You're so awkward that you have to change your name just to be comfortable in your own skin." And there it was. Whatever politeness that was the gel holding our relationship together just got stripped away.

"Thanks. Thanks for holding on to that and throwing it in my face." I got up and put the dishes in the dishwasher, making sure I rinsed them so they wouldn't stain. He sat there and stared into the candle with dark and glazed eyes, probably summoning the gods that made him stay handsome and graceful.

We went to bed without speaking that night. I thought maybe our relationship was over then. The masks had been taken off. He was a broody, spoilt kid. I was the great pretender. And we both knew it. How could we possible stay together?

But in the morning, I went into the kitchen and he was making buckwheat pancakes and whistling to some weird Italian music.

"Hey." He kissed my cheek, poured me coffee, and told me to forget about last night. He was back to being the self-assured bartender I met the very first night.

We continued on for a couple of days and it was okay. He left me on my own a bit because he had to study and work at the bar. I suggested coming in like I used to, but he said it was too distracting and seemed bothered by the idea. It was subtle, but somehow things were a little different between us. I guessed that it was what a normal relationship was like after being around each other for a while. This was the most time we had ever spent together. I couldn't gauge anything from my relationship with Sunny because it was sort of flat from the beginning and didn't really get any better or worse until the end. I felt our judgements towards each other growing, or maybe they were always there but just more visible now.

Point Grey was expensive, and I found it a bit ostentatious that he wanted to live there. He said he wanted to be removed from downtown and was willing to pay for privacy.

"Privacy from what?" I asked. "You're not a famous DJ." He glared at me when I said this. He really didn't respond to my jokes and was still definitely not a fan of being teased.

Even my own self-deprecation bothered him sometimes. "You shouldn't do that so much. It's not very attractive to make jokes at your own expense."

"So, arrogance is better?"

"Are you implying I'm arrogant?"

"No, but you could lighten up a bit."

"That's not what you said."

I felt weary and tried to change the subject. Steven reminded me of Mom sometimes. We would start having one conversation, and then it would just turn into some sort of twisted argument; he'd miss the point and then convince both of us I had said something else completely. He always won.

Also, we were starting to feel more like siblings. I only saw him once a month, so I figured he'd be into me, but we had gone through two visits without any physical intimacy. Yet he was adamant that we were serious – that I would be in his future.

I popped into some random church one evening while he was at work. I wanted to say a prayer or something to figure out how I might be sabotaging myself. I was hoping for quiet, but it ended up being a very loud service in Chinese. I had no idea what the minister at the front was saying, but he said it with so much conviction that I felt deeply moved and alerted to how vague things seemed. I prayed that night in a logical way, for clarity and progress in my life like I was praying for a political campaign. *Jesus, let me move forward in the right way, whatever that is. Let it be clear.*

I imagined Steven asking me to move to Vancouver with him into our own condo (a house was too unrealistic), with dishes we bought together and only just a couple of his ugly paintings on the wall. I would go back to school, and in the evenings, we would talk about class and drink tea. Maybe, I would even sell the house. I listened for Jesus to confirm my vision, but he didn't have a lot to say. I told him he was a good listener, but his silence was starting to make me question our friendship. What might Guru Nanak say? He'd say I never should have scared away my first husband to begin with.

It was my last night in town, so I decided I would just go to his workplace and have a talk with him. I didn't care that he didn't want me to be there and sat on my favourite bar stool. Everyone greeted me and asked where I'd been. I ignored the implication that he didn't discuss me. Instead, I focused on the memory of the first night that marked the transformation in my life, when I'd worn bright lipstick and a pencil skirt for the first time. I could do this too. Steven ignored me until the very end of his shift. I knew it was a power thing because he wanted to show me this was the consequence of not following his wishes.

He wasn't unpleasant though. "Let's have a drink," he said. He made us spectacular fizzy drinks with blueberries, basil, and rum. Then he poured us two shots of tequila.

I was surprised. "What are you doing?" He never really drank that quickly.

"It's your last night. Let's have some fun. You know, fun?" His blue eyes lit up when he smiled and I felt like the most spectacular person in the room. "Let's go for a drink, okay?" He grabbed my hand and whisked me out the door like he did the first night.

"Okay, but I want to talk to you about a couple of things before we get drunk."

"Yeah, sure. I do need to stop at a friend's place though at some point. He owes me some cash."

I found it funny that he was like this – so posh and stoic about status most of the time, pretending money was a non-issue and glossing over his need for it. But I usually picked up the bill when we ate out, and he usually pretended to look out the window as if I was sorting myself out in some uncongenial manner, like picking food off my clothes.

We walked for bit. There was a cool breeze in the air. It was October. The leaves were illuminating the streets with all different colours.

"Remember the first day we did this?" he said. "Cherry blossoms were blooming."

"You remember?"

"Of course I do."

We walked through the West End, and I could hear loud music thumping Pet Shop Boys from one of the bars.

"Let's stop in here."

"Really?" It was a gay bar. A really gay bar. The kind that was known for naked, sweaty bodies grinding at eight o'clock at night.

"Come on, it'll be fun, don't be a drag . . . queen." He laughed and pushed me past a group of topless men all wearing matching leather pants. "Let's get a bottle of wine. You like red, right?"

I hated red wine. I thought he knew this but I watched him go to the bar and bypass the line-up. The bartender squeezed his arm and gave him two glasses and bottle. He didn't pay for it.

"So, are you a regular here?" I was trying not to be judgemental. He filled my glass and pointed to the stage. There are small, spectacular moments in your life that you don't forget, especially when you're me and your life has been fairly predictable. This was definitely one of them. On stage was a gorgeous, muscular man dressed in a tight, red, buttoned-up shirt and jeans. He was dancing and stripping to Cher in a shower stall encased in glass. Everybody was clapping as the clothes came off his wet body. I watched Steven, who downed the wine and refilled his glass, clapping and cheering louder than anyone else. It was the most animated I had ever seen him.

He couldn't take his eyes off the stage and just kept refilling his own glass. "Isn't this fun? It's shower power night!" He moved his hips in sync with the guy on stage like he was in a trance.

"Wow, shower power night. So, you *do* come here a lot?" There was an uncertainty in the air that hovered against the disco balls shining their chaotic light. The air was thick with Steven's glee.

"Are you being judgemental? Who needs to lighten up?" He winked at me instead of being annoyed. His eyes looked a bit different – vibrant in a new way. He kissed me then, but it felt detached – like he wasn't sure who he was with. Then he started talking *a lot*. He told me how I inspired him because I felt so much. And that it was difficult to meet people who had the same capacity to take in the world around them, much less feel it with the same intensity and express it.

"Steven, I'm the most disconnected person you'll ever meet." He really could have been speaking to anyone and said the same thing.

"It's good wine, isn't it?" He emptied the bottle into his glass and drank quickly, not noticing I hadn't really touched mine. His lips were stained red and he looked girlish.

"Yeah, sure."

"Let's go." He grabbed my hand again like he was in a frenzy and pulled us out the door into a taxi. "I gotta see my friend."

We somehow ended up in a penthouse apartment overlooking the beach. The elevator doors opened right into someone's living room, and a handsome man opened the door. He was wearing all white. A white blazer and white jeans. His apartment was also really white: white couches, white carpet, and white walls.

"Hi, nice to meet you, Maya." He leaned in and gave me a hug. He greeted me warmly – but in a way that made me feel like a seven-year-old first to arrive at a birthday party. I was a bit taken aback – finally someone who knew about me. He was ultra-confident, in the way rich people are, and beckoned us to sit down. He poured us wine – more red wine. I sat next to Steven across from All-White Guy (who was actually called David).

"She does have lovely eyes, like you said," David said to Steven. It was like I was a new accessory or maybe a new bike.

"I know, right?" Steven was beaming at David, and they started chatting about art and some sort of auction, which amused me because Steven didn't have any money.

"How do you two know each other?" I asked.

Steven looked at David and waited for him to speak.

"Steven works for me sometimes," David said. He then quickly changed the subject and told me I looked great in red – that it was definitely my colour – as if he saw me all the time in other colours.

They mostly ignored me after that, so I forced myself to drink the wine. I downed it, the way Steven did at the club, and David politely poured me another while continuing to talk about his property in California. I don't really know what happened after that, but there was a reason I never drank wine. It made me sick and drunk quite quickly. I got up at some point to go to the bathroom, but I stumbled and the wine went flying across the carpet. Red on white.

"Oh shit! Sorry." I expected them to laugh or for David to tell me that it was okay and his cleaner would deal with it. But he didn't. There was a silence like I had just announced my pregnancy.

Steven got up and said, "I'll clean it." He ran into the kitchen to look for paper towel.

David followed him and put his hand on Steven's neck. "It's okay, it's okay, just leave it." Steven held his gaze with David. His eyes softened and he raised his hand like he was going to reciprocate, but then glanced over at me and decided not to. It was *that* moment – not the gay bar – that I realized Jesus had answered my prayer for clarity. We left shortly after that. I had ruined the vibe.

We were both in the fetal position when we awoke the next morning facing opposite directions. I had a faint recollection of being in his arms earlier. My hand prickled against the tiny cactus plant next to me as I reached across to check my phone. Noon. I looked at the salmon coloured wall across from me and gazed into his closet – finely pressed shirts perfectly lined up, straight rows of pants on the shelf, also neatly pressed and folded. Loads of shoes, too many, were stacked with care on the floor. On the wall were three landscape photographs he took in Africa framed in beautiful red mahogany. There was a big red canvas to the left of me with ugly red and orange sploshes of paint. "Abstract Anger," he called it.

He turned onto his back, still asleep, and without thinking I did the same. I glanced over and stared at him. Long, lovely eyelashes. Eyebrows that I was positive he tweezed. He had criticized mine one time, saying they were uneven.

He opened his eyes. "You're looking at me," he said. I looked away. I wanted time to think. "You know red really stains. It's hard to get out of white. It's the worst."

"I know that."

There was something rather magical about the days when you were first discovered by Steven. It was like being singled out in a crowd by some talent agent, who then whisked you into celebrity status. Suddenly, everything changed. He would sweep you away, and you wanted to be there with him. Because if you weren't, you were missing something vital and life altering, or some dimension that only he knew how to get to. He never justified it with reason, but always with urgency.

Now, his lacklustre eyes told me the urgency was gone. I had been taken off the guest list to the most elite party in town. Suddenly, I was in the back of the line waiting my turn, hoping to make my way in before it was too late and the moment was gone, knowing the decision was never mine.

He loved shopping at Gap, had a silver tea set on his coffee table, and performed as the lead in the Nutcracker. Of course, these were all stereotypes, but what was I thinking? One time a man had approached us while we were holding hands, told me he thought my boyfriend was handsome, and then winked at Steven. I remember the beaming glow on his face. It all made sense. A long-distance girlfriend who was pathetic enough to settle for what she could get, but someone he could still introduce to his family. He was a charlatan like me.

"I'm hungry," he said, bolting out of bed. "You should brush your teeth." He was expressionless when he reprimanded me.

When I went into the kitchen he was setting the table, folding napkins, and laying out cutlery. He grabbed his silver tea set off the coffee table.

"You really don't have to do all this."

"There's no point doing anything without passion." He gave me his whole cooking with passion spiel, and I tuned out and started counting the asparagus that was in a bowl on the table. Who had fresh

asparagus on their kitchen table anyway? What was wrong with
bananas? He placed an apple that he carved perfectly into a tulip onto
my plate and told me not to touch it. He kept ranting on about this
and that, about how he was annoyed that his roommate didn't cook,
and that he wished Kevin had the drive to do something creative.

Kevin had been mostly absent all week, slamming doors and only
entering a room after we had left it. "Are you okay, Kevin?" I had
asked when I finally saw him. "You've been hiding."

"Well, some of us have to hide," he had said cryptically.

"Is there something going on between you and Kevin?" I asked
Steven. A squirrel jumped from one branch to another outside the
kitchen window. A few leaves fought to stay on their branches; it was
autumn again.

Steven paused from chopping but wouldn't turn around. "He's
needy. You know how foreign people are. I try to spend time with him
when I can, but he has a hard time accepting what I can give him. You
never told me what you thought of my latest painting – the one in my
room." He continued chopping.

"I think you need to finish it. It looks like an abandoned ware-
house. Like you poured yourself into it but it doesn't measure up
somehow, so it's just a bunch of paint on canvas. But I'm no artist,
Steven."

He was silent when I said that. I had hurt his personal beauty that
he had so generously framed for me to observe this whole time. He
had always been ensconced in glass, just like the guy at shower power
night. He made me the breakfast of a lifetime: omelette, bacon, and
pancakes. His teapot shone in the afternoon sun. The Last Supper.

I chopped his apple-tulip into a million pieces with a knife before I
ate them one by one. I ate everything, and for the first time in a long
time I didn't care about the calories. Then I made a decision. "You
know, Steve, I used to be really fat. Like really obese."

He looked up from his newspaper. "I told you not to call me Steve
– ever."

"I was really fat. When you and I go out, I often have to throw up afterwards, and you've never noticed. I only eat rice cakes at home. And I hate sushi. I really hate it – so much. And this cross I'm wearing is because I'm Christian. It's not because I'm trying to be hip and trendy. I was Sikh but then I became Christian, and I don't even really know why. And I laughed at my brother's funeral. And I'm forty-one years old. And there are twenty-four pieces of asparagus in this bowl."

I wanted to say more – like how I recorded three soap operas a day at home, but I stopped when I saw he was finally looking at me, maybe for the first time. I wasn't sure what he was seeing. Was he imagining my face being much bigger and slightly distorted?

I stood up and told him it was time for me to go. He stayed seated and nodded his head, speechless. "Do you know what my name means, Steven?"

"No."

I observed his face again – his tortured, dissatisfied beauty – knowing I would never see him again.

"Illusion."

I left – feeling quite full.

# SARIKA

2010

WHAT WAS it about the sky? It was so unpredictable and full of contradictions. Sometimes there were too many stars and they shone an invisible spotlight that exposed you and other times there was nothing.

And then there was the sun, which actually shone a lot more frequently than one might have thought in England, but was horribly cold in February. It sometimes lied and made everyone think it was going to warm you up, but it just illuminated the stains on your walls. It was invasive and watchful, especially in the morning when it cast its glare on you.

I trusted the moon. She was like a cat who didn't reveal everything. She knew it wasn't useful. And if you were a block of ice, you could stay that way in the shadows and not lose your shape.

These were the things I pondered, while I lay on the carpet on the living room floor in the mornings. I did this instead of laying down in bed, so I could convince myself I had begun my day. My doctor, a soft Polish woman with three kids, wrote me a note as soon as I told her I was depressed because I was barren. I felt like I was lying when I cried because I wasn't sure of the truth of my performances anymore.

I processed Tom in segments of getting drunk and getting high. It had been a year since I'd met him, and it felt so fast. Parts of it were vivid, detailed. I could see the wrinkles around his eyes and the way they changed from amber to gold depending on what mood he was in. I could script out certain conversations we'd had about the future and the house we would build. Other big chunks of my memory disappeared though like bits of rubbish dumped in a flowing river. These pieces dissolved, but they were important. I couldn't see them anymore, but I know they had contaminated my reality, and I kept trying to piece them together now. What led to what?

I'd had an affair with a married man. He kept saying how unhappy he was, how his wife was like a sibling, how she had cheated on him with his best friend and he was stuck because of family and money. What was I thinking? He made me feel visible. That was really the thing. And he suggested the possibility of a stable, normal future despite the reality of the chaos we had created together.

I spent days in a haze of equations over the various probabilities in my life. If one thing had worked out, wouldn't I be better? If my brother hadn't died, if my parents had looked after me, if Maya had been a good sister. Or if I had gotten one decent acting gig. I distilled every event, trying to turn each failed possibility into some pure potential that simply never got to take place. Magic was off the table now completely.

When I looked in the mirror I heard Mom's voice in my head. "You're the dark one, Sarika. Dark." My teeth were stained from cigarettes, coffee, and regret. There was nothing sexy or mystical about what I'd become. I had thought the world would make me a strong woman, but instead its enormity made me feel small and disoriented. I pretended I was searching for mystery and wonder, but really, I was just too afraid to look in the mirror. It was staggering – the gap between what was real and what never was.

In the end, my summation was that regret was perhaps worse than despair, as it required accountability. I had to get professional help for my addiction issues though, regardless of my existential pondering. But I kept putting it off each day, clinging to the romance of despair because it was the only thing I had left.

One day I was reading *Twilight* for the third time when I received an email from Wan's Wild Ride asking me to confirm my presence for a psychic reading the following week. I had booked it over a year ago before I'd even met Tom. Wan had a waiting list with an online booking system – modern times in the world of psychics. No more hiding behind a circus curtain or outside a tent at a craft fair while people stood sheepishly in a line-up to pay ten bucks. Apparently, he was very accurate and even guessed the name of Bonnie's aunt who had passed away. I had gone to several psychics in the last few years. Some of them were awful clichés with cats and moon rings and beaded curtains. They told me things like, "You're popular and have experienced hardship." But others told me tidbits that actually came true.

I was always interested in the occult as a means to access universal energy or to answer my questions about when I might find love. But my driving force was usually to find out what happened to my brother. If I could find out where he was, maybe I could have a deeper sense of my own place in the world. I thought we were magnetically connected and when he moved around out there I got displaced and that's why I always felt lost. I would ask people if his manifestation was real – not telling them the truth about the drugs that often evoked his presence. They always said something very general about how he was there to comfort me, and I would argue about how he actually aggravated me.

One time I saw a therapist and I asked, "Do you believe Jeevan is real?"

And he replied, "I believe you want him to be."

Wan had office space in a seedy part of East London on top of an antique shop. When he opened the door, he was chomping into a Subway sandwich. "I love Subway!" he said like he'd just won the lottery. I expected him to look more spiritual, whatever that meant, but he was wearing jeans and a green polo shirt. He had shoulder length hair that was unkempt, but his face was wide and mesmerizing. His eyes were so big I thought he looked like an alien.

The whole office smelled like his sandwich. There was a picture of some monastery on one wall and a picture of a cactus on the other wall, with the words: "Life is prickly and sharp! Stand tall."

He beckoned me to sit down and wrapped up his sandwich. "You want to rub the Buddha's belly?" I looked at the Buddha figurine on his desk who looked fairly amiable. It occurred to me right then how outrageous my life was. I was on the verge of rubbing a figurine's belly on a strange man's desk after losing everything.

"So, why are you here?"

*Why the hell does he think I'm here?* "I want to know what's in my future."

"Ha-ha! *You* tell me what's in your future." He laughed like I had made a really funny joke.

"I'm not here for therapy. I came here for a reading. What's my path?" I was normally never abrupt or sharp. I noticed this had been happening for a while. An irritability with people in general, especially jovial people.

"There are many paths for you. Many possibilities with many outcomes."

I crossed my arms and stared. Worst answer ever. "Well, I've had accurate readings before."

"Like what? Tell me what they said."

*How does this man have a waiting list?* "Like I was told I'd move to London and fall in love with a business man and be successful."

"And then?"

"And it all came true."

"And then?" He knew I was annoyed and smiled at me. His eyes were kind. "Take a breath. You are not breathing." Somehow the awareness to my breath felt like an invitation to admit that I had failed to live properly. He handed me some water in a mug that said, "Best Mother" on it, which I found ironic. And then he insisted I have some gum, which I found quite strange. I took a couple of deep breaths. "Good," he said. "And then?"

"And then it all went terribly wrong."

"What do you want?"

"I want what everybody wants." If he was going to speak in clichés, so would I.

"What does everybody want? People want different things? No?"

*What do I want?* "Peace? Love?" I didn't believe that. Wasn't life simply a dream of something that either did or didn't come true, followed by the listless ache of another dream?

"Peace is state of mind. Love is a feeling inside of you." He opened the drawer next to him and took out a packet of incense and tried to light it with matches, but none of the matches would work. I pulled a lighter out my purse. "No! Always with matches. Using earth's energy." He finally got it after six tries. "See. Patience. Stilling the mind. Waiting." Then he laughed again at me. "You are so stressed."

"Okay, so I'm not peaceful. And I don't have any love."

"You don't know what love is. Not giving, not taking – *being. You* love from here." He pointed to my abdomen. "Empty."

That stung. "Well, there's nothing down there. I know that."

"Yes, that's the problem. You need to fill your belly with other things. Then you love from here." He poked his finger at the centre of my chest.

"Fill my belly with what?"

"With you! With you, always with you. Stop looking. Looking, looking. You're always looking. It's making you more empty. How's the gum?"

"Huh? The gum?"

"Still sweet?"

"No, it's chewy and hard."

He laughed again. "Yes, we look, we find. And use the things we find. It tastes good for a minute, until it stops being sweet, and then we look for something else."

"I didn't even ask for gum."

"No, but you look for things to fill your belly. Always looking."

"I don't even like gum. It makes me get headaches."

"You have a voice. Use it."

"What do you mean I have a voice? I have a terrible voice." I was starting to get annoyed and needed to redirect him. "When will I get married? What should I do for work?"

"Find your voice. But first feel the pain. Let it in. Then use your voice. Hmmm." He was staring at the cactus on the wall like it was a muse. "Something happened when you were very young. Very bad. Oh. You need to see a healer."

"A few bad things happened. And I feel pain all the time." I was unimpressed by the lack of new information.

"You must forgive, not forget. Here." He pulled out a card from his drawer. "Call this lady. She will help you."

The card had a picture of a ladybug on it with the name "Jenna" and "Energy Healer" underneath it and a phone number. I liked the ladybug but couldn't imagine seeing a woman named Jenna for help. I hated that name. It reminded me of server who used to flirt with Tom at his favourite Indian restaurant. "But I came to *you* for help and you're sending me somewhere else?" I had already paid this man sixty pounds online.

"You need to heal the past. Then make a future. Go. That's it."

"What? I paid for half an hour." I felt the pathetic tears coming on again.

"It's not up to me. That's it." He started unwrapping his sandwich.

"I can't believe I paid for this." I got up and stood by the door but couldn't quite leave. My fragility was desperate.

He glanced up at me briefly and laughed again. "Life is unbelievable! But we must believe anyway. That is trust, that is love. And then maybe later we look back and say 'Oh, I understand,' or maybe not? Go." He focused on his sandwich again, taking a hearty bite. He looked elated as an onion fell out onto the floor and mustard glazed his lips.

I was halfway down the hallway when I heard him shout, "Wait!" I turned and he was standing in the doorway. This time his eyes were wide and piercing straight through me. "Say hi to the moon. And then let it go." He turned and shut the door before I could say anything.

I met Phil for dinner afterwards. I hadn't seen him in months. It was he who had reached out. "From my self-absorbed haze, I managed to wonder how you were doing. I was even worried about you," he said as he picked mushrooms off his pizza.

"That's kind of you, Phil. Maybe you even have a heartbeat now."

"You look terrible. I told you how it would go down with that married guy."

"Oh, Phil. Sometimes I just want to eviscerate everything from my mind, you know. Start over in this life." Phil looked at me blankly while I shared my story about Wan.

"Look, I'm not really into any of that weird stuff, but I'll tell you what to do. I think you should go home, Dorothy."

"What?"

"You're always wandering around, looking for the next drama. Nothing here makes you happy. This life doesn't suit you."

"How am I any different than you – you big man-whore. You're such a hypocrite. You bring home a different girl every night."

"But I'm content. I don't lie to myself or anyone else, and I sleep like a baby at night." Phil put a generous helping of parmesan cheese on his pizza and took a big bite. "Maybe you should go home."

"How do you do that?"

"Do what? Are you going to eat that garlic dough ball?"

"You just don't really care." He had a dysfunctional family like everyone else. I could hear it in his voice when he spoke to his mother.

"I do care. Life is shit. I know that. Which is all the more reason why I get on with it. What else is there to do?" He shrugged and shoved a dough ball into his mouth.

I went back to my apartment and ruminated over every word Wan

said. Sometimes when I lost faith completely the universe would
throw something at me – some weird nugget that made me believe. I
put my hand on my abdomen – my empty abdomen – and thought of
the night that had changed my life.

I had been doing kundalini yoga at a studio where the white
instructor had changed her name from Vicki to Pramjeet. Why would
she willingly call herself that? That blew my mind. She said her new
Sikh name expressed her devotion to the kundalini practice. We
always observed each other with judgement, both of us wondering
why the other had subscribed to some suspicious foreign culture
when our roots should have been enough. She could see I wasn't
properly Indian, but that I was just there because yoga might be cool.
When she talked about the origins of kundalini to the class she always
looked at me when she spoke, hoping to convert me back to who I
should be.

One evening she asked me if she could put her hand on my belly.

"Why?" I had asked.

"You need it. You have a block," she said. I didn't know what that
meant but figured since she had the guts to call herself Pramjeet she
might know things I didn't know, so I let her. She closed her eyes and
asked me if I felt anything. I wanted to, just like how I wanted to see a
face in Jeevan's moon, but there was nothing. "There," she said after a
few minutes. "Something will happen now. Something will be
released." I left, certain that my lack of feeling implied the universe
could never reach me, so why did I ever think I could ever reach it?
The other part of me thought there was no design to the universe, and
that God, like Pramjeet and the Wizard of Oz, was a phony and all of
this was a hoax.

Two hours later I was in emergency doubled over in pain. I
initially thought Pramjeet might have been evil and put some weird
curse on me. But really, I had been avoiding my illness for so long in
so many ways. The painful irregular periods, the swelling of my
abdomen that I'd been masking with alcohol and drugs. I searched for
Pramjeet a few weeks later, but she had left and moved to Toronto.

I don't know what made me think of all of that. I felt like I was on the edge of some awareness – like I could touch something but couldn't get inside it. I didn't drink that night or take sleeping pills. I stayed awake and stared at the moon, which that night was such a thin sliver I could hardly see it.

"Jeevan?"

He never came when I asked him to. He only showed up when he felt like it – a bit like Tom. But I was starting to think maybe it wasn't Jeevan I was calling. I didn't believe in a God, as in a fictitious man in the sky with a grey beard who had all the answers. Though I supposed if there was a God it would be a man; only a man would take my womb and rip it apart.

But there was something else. What was Einstein sure about in his equations? Sometimes when I closed my eyes I could reach out to this and grab hold of it for just a second. I would know it deeply, but then it was gone. I kept my eyes closed. I was asking for something. I stayed like that for hours, sitting upright with my legs crossed on the floor and facing the window. Eventually the dark sky gave way to listless, puffy white clouds, and I could hear cars start rumbling in mundane certainty. Outside, people were following rules of discipline and order. Traffic itself offered a sense of rightness.

I opened my eyes and looked around, unsure of what to do. I didn't want to lose this feeling. I wouldn't say it was peaceful or even hopeful. It just felt more grounded. The dust on all my furniture sprung out at me along with coffee stains and crumpled clothes scattered everywhere. God – whoever she was – was telling me I needed a shower and a clean flat.

The phone rang, and my whole body jerked. No one had called me in days.

"Hello?"

"Hi. It's me." My sister. There was a long pause. "I'm downstairs."

"What?"

"I wrote down your address, but I can't tell from my own writing if it's 1E or 1F. Are you home? It's only seven in the morning so I thought you'd be home still."

My sister, who I had been asking to come for years, was here at my doorstep. I guess I had summoned something in spite of myself.

# MAYA

2010

I ONLY PUT on ten pounds before I knew that I was spiralling. I gained it all in a month. It was like meeting old friends, buying bags of chips, chicken wings, and whole cakes. It was a relief having sugary break- fast cereals as a snack while I watched *The Young and the Restless*. I had to buy a few new clothes again. I wasn't sure what to buy or how much my body would revert back to its original form, so I bought legging and loose tops. I wasn't planning on keeping up with this eating, but I knew that if I had to look at another rice cake, I would have an even bigger meltdown.

Kelsey warned me not to let myself go back to that place. "Look, I know you're upset about your break-up honey, but if you get fat again, you'll never recover."

Riley called me too with panic in his voice. "Girl, you have worked so hard. Get your ass in here."

"Okay, I will . . . soon." I tried putting him off, but he wasn't having it.

"No, he said firmly. "You will come in tomorrow after work, and I'm giving you a free session."

"I can't tomorrow."

"I will see you tomorrow, or I will come straight to your house and look through your fridge." Riley was one of those lovely people who never demanded much, so when he got a bit mad at you, it reduced you completely.

When he saw me the next day he was pleasantly surprised. "Oh, you don't look that bad at all. You just look a little fuller."

"Well, Kelsey told me I was getting fat again." I felt like I was tattling on Kelsey to our grade five teacher.

"Well, Kelsey's a little bitch." He took me into his office and got a notepad out. "Right, tell me what you've been eating. And tell me the truth about what you were doing before."

"What do you mean? You know what I was doing."

He looked at me squarely. "Were you taking diet pills? Were you even eating at all? Were you throwing up? Tell me everything."

I was about to lie like I had been so good at doing, but I couldn't. Riley's loving urgency to know the truth forced me to tell it. It was cathartic to be so blatant and lacking mystery. Telling him about my eating history was essentially about me relaying all the strange failures of the past few months. Riley listened with devotion as I told him about the stress of eating white rice all the time with Steven, and how I hated the smell of grapefruit now.

"I was pretty sure you were doing all this. Well, not all of it. I didn't know the extent of it." He took my hand and said, "Okay, no more grapefruit. And no more lying to me, okay?"

"Right." I was relieved to admit to my crimes. I squeezed his hand back, maybe too hard.

"Maya, it's not about being a stick. You don't need to be skinny. It's about being healthy, eating well, avoiding disease. You need to feel good. That's it. Do you understand that? We're going to try a new approach. We're not going to weigh you anymore. But you need to stop eating all that crap. And you need to come in here three times a week. Okay?"

"Okay." As I agreed, I thought about the half-eaten lemon meringue pie in my fridge and the idea of it going to waste.

"I want you to keep a food diary. A real one where you tell me the truth. Okay?"

"Okay."

"And what about therapy?"

"I am not doing that again, Riley." I felt a wall go up immediately, as I thought about Sally Field and her patronizing voice and pearls. "It doesn't work for me."

"See someone else."

"I'll see."

"No, you won't see." Riley sighed and let go of my hand. "Maya, you know weight issues are about other things. You're not a kid. You've been around the block. There's no point to any of this if you don't try to work through your demons. I have someone who I think might be able to help you. He helped my family through a lot of stuff."

"You're Chinese. You don't go to therapy, do you? And I'm not going to see a man."

"He's different. Trust me. I'll send you his details." He stood up and told me to go do a light workout just so I could feel like I was back in the game. I went out the door feeling relieved about admitting to lies I had totally forgotten about. There were so many I couldn't even remember anymore, and they'd been stored in my body like fat cells waiting to be released.

I made my way to the treadmills wondering what might be on TV when I tripped over my undone shoelace and collided into someone. "Oh shit, sorry." My heart fell into the sweaty floors as I stared up at Brody and his blonde tips, which were only slightly less gelled than they used to be.

He looked at me obliquely, like he was shocked I still existed. "Maya? Is that you?"

"Yes, it's me."

"You look so different." He smiled and I just stared at him, thinking I might throw up in his face.

"You look exactly the same."

He stared at me, unable to digest my sarcasm. "Um, Sunny is actually over there." He pointed to the weights, and I felt myself leave my body like I used to when we were together. There he was sipping water and texting someone on his phone. He looked the same but different. His hair was less gelled, and his body was solid and full. His presence echoed across the room, keeping me separate but informed. Who was he texting? I wouldn't know who was on his phone anymore or what he ate for breakfast. Maybe he smelled different.

"Do you want to talk to him?"

My gaze went back to Brody, who I had once mistaken for a trivial event in my life, like a brief rainstorm. But he was now granting me permission to speak to my husband.

Then it happened. I imagined Sunny and Brody together, grimacing and admiring each other's beauty at the same time, under heavy but insignificant weights. Red-faced, they'd grunt praise at each other, both trying to make up for their mutual lack of wit. Sunny's skin was different then Steven's or Brody's. It was the colour of honey. Sunny and Brody – honey and milk – together. It all made sense: a moment of recognition.

I walked towards Sunny just as he looked up at me.

"Maya, I've been trying to call you."

It was true. I had ignored his messages and the notice that had been delivered saying I was being served. Sunny wanted a divorce.

I imagined ripping his heart out along with each sinewy muscle, one by one. "You . . ." I couldn't find the words. "You and Brody?" I accused him loudly in front of everyone over the sharp house music that played in the background.

"What?" Sunny looked confused. He used to have the same look when I told him the bread he was eating was starting to mould.

"You're with him, aren't you?"

He looked at Brody and then back at me, and then his face contorted in shock as he realized what I was implying. "Maya, are you insane? You think I'm with Brody?"

I couldn't speak then. A woman had taken her earphones off and blatantly turned off the treadmill so she could witness our exchange. "Maya" – he said my name fully, with conviction – "I'm dating someone now. I'm dating a girl I met in Vancouver." His eyes were so kind, in a way I had never appreciated, and so full of pity for me. He wasn't supposed to see me like this. He was supposed to have seen me with my bright lipstick, short hair, and skinny jeans. I was supposed to have made him jealous with my gay boyfriend, not the other way around.

"Oh." It was all I could say, and then I turned and bolted. He didn't even come after me, which was a relief, but I think I was offended. In the past, he would have.

I went home and ate the rest of the pie that was in the fridge. Sunny had a girlfriend. *Was she Indian? Was she skinny and graceful? Maybe he was with a female version of Steven, or worse, someone soulless that Brody picked out for him at a bar.* He had become really polished. I could see him living a whole new life with no reverberations of the past haunting him. Men could do that. They were different. I couldn't discern how I felt about him moving on; it felt like jealousy more than the ache of love.

Four days later I was sitting with my new therapist, Carl Green. When he greeted me, I tried to not look surprised. He was black. There were very few black people in Prince George – maybe one or two families when I was growing up. Because I never travelled, I never saw them unless they were on American television shows. There weren't really that many in Vancouver either. I think they were mostly in Toronto. I had always been sad about this, thinking I'd missed out on some sort of camaraderie.

Carl was really tall – taller than Dad – and he had short grey hair and a closely shaved beard. He was so tall that I wanted to ask him where he got his pants from but didn't think it was appropriate.

"So, your friend forced you to come here?"

"Yes, how did you know?"

"He forces everyone to come here. That's how I get all my business." He laughed then with a bellow right from the bottom of his belly. It was nothing like my stilted and weird laugh. His was full of life and jovial. It lifted the whole room. I wasn't sure before how I was going to speak to a man about the things I needed to, but somehow his looming presence provided some sort of comical refuge.

"So, Maya, what should we chat about? Where should we start?"

"I don't know where to start."

I took a deep breath.

"Do you like music? Do you mind if I turn some on?" He could tell I was nervous.

"Sure."

"How about Sade? I love Sade. She has my heart." He smiled and pointed to his bookshelf. "Some people have books. I have records." There must have been at least three hundred records there, but he knew exactly where to find Sade.

"Wow, that's cool that you have records." The crisp sound of the record player brought back a comforting resonance from the past, from days when Jeevan and I threw water balloons at each other and made homemade root beer popsicles in ice trays.

"Do you want a cigarette? Or a drink?"

"Really? Can I?"

"No, of course not." He laughed again. "That was a test."

I laughed too, like him. It was infectious. "Those are not my vices. Mine is food."

"Savoury or sweet?"

"Both."

"Oh, I'm savoury all the way. Give me a platter of nachos and spicy chicken wings and I'm good to go." He clasped his hands together. "Oh, I might make some tacos tonight. Pulled pork. I make really good pulled pork. But that takes time."

We talked about food for a few minutes. My impulse was to suggest going for lunch and sharing recipes. Then I imagined Riley standing at the end of my treadmill shaking his head with his arms folded.

"I should tell you why I'm here."

I told him everything about my marriage, Steven, and my weight issues – even about the rejection from my first fiancée.

"Wow." He paused, staring into space. I wasn't sure if he was thinking about Sade or pulled pork. "So, why are you here, Maya?"

"Huh?" I was feeling rather proud of myself. I had told him about my life history in twenty minutes. He needed to step up and fix me.

"Are you here because you're afraid of gaining weight again, because you have OCD, or because you don't know how to have healthy relationships?" I imagined Carl at home later that evening chopping lettuce and tomato with careful tenderness and placing them in small serving dishes, the kind Mom used for chutney and spicy nuts. "It seems like you know the obvious stuff."

"Do I?"

"Well, what do you know, logically speaking?" He was drumming along to "Smooth Operator."

"Well, I know that I chose an unavailable man after Sunny because I had low self-esteem and low expectations. That's fairly obvious. And I had to starve myself because it was the only thing I could control. I knew all that while it was happening though."

"And what don't you know?"

"I don't know."

He waited. Then he turned the music down and smiled. "What don't you know?"

So I told him about Jeevan, about the hole he'd left, and the urn in Mom and Dad's closet that we never spoke of. "It feels like no matter what we do with our lives we just can't seem to be happy."

"Did your family process this properly? Did they have support?"

I was quiet for a moment. I'd never spoken about the details of Jeevan's death to anyone. Indian people never went to therapy or spoke about trauma. Carl turned off the music. He could tell he was hitting some sort of edge.

I looked over at the clock. "I think time is up."

"It's okay. I took up some time talking about food. Keep going."

"He got into a car accident. He was drinking and driving, and he hit a pole. I think he was stoned too. It was so fast – the whole thing. I think he was trying to run away that night. He wasn't happy at home."

"Why?"

"He didn't really fit in."

"Why didn't he fit in?"

"He was artsy. My parents wanted him to be a good Indian son and go into science, but he liked to draw. He wanted to go to art school when he was older, but that was never going to happen. And there were lots of other things."

I was starting to feel anxious talking about this. My hands were turning into fists as my mind gathered up all of those old images. Jeevan flying around the house with his sketch pad. The time he drew a picture of the tree in our backyard and had drawn some of the branches as human limbs. He had asked me what I thought of it and I tore it into pieces. I told him it was creepy.

"What other things?" It took a moment for me to realize Carl was talking to me. "Maya?"

I started playing with my wedding ring. I was still wearing it. I didn't know why. I felt feverish at the memory of Jeevan's torn work being strewn all over the floor – a branch here – an arm or leg there.

"I think you're a bit tired. We did a lot today. Should we stop and carry on next time?"

"Yes."

I stood up abruptly, ready to bolt.

Carl stood up too and shook my hand. He smelled like fresh laundry. I wondered how he saw the world from up there – if he saw things other people didn't. "Come back next week. Same time."

"Okay."

"I want to get more into your feelings about things next time."

"Feelings? I just told you a bunch of stuff. I thought I did pretty well."

"I feel like you've told me about events in your life, but I don't really know anything about what you feel, only what you think.

That's not a judgement. It seems, Maya, that you're in your head a lot because that's safer for you. That's the sense I'm getting."

"Sure."

I was having trouble receiving his kindness. It was making me spin.

I walked to my car feeling numb and unsettled at the same time. I had been trying to hold it together for Carl there at the end, but all I could see in Carl's face was Jeevan's. They had merged into one other. Something about their kindness was similar and made me want to wither.

When I got home, I made a cup of tea and folded towels. It seemed important to do something ordinary because being ordinary implied normalcy. I wasn't sure how to make sense of the other things I needed to tell Carl, but a strangeness settled in my body – like I could feel my weight through my history.

It takes the mind effort to bury memories – to mix them all up seamlessly so one doesn't dominate the other. There were glimpses of white girls standing in circles at recess, excluding me in the freezing cold, watching while I fumbled with my numb fingers to fix the broken zipper of my outdated winter coat. I still remember that coat. It was burnt-orange. It looked like I had never quite made it out of the seventies. There was the dippy bird that Jeevan ruined, and my Stevie Nicks poster that had turned the colour of fall leaves over time as bits of her hair fell off. It's amazing how we compartmentalize memories in our minds to control the stories of the past in the same way we might arrange seating at a dinner party so things don't get out of hand. You never know what one might say to disrupt the whole flow of the party; it could just take a small word or a mannerism.

There was the time I walked into my room and found Jeevan wearing my clothes. He was dressed in a black skirt and purple blouse, with a big black belt that buckled in the middle, and purple suede high heels to match. He was putting on sparkly eye shadow that matched his skin tone perfectly. I recall being so shocked, not knowing what to say, and instead of yelling at him I walked out. He was eleven then. I remember all the dolls he played with as a kid and watching Dad rip them from him one by one in disapproval and put them in a bag by all the onions in the garage.

Then there was the day before he died. His friend Ricky was over. Ricky was scrawny, didn't talk much, and always had his skateboard with him. They would sit in Jeevan's room and smoke weed with the window open. I had stormed in while Ricky was doing up his pants and Jeevan was sitting on the floor. Jeevan had a frightened look on his face. He was frozen like a mime artist holding a pose. Ricky turned red and left abruptly. That night Jeevan stood in the kitchen and watched me as he used to when he was a kid. I was making a Victoria sponge cake. "You're really good at that, Maya. I was thinking of getting into baking. But then I think it would put Dad over the edge, you know, me baking on top of everything else."

I distinctly remember putting a thick layer of raspberry jam in the middle to cover the white icing. I recall the smell of it – homemade and fresh. I didn't say anything then. I kept slathering that red jam back and forth on there in straight smears. And that was it. That's how goodbye with my dead brother went. Just an ordinary event.

"I didn't see him the next day. I was at work, and when I got home he had already left."

I was in Carl's office three weeks later.

"So why is this important, Maya? This incident before your brother died?"

"Well isn't it obvious?"

After three sessions and a lot of build-up, I expected him to understand the intricacies of my weird family by now.

"Are you suggesting your brother might have been struggling with his sexual identity?"

"I wouldn't even look him in the eye."

"Well, who knows. I mean we don't know, do we? We don't really know what was going on in his head, or what was happening between him and Ricky, or even how he was processing that. I think what's important here is how *you* process what happened."

"I wasn't there for him. He reached out to me so many times and I was uncomfortable and scathing towards him. He was embarrassed. And then he died." I was almost yelling. Yelling at Carl for making me spell all this out to him and for making me admit out loud that I was a horrible person.

"Maya, are you listening to yourself? I think you're saying if you'd responded differently to what you'd witnessed, he'd still be alive? Am I right?"

"Maybe he wouldn't have gone out that night." I thought of the crematorium, the ashes in the jar, and me laughing.

"How can you know that? How can we know what leads to what?"

"What leads to what? I could have . . . should have been there for him many times. He didn't have anyone to talk to and I just ignored him. I made him feel like a reject all the time." My chest hurt – weighed down by each admission of all the different ways I had killed my brother, slowly.

"Maya, didn't you feel like a reject all the time yourself?" I stared at my feet, thinking of Jeevan in my heels. Why couldn't I have just said he looked great in purple? "Maya, you were a young girl yourself, trying to navigate through the world as the eldest child in an immigrant family. Maya, look at me."

Carl's broad nose was the colour of milk chocolate. His skin was still smooth and supple. Jeevan might have looked like this as an older man. I would never know. "Maya, maybe you could have been nicer, but it wasn't your job to work out if your brother was gay just because you caught him wearing your clothes, or however else you saw him with Ricky. It wasn't your fault that he was drinking and driving. Those are the choices he made. And it's certainly not your fault that your brother died."

All I could see was Jeevan's ripped-up tree.

"Maya, do you hear me? It's not your fault your brother died." I looked at Carl, allowing myself to receive his compassion fully.

"I think I need to go."

"Okay. See you next week, okay? Or let me know if you want to come before."

"Okay," I said. I went home and felt things – things for my parents I had never wanted to feel before. There were lost gardens, train sets Dad couldn't afford to buy, and the disappointed looks on people's faces.

I didn't see Carl for a couple of weeks. I had to go out of town. It occurred to me when I got home that day that there was one person I could still save.

# SARIKA

2010

When I opened the door, Maya was looking around like she wasn't sure where she was.

"God, there are so many people here, walking so fast. I almost got run over by some kid on a scooter."

I hadn't seen or heard from her in months. She looked different. She had gained back some weight and her hair was longer.

I stared at her for a while and then realized I was being rude. "Come in." I grabbed her suitcase and slowly dragged it up while she pushed from the bottom.

"What's with these stairs? They're tiny. Have they ever heard of elevators?"

"Welcome to England. I would've warned you if I'd known you were coming." I waited for an explanation for her unexpected burst of spontaneity.

When we got to the top I suddenly became aware of what she'd see when she came in, but there was nothing I could do about it. She tried to repress the look on her face.

"Yes, I know it's a bit messy at the moment. I've kinda been going through stuff."

She took it all in and tempered her reaction. "Can I take a shower? And then, can we clean this?"

The next couple of days were strange but fabulous. She didn't tell me why she had come other than she felt it was time. I didn't tell her right away why I wasn't working, and she didn't push for an explanation. We toured around London, and I got to see it again through her eyes. They were wide and full of wonder when I took her through the parliament buildings and the old witchy streets around London Bridge. She seemed different to me – softer – less contained.

"I've never travelled." She said this like it was a revelation.

I took her to outdoor food stalls. I thought she would appreciate that. "Try some cheese samples," I said, as we walked through Borough Market. It was Friday morning and it was packed – not just with tourists, but locals too. *Don't people have jobs?* There was fresh fish everywhere, bins full of olives, grilled sausages and kebabs, and pastries lining every corner. "What do you want?"

"Can I just get a salad or something?" Words I had never heard come out of Maya's mouth. It occurred to me now that maybe I had brought her to the wrong place.

"Sorry, should I not have brought you here? I thought you'd love it."

"You mean because it's a bunch of food?" She smiled. "It is okay, I do love it. It's just that I gained some weight back, and I don't want to gain anymore."

"But you look great, Maya. You look better. You were too thin before. You look normal now."

"Ha." Maya shook her head and looked at me. "Now those are words I have never expected anyone to say."

"What – that you're normal or thin?"

"Both." She smiled again. It was so strange to see her smile, but somehow, she looked sad at the same time. "Actually, my personal trainer told me the same thing."

"Good. Great." I felt awkward – worried that I would do something to mess this up. I had never spent time with her like this before. I felt like I was on a second date with someone who hadn't called in a while and they were giving me a second chance. "Don't be so hard on yourself about food. We've been walking around all morning, right?"

"Yeah. You're right." She got a Thai curry in the end and told me about how great coconut milk was. We never got to eat it because Mom and Dad thought it was fattening, even though they threw dollops of butter into our dhal every night.

"Wow, you're so healthy now."

"Trying to be." We sat on the bench at the Southbank gazing at the murky river. The sun colluded with thick cottony clouds to cast a hazy glow on us. Maya stared straight into them. "It's nice, your life here. I wish I had made it earlier."

"Well, you made it." I thought I could cry then, but I knew that would freak her right out and break the invisible cord that might be forming between us.

"How are Mom and Dad?" We hadn't talked about anything real in our personal lives up until that point. We knew how to contain our roughness. We were adults now and the western world had taught us how to be polite.

"They're fine. They're obviously upset about Sunny. I had to tell them we're getting a divorce. They're old now, right? They can't handle much. They shouldn't have to."

"Oh, so it's final?"

"Yeah, I was all revved up to do it myself but then he beat me to it. He filed. And then I did some other stupid things." She flinched a bit. "I have a lot to tell you." I felt some sort of jealousy creep in as she relayed her story. Even though the man had humiliated her, she got to be part of this western family for a while. She got to go on real dates and experience a real relationship. Looking back, Tom only ever took me to Indian restaurants in Tooting, where he knew he'd never run into anyone. And that was only for a short time.

"Wow, it sounds like a movie, Maya. It doesn't sound real."

"It wasn't. I remember thinking he might be the kind of guy you'd go out with."

I didn't know what to say to that. She had this image of me that on some level I tried to leverage against her all these years to punish her.

"I'm not all that glamorous, Maya. Really."

She looked at me and waited. It was strange having my sister be this open with me. I had always wanted this, yet I couldn't seem to reciprocate. How could I tell her what I had done to myself – to my life? Her story was redeemable.

"So why aren't you working?"

"Oh, Maya."

I looked out at the filthy river. Under the surface of it was centuries of rotting ancient objects – all irrelevant now.

"I came here because I was worried about you."

"Me? Now?" I felt some anger spring up.

"You've seemed really tired and strung out the last few times I saw you." She paused. "I don't know, I wondered if you were drinking too much." I didn't say anything. I watched a pigeon wrestle with a chip and try to pick it up. "I know I haven't been a very good sister. But I was such a mess myself, you know? I'm just starting to deal with myself. I'm trying, anyway. I'm going to therapy now."

"Good for you." That's all I could say. I couldn't look at her. I wasn't sure why I felt so angry all of a sudden. How was I supposed to engage this way after all these years of apathetic disapproval?

"I'm processing lots of things. Things I've never told you about. Sarika, a few years ago I had an abortion. I never told anyone except my therapist. I never even told Sunny. And I've felt so guilty about it. And then we sort of tried to have a kid, though I just don't know if I was into it. I don't know. I'm still trying to work it out."

She blurted it all out like she was released from it now by saying it – like it was compost and it could be used to replenish the present.

I wanted to slap her. "*You* were pregnant? And you got rid of it?"

"Why do you look so angry? This has nothing to do with you."

Her eyes shone green against the river. They flowed out and asked me to join them now, in spite of the past, in spite of everything.

I stood up and started pacing around. Two German tourists trying to take photos scuttled to the side – unsure of what was unfolding.

"I lost my ovaries."

"What?" Maya thought she misheard me. "What did you say?"

"I'll never be able to get pregnant, like *you*."

"I didn't know that." Maya looked at me sympathetically, maybe for the first time ever.

"No. You didn't. You don't know anything about me." Then I told her, or rather I screamed at her, about all the invasiveness I had to endure: how I lost both ovaries within a year because I had cysts the size of melons. The male doctors poked and prodded at me to figure out what was happening down there. None of them asked my name. They put me on the maternity ward and new mothers asked me if I'd had a boy or a girl. I named my first cyst Bethany and they put it in a jar for medical students to study.

"Why didn't you tell us?"

She looked scared, like she didn't know what to do with me. For once, she couldn't walk away.

"And what, you would have flown over here and looked after me? You barely spoke to me." Phil was the only one who had shown up, bringing tulips because he said they looked like lady parts.

"You can still have children though, Sar." She said it weakly. I was pleased she couldn't console me.

"I probably can't. There are other problems too. Let's go home. I'm tired."

I stood up and she had to follow me. I couldn't be expected to let everything out when she had expected me to keep it in for so long.

We clung to metal bars on the Tube in silence during rush hour on the way home. Maya was getting anxious and claustrophobic among throngs of grumpy, sweaty people. But I didn't care. I couldn't help her. I picked up two bottles of wine on the way home and poured myself a glass as soon as I got in. I didn't feel like hiding anymore.

"Do you want one?"

She was about to tell me off but knew better. Instead she took a glass and made a face as she had a big swig. "So, you're mad at me now," she said, "because I could've had a kid. Is that it?"

"I don't know. I'm just mad."

"At what? That I had everything you ever wanted? That I was expected to get married to a boring guy and have kids? Seriously?"

I stared at her face – at the fatigue I hadn't noticed – and I felt ashamed of my self-absorption. The burden she had taken on so I could leave was visible in her posture and her eyes.

"It's too much, Maya. Isn't it? Look at the world. It's gone mad. Everyone's turning on each other. The earth is turning on itself, and we're meant to navigate through all this shit. Sometimes, I don't even want to be here." I finally said it out loud, reducing all my problems to a wish that had always sat on the edge of the moon, waiting, gazing down on me.

"Well, you have to."

"Why? For Jeevan? I'm so sick of that story."

I felt angry at Jeevan then in a different way, not for his absence or presence in my hallucinations, but for not explaining himself and the world properly before he left.

"No, you need to for me. Because I'm here." Maya's whole face opened. It was like her pores exploded out bits of herself she'd been concealing and she was ready to be witnessed. "And you have to for you. Because you have no choice. So, you're gonna have to just do it."

"Do what? What am I supposed to do?"

"I don't know. Figure it out."

"I don't have the energy."

I thought about what Wan said, about me being empty.

"Okay, then get better first." Maya paused, hesitant of what she was about to say next. "You can always come home…I know it's not home for you. But it could be a break."

"I know."

Maya grabbed my hand. "You need to get help too."

Her tenderness seemed to be having an opposite effect on me. My body was used to being a container.

"Okay, so maybe we should watch a movie now or something."

"Yeah. Good." It was exhausting for her too. She let go and poured herself some more wine and gave me a loose girlish smile. "Do you have any chips?"

Maya left three days later after cooking several meals for me and putting them in Tupperware containers. I never told her about Tom or the *Wizard of Oz*. It seemed the details of the story were too shameful or irrelevant, or a by-product of something larger. I offered to go with her to the airport on the Tube, but she looked horrified. "Call me a taxi. I do taxis now."

"Okay. You know, you look different. I'm not just talking about the weight."

"It's all the coconut. Try it."

She hugged me – really hugged me – in a way that maybe no one had since I was really little. It reminded me I was still real.

Maybe that was what gave me the courage to meet with the head teacher the day after she left. I surprisingly wasn't that nervous about the meeting itself, but about everyone looking at me when I came in. Part of me was worried I still had glitter on my face from the night of the production. That glitter had gone on for days; I would find it on my face, body, hair, and clothes. It was like a bad hangover I couldn't shake – a reminder of how I had ruined my life.

As soon as I walked in through those iron gates, I realized I was done – really done. I had been trying to release myself from this prison for months, and it was unfortunate I had to use cheap glitter and whisky to do it. I didn't even miss any of the kids. All the ones I was really attached to had left and I just hadn't bonded with the new ones.

I beelined through a back door into the head teacher's office before anyone could see me, and before he could say anything I said, "I need to quit, effective immediately."

He was a stern, incompetent man who didn't know how to forward emails. I could tell he was shocked. "You've worked hard to stay in this country. Are you sure you want to leave, Miss?"

I looked at his pale white skin. He was from Ireland. His accent had only slightly faded from thirty years of being in England. "I think we need to ask ourselves sometimes, sir, why we stay. Perhaps that's the bigger question."

I went home that day unsure of what I would do next. How did Dorothy make her way back to Kansas? In a modern world, I doubt she would ever want to go back there. I was bound by my work permit. I could move to Vancouver, take more acting classes, and try to network. There was a big film and TV scene there now. I wasn't sure. I closed my eyes and asked for Jeevan to show up. I knew I needed help. I didn't feel like drinking or doing drugs. I didn't feel clear or sad, just uncertain.

Jeevan never came. He wasn't going to buzz up to my apartment like Maya. It was up to me now. I could feel him telling me that. *Come on Sarika, get your ass up, and just do something.* So, I cleaned my flat again for the next two days and got rid of old clothes and anything that reminded me of Tom or unhealthy patterns. I even decided to throw away my old, red wallet I'd had since I was sixteen. I'd spent money on too many things that had chipped away at my soul. In the pile of credit and random business cards I found the card Wan gave me with Jenna's name on it. The ladybug on her card matched the one on my wallet. I used this as a sign that I should call her, though I wasn't as intrigued by the coincidence as I might have been in the past.

Jenna sounded syrupy on the phone as if cotton candy and rainbows ruled her soul. I told her I lost my job and I was free anytime. She felt sorry for me and told me to come the next evening. "We'll see you tomorrow, sweetie." I hated being called "sweetie" and imagined Jenna giving me a lollipop to console me.

I wore patchouli the next day to get into the vibe. When I knocked on her door, I heard a bang like something had dropped, and someone shouted, "Shit!" and then feet rushed to the door.

Jenna had long curly ringlets of red hair. Her head looked like an explosion of honeyed carrots. She wore a loose, yellow cotton dress that went down to her feet and an ugly ankle bracelet that had feathers on it. Her flat smelled like burnt toast and coffee. There were a few hippie tapestries on the walls, but overall it looked pretty normal.

"Sorry, it's a bit messy. I just dropped my coffee grinder and there's coffee all over the floor. Hope you like the smell." She smiled in apology. I was relieved at her humanness. She gestured for me to lie on the massage table in the center of the living room. "Have you had energy healing before?"

"Sort of."

"Okay, well I work with chakras, the seven energy points in your body."

"Yes, I'm Indian. I know. Those are from India." I felt my disapproval towards myself for going there. It was a bit like how I felt when I was sitting in Wan's office.

"I work on the premise that we are all comprised of energy. Particles are mutable so they have no edges, right? So, when I put my hands just above your body, my energy is affecting your energy. You'll feel some tingling. Just close your eyes and relax."

"Sure."

I took a deep breath and thought about the bottle of wine I had at home in the back of my cupboard behind the oatmeal. There was a Buddha ornament on the coffee table. He was smiling up at me. I was sure I could see Wan's face there, laughing at his own private jokes. Jenna put her hands just above my forehead, and I did feel some tingling like my head was spinning, but I wasn't sure how this was really going to help me. I opened my eyes.

"You need to keep them closed. You're resisting," Jenna said.

I wished I had just booked a massage. Dust particles gathered around her through the stream of light coming from the window. They created a distorted spotlight around her that made me feel panicky, and I couldn't see her face. She seemed like a trick of vision too; something that came from a swarm of bees.

I closed my eyes again and tried to let her do her thing for a while, feeling tingling and fluttering here and there, mostly through my stomach and knees. I was unsure of what to make of any of it. Then there was a tightness around my throat and chest like someone was choking me.

I opened my eyes again. It felt like I was crawling out of my skin. Her hands were over my abdomen and my heart started beating really fast. I sat up. "I'm feeling really anxious right now. This isn't working."

"Sarika, it *is* working. The pain is coming up to be released, so you're feeling anxious. We hold trauma in our bodies through cellular memory."

She put her hand on my arm and made me lie down. I was having déjà vu from when I was seven and in the hospital with pneumonia. I couldn't place why, but it was her smell. She smelled like strawberries – like the nurse who looked after me every day. I didn't know what she was doing but my abdomen swelled with pain.

I felt dizzy thinking of things but not sure why: Jeevan flying me through the air, my doll in the dumpster, Jesse James groping me, and me being alone in the hospital all the time.

"I'm sorry, I can't do this." I sat up again and swung my feet over the table to get up.

"Wait, Sarika. I was picking up on things. Something happened when you were around seven or eight, something you haven't dealt with." Jenna put her hand on my arm again. Her yellow dress looked like the sun, not the moon.

"Look, I already know what happened. My brother died and I was sick with pneumonia in the hospital, and no one really looked after me. I have huge abandonment issues, so I make poor choices. Classic textbook scenario." I had never labelled myself in such an honest way before. "Thank you for this, whatever it was, but I get it now. I understand."

"No, there's something else." She pointed to my throat. "It's been blocked." I thought of Wan and his dripping Subway sandwich. Under my confused cynicism in all these silly mystical things, was a thirst for something sacred; magic beyond Jeevan and what he knew.

Jenna leaned in and the strawberry smell wrapped itself around me. "There's a secret you've been keeping, even from yourself. It has set the tone for the rest of your life. I think I know what it is. Please stay."

I looked beyond her carrot-coloured hair to the wall behind her. There was a painting of an owl with big brown eyes whose stare seeped right into mine. Right behind the owl was a big yellow moon that was blurry like it was a reflection off the water. It had an aura of light around it like it was pulsating out and pulling me in. My abdomen was throbbing in sync with it. I felt dizzy.

Jenna proved herself that day. It was the craziest thing. She was able to name, without me saying, the most unspeakable thing that had ever happened to me – the pain underneath all the other pain – the original wound that kept swelling and reinfecting itself.

# MAYA

2010

WINTER THAT YEAR saw a little more snow. I was happy about that. I'd
been worried about the disappearance of reliable joys and irritations.
As I aged, I could see that was all I could hold on to. I wasn't sure
what I was going to do. Mom and Dad were talking about moving to
Vancouver. Even though the winters had become milder, it was still
hard for them, and most of their friends had left. It was strange to see
them move on when I was so unsteady; they had unknowingly moved
with the times. Dad played video games on his iPad with his Black-
berry close by as a back-up. They went on cruises, eating at buffets
and going for tea in the dining room.

"Don't you feel uncomfortable there?" I asked, feeling slightly
betrayed but not knowing why. "And how do you drink that tea? It
doesn't have any of the spices in it."

"We both like it," said Dad. "It's nice and light, with just a drop of
milk."

"And we like all the cakes," Mom piped in. "All different kinds
shaped like diamonds. Some of them are crunchy and have cream in
the middle."

So, they liked the same tea. They were united. I was happy for them. Sarika had quit her job and went travelling through Asia to meditate and find herself (whatever that meant). She threw away her pencil skirts and bought loose dresses with colour.

I could barely find myself anymore in my own house, much less anywhere else. I could feel my loneliness like a heartbeat sometimes, staring out the window at the houses down the street that cast a glow on my solitary confinement. I used to admire my two thousand dollar curtains. They were lavender and shiny and shielded me from the neighbours. Now they seemed oppressive, like unkempt hair and bangs that were too long. They reminded me of Mom combing my hair when I was a kid. It was sort of the only time she really touched me. I reflected on so many things during those months. It was a necessary season. I learned how to cook fish, I took psychology classes at the university, and I made friends who thought I was normal.

I had continued to see Carl for months, unravelling things from my childhood in stages and learning about music in the process. We would talk, and then he'd make me listen to the lyrics of his favourite songs – Joni Mitchell, Cat Stevens, and James Brown. Sometimes we'd chat about food and what I was cooking to maintain my weight. I had put some on again but I was okay with it. I was curvy, healthy and was never going to be skinny like Sarika and that was fine.

I hadn't been connecting to church as much as I used to. I wasn't sure why. Maybe Carl was my saviour now. I went to my last church event on Easter. There was a sermon about new beginnings and hope. Jesus was dead and then he wasn't. "There is always hope," said Daryl, the minister. "That's how quickly things can change." I personally thought Daryl was a sleazy letch who took every opportunity to touch women while making a point. It was something I had always noticed, but I didn't want to impose jaded stereotypes on him in fear of giving into a pervasive cynicism that I'd been working on releasing. His wife was this skinny little Thai woman who looked fresh off the boat. I was sure there was a story there.

After Easter service we had tea, and cake of course, in the foyer. I had been getting a little tired of all the Raisin Ladies. I called them

"Raisin Ladies" because they all seemed dried up like they got even less action than me. Nicola, a woman who spoke like a teacher, came up to me wearing a yellow sweatshirt with three little chicks on it. Her hair was dyed blonde, and she had really bad roots.

"Have some cake, Maya," she said.

"I think I'm good. I don't need cake, and I need to leave soon." She looked at me like I was rejecting Jesus.

I could sense Daryl gazing at me from across the room. He probably felt my growing ambivalence and was wondering how to entice me back into displaying the same fervour as the others. My resistance pulled him over to me. I tried thinking of an escape as he walked towards me, but Nicola and her three chicks were all blocking me. "Maya," he said. "It's lovely to see you here. Where have you been?"

"Oh well, I've been busy with the religion I grew up with. I've been at the Sikh temple." I didn't know why I said it. I think I wanted to be controversial. It worked. Nicola and Daryl didn't know what to say.

"Oh, well that's nice," said Nicola. "Does anyone want coffee?"

Daryl leaned in a bit. "Maya, are you experiencing any doubt or confusion about God? Are you searching?" He furrowed his brow in an attempt to feign genuine concern, like a bad soap opera actor. He had a big gap in his front teeth and his hair was a strange rust colour. He looked like a white rabbit that needed a bath.

I heard the Blondie song, "The Tide is High," playing in the background, so I focused on that.

Oddly, it was the only English song my mom recognized. She always revealed a half-smile of recognition when it started playing. I think it reminded her of something nice when she immigrated, like eating Neapolitan ice cream for the first time.

"No. I'm not having doubt. I just like to keep my options open. Also, I'm seeing a therapist, going to school, and getting divorced." I stared at the piece of cake in his hand. It was Black Forest – my favourite – and there was a generous amount of cherry in the middle, which was important. I hated going to a cheap bakery as they didn't put enough inside.

I couldn't take my eyes off it, so much so that I missed seeing him put his hand on my forearm and giving it a little squeeze. "Maya, you seem to have lifted some burdens."

I was wearing a blue dress that made me look pretty good and he was looking at me up and down. I forgot that to everyone else I was still remarkably thinner – a transformed woman. Daryl was too close. He was glancing at my chest. I shoved his hand off me, and his whole body jerked. I didn't mean to. It was just a reflex response. The cake that was in his other hand went flying through the air. It was dramatic like a Bond film – maybe fast for everyone else but in slow motion for me. It landed behind him on his wife's shoulder. Bits of cherries dribbled down her pink dress. No one said anything.

Everyone was looking at me now. "Maya," said Nicola disapprovingly, like she was going to tell me to have a timeout in the corner. As I looked around, I could tell that this minor incident was, in fact, a major infraction I would not be able to recover from. I wasn't capable of feigning remorse, so I failed my probation period. Daryl stood protected by his harem of women, and I was a misguided sinner. Good. I felt like my old self again.

"You know, you guys all eat way too much sugar. I'd cut back if I were you." I walked out, pondering over whether the cherries from the cake were drenched with enough brandy.

I knew on the drive home that I had just re-lived an old pattern, making a spectacle of myself and walking away. I also knew there were things I needed to talk to Carl about in therapy that I'd been avoiding.

When I got home, Mom was standing in my driveway, and I knew something was wrong. I couldn't remember the last time she had come to my house. It was probably when Sunny and I first got married. Her eyes were big and wide. Her whole body clenched up in an oversized brown trench coat.

"Your dad – where have you been? Your dad . . ." I knew the last time I had seen that look. It took a lot to surprise Mom.

"What?"

"He had a heart attack. I tried calling you."

The next hours were a blur of wires, tubes, and Dad's greyness. He had four arteries clogged, and they would have to do quadruple bypass surgery on him. He had fallen over in a supermarket in the vegetable section. They were arguing over ripe tomatoes. "He never picks the right vegetables – the fresh ones from the back. Then he just grabbed my arm and started falling." Mom's lip quivered. I could feel the weight of her emotions – how much she felt that no one could see. It was hard holding it in all the time.

I wasn't looking forward to calling Sarika in Thailand. I pictured her leaving the monastery and getting mini bottles of vodka to drink on the plane. She had a solid voice on the phone that I wasn't used to. "I'm actually in Vancouver. Be home soon."

I waited for Sarika and Dad at the same time. Mom quietly sat in a corner with her scriptures, praying with her new little glasses on. *Not now*, I thought to myself. We all needed to be okay for a little while. I wondered if this was my fault. Or if Daryl or Nicola had cursed me, if Jesus was angry at me, or if Mother Mary had picked sides with the Raisin Ladies.

I left Mom and went to the hospital chapel expecting to get stoned. I didn't know what I was doing there because I didn't know what I believed. I felt my aloneness again; it had been imbedded in my shiny curtains all along. I didn't pray. The tears finally came there in that church. I cried for everyone: for the brother I lost, the sister I found, and for my strange parents who revealed themselves as frail creatures of discipline and order. I cried for the real life I had with Sunny, the fake one with Steven, and for things that hovered in the background like white noise.

I cried so much that I didn't hear her come in until she was sitting right next to me, and I could taste that familiar patchouli coming out of her skin. "Let it out," Sarika said. "Let it all out."

Ridiculous sounds came out of me like I was being exorcised. The past was loud once it finally got permission to speak. Someone came over and asked if we were okay, and Sarika gestured for them to leave. Her tiny body felt strong to me – there in that place where people hoped and mourned for the inevitability of life. It was a place we both had rejected in some way.

When I finally stopped I felt unsettled by her stoicism. "Don't you wanna cry too?"

"Seriously, Maya? Haven't you seen me cry enough? Dad's fine, by the way," she said.

"Why didn't you tell me that when you came in?"

"You were giving such a spectacular show."

There was a rawness in the days that followed, like the vivid green of leaves after a good rain. I moved into my old bedroom, and Sarika stayed in Jeevan's. The stiltedness of the past opened up into a modest quiet. We filled it with the sounds of chopping and frying onions and spices. Mom made lightly diluted dahls for Dad, and I made vegetable soups in the slow cooker. Sarika cleaned a lot and bought fresh flowers to put in the kitchen. "You shouldn't pay for flowers," Mom said. "But they're nice." She awkwardly patted us on the head all the time, like she expected we might pop and disappear.

When I got home one day from work, my white cashmere scarf was hanging outside on a chair. I picked it up, searching for the curry stain. "It's gone," Mom said. "If you put them out in the sun, those stains disappear."

Late one night I noticed Jeevan's bedroom door was wide open, along with the curtains and the window. Sarika was nowhere to be seen. I expected her to be there on her back, like she was most nights, staring at the fake stars on the ceiling. It was an unspoken rule to keep that door closed, even when she slept there. A cool breeze blew into the room, and I took a deep breath. I looked at the window sill and thought about all of us sitting out there together. I soon found myself out there, wondering if Jeevan had ever really been with us to begin with. And what his sudden departure was meant to teach us.

There was something about wholeness that I could only touch the sides of. I stared at the moon and the tapestry of real stars my sister was so obsessed with. The moon was almost full but not quite. I wanted to fill it in with a crayon right there at that moment and give it its fullness for my siblings. I looked down at the front yard as bits of snow shimmered up at me. Most of it had melted, and it smelled like shit and dry grass. I never really liked spring for that reason growing up. I remember trudging to school through the dense sludgy mess every year as it melted. I cussed and swore as I tripped over stuff that got buried over winter – like tennis balls, broken toys, and random pieces of plastic.

One spring, Dad decided he would try to revive the garden for Mom, but then he gave up. "It's just too hard," he said. "The dirt is too hard. Here – I found this." I couldn't see what he was handing me. It was covered in dirt. "It's your Barbie." There she was – her hair still shone underneath all that dirt. I'll tell you what I did with her: I washed her under the sink and cleaned her right up. I combed her hair and took the tangles out, and then I twisted her head off her naked body and threw her in the trash. When garbage day arrived, I made sure to watch her leave.

I thought Sarika might join me out on that ledge, but she didn't. I said a prayer for Jeevan and wished him peace and happiness without having any real belief about where he was.

It was late when I closed the window and shut Jeevan's door behind me. The room was not empty anymore. It was full of memories – of everything we thought we could have been in that moment when we all sat out there. The potential that was in all of us still filled the air like the smell of Jeevan's weed.

When I got to my room, I was surprised to find Sarika in my bed. "What are you doing here?"

"I thought it was time to officially move out of that room." She smiled at me as I crawled into bed. It had been years since we had done this. When she was little she had nightmares. I used to threaten her by telling her she had to make me popcorn if she wanted to sleep in my room. Eventually, she wised up and got bigger dolls. "Where were you?"

"I was in Jeevan's room, on the window sill."

"Oh." A look of pain flashed across her face and then it was gone.

"I was looking at your stars. And your moon."

"I don't know if they're mine anymore. I used to believe in constellations mapping out our destiny. I just don't know anymore."

"What about meditation? You've had some good experiences, right?" I was like an awkward father discussing puberty with his daughter. I wasn't sure how to console her about things that were hard for me to consider.

"I have. But I don't know, Maya – what's real and what's not. Maybe we all just see what we want to when we want to." I didn't know what to say.

Sarika closed her eyes and fell asleep without any fake stars on the ceiling to keep her awake. Her loss – the failure of mysticism and optimism as driving forces in her life – made me cold, and I pulled the covers over me.

I woke up in the morning to find Sarika perched on the edge of my bed, shaking my arm. It was early. The birds were chirping, but the sun hadn't quite risen yet. It was still a little dark.

"What's wrong?" I asked.

"He's dead," Sarika's voice was monotone. Her hair cascaded perfectly around her face, somehow making her look like a serpent.

My heart quickened and I sat up. "What?"

I had plans to plant a garden with Mom and Dad, to get new soil, to plant cucumbers.

"Uncle G. He's dead."

NONE of us had to go to the funeral. My parents had lost touch with him years ago, and they decided to preoccupy themselves with the business of living for once. We were relieved. There was an under-

standing of the delicateness of our situation – not just Dad's health –
but a cementing that was happening between us all that needed time
to dry.

Uncle G died falling off the roof of his house trying to clean
gutters. He was only fifty-five and had two kids, so people saw it as a
tragic death. I had kind of hoped he would die in a more interesting
way, like being struck by lightning. The relevance of Uncle G in the
formation of who I'd become seemed too obvious for me to deal with
all those years. He was in the centre of the painting – the fruit bowl
that shouldn't even be considered. I'd become more interested in the
background – until I had become part of it. My anxiety mounted in the
days following the funeral, even though no one was talking about it. I
thought about telling Carl, but I got really sleepy every time I considered it in a session. It's funny how you can filter the past in a deliberate way when it suits you, and other times deny yourself access to it
completely.

Sarika continued to sleep in my room after I went back to work.
She looked exhausted – like she was recovering from surgery herself.
She went to rehab meetings and made me peppermint tea every night.

There was a storm one night that hit every edge of the house. The
rain blew sideways at the windows and Sarika leaned into me in bed.
She whispered in the dark, "Maya, are you awake? I can't sleep."

I turned to my side, making myself available in an attempt to
redeem myself for being cruel when she was a child. "Yes."

"I have to tell you something."

"What?"

I reached over to turn on the bedside lamp.

"No, leave the light off."

"Is this another ghost story, because it's stormy?"

"Sort of. After Jeevan died, Uncle G came to stay with us. Do you
remember?" Her voice sounded even and dense in the dark. It punc-
tured my gut. She knew something. I wanted to get up and run out onto
Jeevan's windowsill just then. I sniffed the covers, the smell of freshly
washed sheets. "I was only seven. And Mom and Dad were in the

garden, and you were out or something. He made me sit on his lap, and I didn't want to. And he started feeling me up. I was uncomfortable, but then, I don't know, maybe it started to feel good..." The words started to blur for me then but they wouldn't go away. They raged in the darkness. They were invincible, beyond the continuing history of the world. "And then he put his hand..." More words – about Dad coming back – about Uncle G pushing her away like he was finished telling her a story.

I felt overheated – almost combustible – and I thought I might throw up in the clean sheets. Sarika didn't cry. She just waited for me to speak. My silence was a curse that been wrapped around my throat my whole life. I wished Uncle G were alive so I could spit in his face. I wanted to name him – to persecute him in front of everyone. Up until now, Uncle G had just been an idea to me, a construct. I had forgotten he was a real person who had done real things.

"Sarika, I'm so sorry. I'm so sorry this happened to you." There was nothing else to say.

She told me about her experience with the healer – how it had been under the surface all along. "I know you don't believe in that stuff, Maya, but somehow she knew. I've never wanted to deal with it."

I wasn't sure what to make of her experience, or if I believed someone could see something like that in someone else so easily. If it was true, how self-absorbed was I not to see it? I did know that my sister sounded like a woman. Her voice no longer sounded like an echo. It had a deep thick resonance. She had done something I hadn't been capable of yet – she had gone into the forest and faced her demons. I was still a girl.

"How do you feel now?"

"I feel different. More solid in my body."

She looked different too. She didn't look like a shadow anymore.

"Good, I'm glad." But, where was I?

"I'm tired now. I don't want to talk anymore."

I was relieved but I could see she might not sleep. Both of us would probably roll around all night listening to the storm. Maybe there was no wind – maybe that was just me – the restless spirit of the house, running through the wood, creaking and mourning over unspeakable things.

We reconvened every evening in my room as she told me about her affair. There was a new devotion between us now that was based on our mutual incompetence to cure our imperfections. I observed her in a new light, reflecting on things from our childhood – how much she needed love that no one gave her. Of course, I was neglected too, but I always had Jeevan. And something about starting off with the soil in India gave me some sort of grounding that she never had. There seemed no time to tell her what Uncle G had done to me. It seemed an indulgent afterthought that someone from my generation should need to confess such a thing.

It was strange going to work during this time. All my senses were heightened and everything was getting to me, even the synthetic smell of dental floss. The sound of drilling was making me gag and the dentist, Dr. Leon, a man who always smelled like coffee, was so boring I thought I might die. I complained about these things to Kelsey and she said, "But dental floss doesn't really smell like anything, and Dr. Leon has always been boring."

"But what do we really know about him?"

"What do you mean, honey? What does he know about you?" She looked at me quizzically, wondering why I had to make everything so complicated.

One afternoon I was cleaning some woman's teeth, and all I could smell was her horrible feet. They were grubby, scaly on the bottom, and her toenails were too long. She kept trying to talk while I was cleaning which was annoying. She was disappointed her eldest son was not going to law school and that he wanted to be a nurse. Her husband overspent on renovations, so she couldn't afford new sofas. Her lawn was drying out from an early spring and too much sun. "Life is so hard," she said. I stayed quiet until I was done with her, making sure to nudge at the edges of her gums with my scalpel while

I scraped plaque off her teeth. She would wince but that didn't stop her from talking.

At the end of the cleaning, I smiled sweetly and said, "Okay, you're done. For the record, life is not hard. Not for you. Mental illness, cancer, and poverty are hard. We actually need more nurses, and having an early spring is really lovely. What colour of toothbrush would you like? And have you thought about getting a pedicure?"

Do you think you need to make a change?" Sarika asked me later after I told her the story.

"I was trying to tell you a funny story."

"Yeah I know. It's funny. You've just never talked about your work."

It's true I never did. "What is there to say about teeth? They're smelly, crooked or coffee-stained. Or sometimes radically impeccable."

"I feel like you don't tell me everything. You pick and choose what you tell me. You always have. Which is fine, I guess." She had a certain tone, the one that usually made me lash out or shut down.

"I told you about Steven."

"Yes, you did. I don't know, it's just a vibe. Can I have a cigarette?" She was already done with her accusation and looked antsy as she opened the window. She didn't hold on to things so much anymore and moved on. She seemed more matronly now that she couldn't have kids. One of the many ironies of life.

"No smoking. You stopped."

"No, I stopped drinking. I do have some cigarettes though." She pulled one out of her jeans and I thought about how I could stop her.

"Sarika, Uncle G did stuff to me too. And to Jeevan."

I didn't know I was going to say it.

She dropped the cigarette on the floor. "What?" We both looked at each other in surprise.

I told her everything as I remembered it, including the guilt I felt about Jeevan. I felt disconnected from it like I was telling her about a documentary I saw. It felt worse for me that it happened to Sarika. "Who knows who else he did this to."

"You've told your therapist, right?" I couldn't speak. "Maya, you have to. You know that, right?" I could feel her urgency fill me up, and I wanted to laugh, only I knew that impulse was gone.

"Yes," I said. "I should." I picked the cigarette off the floor and told Sarika to give me a light. She opened her mouth to speak but then handed me her lighter. I went to the window and perched myself on the edge of the sill, and my sister watched me have a cigarette for the first time. It wasn't very tasty, not like an éclair. I didn't even cough.

I EXPECTED Carl to be angry for keeping it from him – like I had been playing games with him all along. He told me he had wondered but didn't want to push or make assumptions. "Was it obvious? Because I was fat?"

"No." He laughed. "It's not that simple. You know that."

"Sarika is so different from me and I didn't see it. She slept around and looked for all the wrong things, and I . . ."

"And you what?" Carl smiled. "You slept with hardly anyone?"

"That's not what I mean. I just . . . it stopped me from doing things I wanted."

"You're two different people, Maya. There are so many variables. Though I think you'll find, if you look deeper, you're much more similar than you think. Let's make that a homework exercise for you. See if you can come up with how she fundamentally mirrors you." He said this with a grin on his face, knowing he was irritating me.

"Do I have to?"

"It'll be good for you." Carl stared at me for a while, which he seemed to be doing more these days. He wanted me to drive the sessions, but I didn't know what to say. I randomly felt like eating a turkey sandwich with fresh crispy lettuce and tangy mayonnaise. "How do you feel about telling your sister and me this big secret. Do you feel relieved?"

"No."

"How do you feel?"

"I don't know." I felt like cranberry sauce and stuffing would be good in the sandwich.

"I think you do. How do you feel?"

"Hungry." I took a caramel from the bowl in front of me and started unwrapping it. "I want to know why."

"Why you're hungry?"

"Why all this happened to us. Why? Why are all these things allowed to happen? Why?"

I could feel the anger burn through my blood and up into my flesh as I bit the side of my mouth trying to chew on the caramel. It started bleeding – salty and sweet together – like kettle corn. Suddenly, Carl seemed oppositional to me because he could never understand.

"You want reasons, Maya, and I don't blame you. But you can't rationalize your way through the atrocities of life. It takes courage to accept that – to let yourself feel it. A feeling won't kill you. Though sometimes it feels like it."

"I'm tired of feeling. You don't know what it's like losing what I lost."

I caught myself. This is what Mom always said. *You don't know what it's like.* Some sort of awareness washed over me. Something to do with age hardening your grief.

"I do know," said Carl. "You know, my son died."

"What?"

"He died falling out of a tree trying to get his soccer ball. Would you believe it? He was only nine. I called him to come down, but it actually caught him off guard. It was because of me that he fell."

Carl looked off into a spot on the wall.

"I'm so sorry." I could not believe how bad I was at reading other people's pain. He had hidden his grief under stacks of happy records and dead people singing.

"It's okay. I mean, it's not okay. And I shouldn't even be talking about myself. But this is important for you, Maya: the legacy the dead leave behind." It was my first time seeing sadness in his eyes. It was like finding out Santa Claus didn't exist.

"What legacy? To remind us that life sucks?" This nice, overly tall man would have been a great father. Anger should have trumped anything Jung or Freud had to say. "How are you so happy all the time?

"I'm not. You know, they say the hardest thing a parent can go through is to watch their child go before they do. Oh, Maya, he had such a great laugh, and he loved music too. His name was Arthur, but I called him Art because he was a work of art." He smiled like he knew how to keep in sweetness. "I enjoyed my time with him. And then he was gone."

"And then what?" I stared at him and waited for the punchline – the answer to everything.

"And then I had to grieve and feel guilty. And then I had to live. He loved records, you know. He used to take them out of their cases and spread them all around the room." He laughed again. I looked at him in wonderment. Maybe he was Buddhist or something. Maybe he meditated for hours under a tree every morning.

"Do you believe in God?"

The question took him by surprise. "No." He could see the disappointment on my face. "Do you need me to believe in God?"

"I don't know. I just want to know what sustains you. How do you sleep at night? How do you laugh the way you do?"

"What do *you* believe in?"

I hated it when he answered a question with a question.

"I thought I believed in Jesus. Or Mary. I used to believe in Sikhism when I was a kid." I thought back to the boiler room, the giant looming pictures of Gurus, and *Bibi* with her rosary beads. I couldn't remember why I had left it.

"And what happened?"

"They all let me down." I felt like a child. "My sister's different. She believes that God is light or energy, like quantum physics type stuff."

"Does it work for her?"

Carl picked up a stack of records and started looking through them.

"I don't know. She's always looking for signs or synchronistic events to validate that there's something out there."

"Well, if it works for her that's great. So, what do you believe in now?"

"I don't know. I want to know what *you* believe."

If St. Carl could just answer this one question, I might be okay.

"It's funny, no one's ever asked me this before." Carl took a deep breath and rubbed the front of a record on his lap with his long slender fingertips as if he were reading braille – as if it had all the answers. "I believe in *this*" – he motioned to the space between us – "this exchange that's happening between us as humans. I believe in love. Love and levity. These aren't tangible, but I can feel them." He said this with a zeal – like it was groundbreaking. "I believe in dancing and Freddie Mercury." He stomped his feet a bit. "The old stuff. He's dead too, so hey, why not pray to him? He's a god! Do you ever go dancing, Maya?"

"No." I thought of my heaving sweaty body under hot strobe lights.

"I highly recommend it. When I dance, I mean really dance, I feel like I'm soaring. Like something's come over my body and that's when I'm convinced I have a soul. I feel part of everything and I feel like I don't even exist at the same time. You know?" Carl's face was happy again. The flicker of sadness was gone as if we hadn't just spoken about his dead son – but rather a meal that had gone wrong.

"No, I really don't."

"Try it. It's free. Better than any anti-depressant."

He finally chose a record, gently took it out of its case, and started blowing the dust off it.

"I'll take your word for it."

"But hey, don't listen to what I just said."

"Huh?"

Carl leaned in like he was telling me a secret. "In fact, don't listen to anyone, not even me."

Maybe my madness was rubbing off on him. I seemed to have that effect on people. "You really are a strange therapist."

"Follow your own heart. Believe what you want to believe and what gives you comfort. Religion has given peace and hope to billions of people. There are studies on the power of prayer."

"Religion has destroyed billions of people too."

"And that is the choice, Maya. The choice is yours. What you decide to let serve or destroy you is up to you. Look at what's happening in the world. Sometimes I turn on the news and I'm horrified, and then other days, I am moved beyond words because someone gives me a free coffee. So, what're you gonna do? You gonna shut down or you gonna stay soft? Go beyond the edges of certainty. Outside of that, there is so much freedom to move." He turned on "Sitting on the Dock of the Bay," unwrapped a caramel, and popped it in his mouth. "Aw, yes." He closed his eyes like he forgot I was still there. He looked like Yoda – but smaller somehow; an old man that had made his peace with the world.

I thought then about the Raisin Ladies and how kind they had been. Although sometimes misguided, they had taught me something essential for living – the beauty of willingness. I had been quick to fling them aside because I couldn't receive what they had offered. At that moment, though, I put aside my disenchantment and observed Carl, with the hope I would learn how to live with the brokenness of what is never ours.

The next day, a funny thing happened. Mom made us pray with her. She said since we weren't going to the temple, we had to reconnect with our roots. "This is your problem," she said (mostly to me because she accepted Sarika's Buddha more than my Christ). "You two have forgotten where you came from." Although she had recently mounted the big Guru Nanak picture on top of the fireplace, I had been avoiding a confrontation with him, as I assumed he must be angry with me. I looked into his eyes deeply, as I chanted with the women in my family, and realized his eyes were never that hard. They were actually quite soft and strong, and they were telling me it was all okay – whatever it was I'd been condemning myself for. The universe, I realized, was benevolent and simply reacted to what was. I was the punishing one. I was the judge.

# SARIKA

2010

I wasn't into birthdays like I used to be. I sensed the fragility of getting older that loomed ahead. I had worry lines now and grey hair. Everything that had happened in the last few months was a reckoning of sorts. The house was still dusty from it but it also seemed new. Maya was back in her own house, renovating her kitchen and her life. Mom and Dad returned to their routines, perpetually adding new ones like buying a treadmill and making veggie burgers. I was reliving high school, being in the house with my parents again. I meditated and did yoga and tried cooking with lemongrass – all things I learned from my trip. It seemed the universe wanted to realign things so we could answer the question, *What if we could do it all over again?*

"Let's get Chinese food tonight for your birthday." Dad patted my head and grinned like a kid. He loved the brightly-dyed red sweet and sour pork, the thick greasy battered prawns, the overly salted chow mein, and the fortune cookies that revealed everyone's destiny at the end. I didn't have the heart to tell him I hated the whole experience. He'd been eating so well and had earned the crappy dinner. "And Black Forest cake," he said.

"No." Maya looked startled and then composed herself. "Sorry, you should get whatever you want."

"It's okay for you to eat a bit of cake," Mom offered generously. "You're not that fat. You look okay. Just don't gain any more."

"It's not that. I had a negative incident involving Black Forest cake." Maya had a bemused expression on her face. "Anyway, Sarika, what do you want?"

That was a good question. I had given up on concrete things like a man and a home. I wanted purpose – whatever that meant in unclichéd terms. There was a wistfulness about not being on the road and externalizing the search. "Remember, you don't need to be on a mountain to find God," the lady in the monastery said. "You don't need to reach your arms up so high. Just close your eyes and go within. All of your answers are there. Everything." I stared at her when she said that, at her orange robe, and at her glowing, wrinkle-free skin. "Close your eyes!" she yelled, saying I wasn't listening.

"What are you going to do?" Mom asked at dinner, adding hot sauce to her chow mein. She asked me every three days or so, suggesting I go down to the school district. As much as she was grateful to have me home, she was worried about me now that I was in her immediate presence. Before, she could conveniently ignore that I was aging unmarried somewhere in a foreign country, even glamorize me a bit to the Indian community, and say I was too busy and successful for everyday life here. Of course, she didn't quite realize the perilous state I had been in.

"Sarika can't stand kids anymore," said Maya. "Leave her alone."

"Then what will you do?" Mom started getting stressed, a noodle quivering on her chin. Maya had just started something.

"Open your fortune cookie." Dad ripped the plastic off and handed me the cookie with anticipation. I wanted to tell him I was really done with all this stuff – that fortune telling led to a self-loathing of all the things I failed to manifest.

I ripped it open only to find there was no little piece of paper inside. I searched in the two little crevices in both pieces of the cookie. "Great, it's even worse than I thought. I actually have *no* destiny." I could hear Wan chuckling in the distance somewhere as he psychically observed me through the layers of his Subway sandwich.

"No, Guru Nanak is saying just pray – pray to God and that's it. I don't know why you get involved in all these things," my mother said as she looked resentfully at my father. There was potential for a rant about religious roots and the futility of idle spiritual searching. I wasn't up for it.

I stood up. "You know, Mom, I really want to get your garden going."

"Huh?" Mom looked confused as did everyone else. There was a panic in my head about my race against time. A sense that Kansas would disappear altogether if I didn't find my way there soon. I didn't want to talk about all this. I wanted to put down some roots rather than look for them.

"I bought soil yesterday, and it's still light out. So let's go dig up weeds and put down some soil."

I didn't wait for anyone to respond. I went outside and grabbed the old, red shovel that had been sitting there for years and started digging alone.

Admittedly this wasn't really my thing. I couldn't even tell what was a weed and what wasn't. I just started digging. Digging and thinking in one spot just like Dad used to. He was right. The soil was hard and dense. My hands weren't cut out for this.

My best friend – the one who'd had the odds stacked against her – was getting married in three days. Marcy should have been a bigger mess than me. I wanted to be happy for her – and in my semi-evolved state I was – sort of. But the emptiness crept in at night and positioned itself in front of me so that I couldn't sleep. It had a shape of its own. There was no booze or drugs to hide it.

"Today is not a good day to think," Maya said. She stood on the edge of the lawn wearing Dad's big brown boots, amused at how I wasn't even making a dent. "Just stop for a sec. This will help you." She handed me a tweed bag with pink tissue lining the top. It was heavy. "It's my first birthday with you in a long time. Open it."

I threw down the shovel and observed her beauty. Her eyes looked jewelled and full – like she had a secret to happiness that she wasn't quite ready to divulge. Her hair was long and wavy and her hips looked big in a luscious sort of way. She said it was her psychology classes. They were validating her madness and giving her hope.

I took out the tissue and pulled out a big clay object. It was a Buddha statue. A big fat smiley one. "I thought you'd be into that after your travels. I got you a fat one because, well, they're better." The gesture took me by surprise.

"I love it. I really love it." I put him on the edge of the garden right where she was standing.

"You don't want him in your room?"

"No. I think he needs to be out here."

I went to sleep that night in my own bed. The walls were decorated with tapestries from my travels. I plugged in the lava lamp only to find that it no longer worked. It had finally died – on my birthday. It was Jeevan telling me it was time for me to find my own light.

The next morning when I went downstairs I could hear banging outside. Mom and Dad were yelling about chili seeds and which kinds were the hottest. I opened the back door to find everyone outside in the garden. Dad was digging, Maya was opening the bags of soil, and Mom was pulling out weeds. Jeevan's urn was sitting off to one side. Maya saw me looking at it.

"It's time, and it's the right place."

I hadn't seen it for years and was too overwhelmed to make a distinction between the urn and the figure who had been visiting me in the night. "Dad, I don't think you should be doing that, you're not up for it," I said.

"Well, who is up for anything?" He had a good point.

"It's okay," Maya said. "He's got the right hands for it. He'll be alright."

"Well, what should I do? This was my idea."

Maya smiled. "You can plant the seeds." I snapped a photo of them all. Three months later there were peas, tomatoes and coriander seeds that turned into fresh ground masala.

I made Maya go with me as my date to the wedding. I couldn't bear the idea that I had done all this spiritual work and I was going to this event as a single, bitter old hag.

"I need you to be cynical and rude about everyone so I can feel better about myself."

"I'm sure I can do that." Maya wore a pink dress that made her look like an angel.

"I'm not sure you can. You're too nice now."

I decided I would meditate before I left until I felt utter surrender and happiness for my friend. I reached up into that quantum space I learned about, where energy moved, healed, and opened your heart. I felt pretty good when I left the house, but it disappeared as soon as I arrived at the venue.

Not only was Marcy marrying the perfect man, but she had also stolen every single idea I'd ever had for a wedding. She got married in a barn with fairy lights and cute little chalkboards with quotes and homemade jars of jam for all the guests. There were sunflowers (my favourite) in vases on each table. I had never wanted an Indian wedding. This was my vision.

Maya could see the look on my face. "She doesn't realize what she's doing. She probably doesn't remember what you like." I looked at Maya with transparent agitation. "Okay, she's a raging bitch. Who does she think she is, anyway? White trash."

"Thank you."

I sat through the service and thought about how proud I was of myself that I hadn't cried for a while. I felt like I was a ghost and this was a wedding being played out for me. I expected famous figures from history to appear next to me in the pews – like Catherine of Aragon or Anne Boleyn. Or maybe the Wizard of Oz himself would come out and reveal himself.

Marcy looked beautiful, even more so than in the photo she'd sent me before. She looked adoringly at her groom and her kid looked adoringly at her. She decided not to have bridesmaids, saying it was outdated and that she didn't want to make me wear a tacky dress. I think the truth was that she was never really good at making friends in adulthood, and I wasn't forthcoming about the wedding.

I wanted to go up to her afterwards, but I couldn't, so I sat at the table and chewed on dry, roasted chicken because I wasn't allowed to drink. It was amazing to me that, as humans, we don't evolve in any linear sort of way. We can survive crisis, death, break-ups, and break-downs, thinking if we've spent some measured amount of time in self-reflection – with deliberateness – that we've grown. But then someone steals an idea, like giving out jam at a wedding, and our whole world is ripped apart. That's how vulnerable we are.

Maya was flitting around talking to people. I wasn't used to seeing her so engaged with life. "Did you see that kid you grew up with in high school, Chad? Didn't you have a crush on him? He's not looking so hot anymore. He's wearing this awful polyester suit and has pock-marks on his face." Maya stood over me with a piece of lemon cake and offered me some. I shook my head and stared at everyone on the dance floor. Marcy had changed into ballet slippers and was gliding around, just like she was the day I met her all those years ago at the roller rink. She was with the cool kids again, and I was stuck at a table. My life was possibly just as it was back then. As Einstein said, time really was an illusion. Maybe nothing really happened in our lives. We are who we are – just like when we began. A series of events are nothing more than what they are: moments. They are so frail, so bound together like arbitrary dust particles and then blown away – making each misery, joy, or sorrow irrelevant. I knew this as a child. I had forgotten.

"Okay, let's go." Maya put down her cake, grabbed my arm, and pulled me up. "We're dancing."

"Are you out of your mind? What's wrong with you?" In all my years, I had never seen my sister dance. "I think I preferred you when you were unhappy. You were more fun then."

"Are *you* out of *your* mind? I'm not happy. I'm bored and I have to stop eating cake."

As soon as I got on the dance floor, Marcy came gliding up to me. "Sarika! I've been trying to catch your eye. I came over to say hi but I think you were at the bar."

"I definitely wasn't at the bar, unfortunately."

"It's so good to see you." I observed Marcy's little face. It looked no different than it had twenty years ago when she sat in my room eating rolled up rotis filled with sugar.

"Is your Mom here?"

Her eyes darkened a bit. "No. She's not well. She has dementia. How's your family? Maya looks so great, really great. You two look close." We smiled at each other. I felt all that was complicit between us – everything that only we would know – and then she was gone. Someone grabbed her and she got lost in the crowd. She had never been my saviour, my shadow, or my nemesis. She was just a girl trying to be okay.

Maya grabbed me and started jumping up and down to "Smells like Teen Spirit" like she was in trance. "Jump!"

"You don't even like this music."

"Who cares?"

She spun me around and I spun with her as images swirled in my head: smoking and dancing to Nirvana in my room with Marcy when we were sixteen; Bonnie, soaring gracefully like an eagle on the dance floor while I stumbled around; and Jeevan, always pulling me off the ground. *Ready for take-off, Birdie? Are you ready?*

A few happy people were jumping around me in a circle, and I let myself give in to it. I could feel the music in my bones and in Maya's eyes, and I let myself feel everything. My sadness was heavy and my heart was open. My jealousy of Marcy at that moment was stunning, but I loved her through it. I realized how what breaks us binds us and rips us open in necessary ways. The pain in that is tolerable if we decide to keep going. I danced for hours and my heaviness transitioned into something else – a grounded knowing of what we can endure.

Maya and I walked outside later following a little trail through a meadow. I wanted to say something to her, but I wasn't sure what. It was an enduring pattern in our relationship.

"There's a lunar eclipse tonight," I said.

"What does that mean? Do you plan on eclipsing me?"

"No, you idiot. It's about change and the sentimentality of endings."

"So, what are you going to begin?"

"I don't know, Maya. That's the thing. I don't know. I have a confession to make. Something I've been hiding."

"You're a lesbian?"

"No. I'm a terrible actress."

I couldn't see Maya's face in the dark. "Oh."

"And a terrible singer."

"Well, I knew that."

"And I'm not sure I even like acting anyway. That's the worst part. I'm not sure I ever liked it." I felt suddenly like I was under a spotlight on stage and it was time for my monologue. "I've been doing a lot of work on myself, uncovering memories and dealing with my past, especially in meetings. And I buried stuff, you know? Like how Jeevan used to smoke weed all the time and throw up in front of me. I pretended it was okay. And once in a while he would twirl me around too fast when he was doing stuff. Sometimes he was such a jerk."

"Oh Sar, is that your revelation? That Jeevan wasn't perfect?"

Maya clasped her hands together and looked ahead like she used to – when she was a teenager in the kitchen thinking of what to cook for Mom and Dad. "You're always looking for something. You're looking for Jeevan or for a husband. Just looking. And I was looking for Jesus or a paper-thin alter-ego. God, I was starving. But none of that is real."

"Jeevan is real."

"Sure, I get it. He's in the moon and the stars, but you can't touch those either. Is he the most real thing in your life?"

"He might be."

I could feel the strangeness of his absence bigger than my presence.

"Really? He wasn't even a part of your life for that long, but you hold on to him – this idea of him – the way you held on to that doll I threw in the dumpster. Stop using him to not deal with anything else. He wouldn't be fond of that. He's not your door."

"Then what is?"

"There isn't one. There never was."

"Then I guess we don't have anything then. What's the point?" My exhaustion was bigger than the grief, and I wanted to lie down there in the meadow.

"We have ourselves and sometimes each other. This flesh. These bones." Maya leaned down and pulled up some weeds and shoved them in my hand. "These are real. Feel them. They're alive and dead in your hand." A rage sparked out of her eyes. It was her essence like I'd never seen it. "Look for yourself, Sarika. Be fierce about it. That's really scary for you. I think you're worried there's nothing there."

She was right. I had invented people my whole life and then I watched them shrivel and disappear in wonderment. I had created my own satirical reality over and over again in my search. I wanted to present a more sure-footed version of myself but I couldn't.

"And you, Maya? Amelia? Whatever your name is? Have you found your missing self?"

"Not really. But I see glimpses of her. I know where to start looking. I know where not to look. I know she's not in a church or a statue or with Sunny. I know I have to start paving a way out for her."

"I really liked that doll."

"I'm sorry. And I never got a doll I liked. Which is worse?"

"I miss our brother. How I remember him in my head. I think of what he'd be doing right now, as a man, but I can't picture it." There it was. The face inside the moon that I could never see.

"We do that with the living too. We try to freeze-dry how we remember them at some point in time because they change and disappoint us. In my head, so many people have died." Maya's eyes looked soft, like melted butter, and a tear came out of her left eye. "If I admit that I miss him, I'll have to admit to other things." I could feel what she was feeling; we were both ashamed of ordinary emotions.

"You weren't a bad sister." I wanted to say more to fix her. I looked up and the moon looked different. It was bright but distant with an orange glow. I sensed that it was just a satellite now and that Jeevan had moved on. It could exist and shine on its own. "I guess he came to teach us stuff and then he had to leave. I guess that's it."

"I don't know. I get that whole thing about the dead teaching us how to live, but I don't know, Sar. Is that it? It doesn't quite give us enough credit, don't you think? What about the dreamers who live among us *now*, who always have that searching quality, who shake up our houses and dig up our gardens?" Maya turned to look at me, as if some big part of her decided to give me what I had always needed. "Don't stop being that. We all need you."

"But I thought you told me to stop searching."

"No, I told you to stop looking outside of yourself."

"So, if I'm the dreamer, what are you?"

She paused and thought about it for a moment, gazing down at the tall weeds for answers.

"I'm the soil, I think. And Jeevan is the sky."

I started calling her Maya Angelou from then on. I told her that she was not the goddess of illusion and that she needed to move with the times. She was now the modern-day goddess of truth and wisdom. She liked that.

"You know, I used to see Jeevan sometimes when I was wasted. I don't know if it was real. And that Jenna lady. . . . I don't know what that was. I don't know what's real, Maya."

"Does it matter?"

"Well, it could mean I'm nuts." I could feel the weight of my confessions – that my spiritual assertions about life had been empty and quivering the whole the time.

"Who cares? You felt something. Anyway, the best people are bonkers. Don't they say something like that in *Alice in Wonderland*?" Maya smiled a little to herself. "No one knows the truth about anything, yet at the same time we all know it so absolutely."

It was true. We didn't always know how to speak to each other. But above logic and reasoning, ghosts and dreams, other things held us. They were palpable. When we walked that night through the meadow and the tear-stained weeds, it seemed that the moon was swelling with forgiveness, and a new language was being formed.

When I got home that night I couldn't sleep. It wasn't because of Marcy's wedding, but a feeling I got a sense of when I was dancing that I wanted to contain and express at the same time. I made a cup of tea and walked around the house until I knew what to do. It started getting light out. The monks in Asia said the veil was thin between this side and the spirit world early in the morning and that's why they got up to meditate.

I opened my laptop and started typing. My shortcoming had never been my darkness, but rather my inability to see it for what it really was. I had wanted to be outlandish but riddled myself with the business of regret. I'd never committed to anything wholeheartedly, whether it be a dream, a belief, or even the darkest wish.

I wrote my first poem that morning called "The Face Inside the Moon." It was a ghost story, but it wasn't about Jeevan – it was about me – how I came to life somehow, grew edges and took shape, and was filled in with force and gravity. I didn't quite realize it then, but that morning was the start of something. I reached in rather than out and finally grabbed hold of myself. I had always thought the biggest day of my life would be my wedding day, but it ended up being someone else's.

For years all I did was fear getting older as stories built up in my body. More important than being told, stories deserve to breathe. Only then can they be set free. Only then can they wander off like loose clouds to create space for new ones. Forgiveness is just that.

These stories – we all have them. I kept mine in my pockets until

the paper crinkled and thinned into nothing, and the words all bled
and wept everywhere. Then I wrote them down again, slightly differently, embellishing certain parts. I read them out at parties or into
empty gin bottles that echoed in the night.

But I forgot to say, even to myself, what it was that actually broke
me. Because I didn't know. I didn't know if it was just one big event, a
series of tiny disappointments, or a gesture from 1996. It could have
been so many things. But it was there for me to look at when I was
ready – to greet its messy face, its wrinkles, its edges. I couldn't force it
to leave – certainly not all at once.

When I finished writing it was six in the morning. I fell into a
loose, quiet sleep and was woken up by birds chirping right outside
my window. It sounded like a flock, singing so loudly it took my
breath away. I looked over at the window and there stood Jeevan. It
was brief, maybe five seconds, but he was clear as day. His eyes
sparkled. He nodded and then he was gone. That was the last time I
ever saw him – at least in that way. I ran to the window and threw it
open – but not for him. I smiled up at all the birds racing across the
sky and heading towards the sun. I swung around the room – by
myself.

FIVE YEARS later I was in London again and saw Wan going into a
Subway shop. It wasn't serendipitous – not everything was. I sort of
stalked him and waited for him to come out of his office for lunch,
knowing he still worked there. I'd planned to run up to him to tell him
I understood now, and that I had found my voice. I'd tell him I had
written plays and a book of short stories that led to a decent bit of
success for me. I'd tell him I met a nice man but I didn't need to give
out jam at any wedding. There would be no riding off into any sunset.
Beyond the horizon, our worlds were full of plot twists that forced our
hands to surrender around every turned corner. I'd affirm that it was
all okay, this silly little life, but that I still wondered about so many

things. But then I realized I didn't need to tell him all this. Not everything needs to be said, and not everything can be. So I let that man eat
his damn sandwich.

There are the things that flourish and take off in an instant, in a
heartbeat without us even noticing, and other things that bind us to
the earth and root us so deeply we can't move. When we hold space
for those things converging in a single moment, we find peace. The
pain of possibility hides in every corner in stillness. Sometimes we
catch it and we feel a glimpse of the all-ness of things. It's enough –
just this, to get us through all the other moments. It's enough to bring
us home.

# MAYA

2015

SUNNY LOOKED like a real man now. That is what I thought when he sat across from me. He had filled out even more, his hair was longer, and his eyes seemed full of wisdom. We were in the West End not far from my apartment. We sat in some hipster coffee shop, with a single blue light bulb dangling from the ceiling, which made me feel like we were meeting in some other dimension. I hadn't seen him in years, but when I heard his father died, I felt a tenderness for him again. It made me realize that all that had been good between us still existed, and I wanted to somehow express this.

"So, you're okay?" I remembered inane questions that people asked when Jeevan died.

"Yeah, I'm good. You know, I'm busy." He had opened his own construction company which was thriving.

"I heard you're engaged." I said it with contrived glee, and Sunny looked a bit taken aback. I lowered my voice. "I'm happy for you."

"Are you?"

"Yes." And I was. And it was good to feel it. "I'm busy enough you know, finishing my psychology degree. I'm getting my PhD. I'm really loving it."

"Right. And there's your kid?" I could see so many questions on his face. He was wondering why he hadn't been enough. I had gone ahead and adopted on my own.

"Yes. She's five, so she's at a pretty great age." I needed to offer him an apology. "I wasn't ready back then, Sunny. I was such a mess. You know that, right?"

Sunny paused, and I could see a flash of pain across his face that reminded me of the time I threw away his old comic books and forgot to tell him. "So, are you with anyone?"

"Well, I sort of have a man friend who has three kids of his own. It's complicated, but I'm really happy with him. We have separate places, and it works. You know me. I need *a lot* of space."

"I do know that." He smiled at me – genuinely – and so did I. We held each other's quirks and misfit identities. He knew my every habit the way no one else would. There wasn't a lot else to say after that. When I watched him go out the door, it was strange. It was like watching someone die. *You go on ahead,* I thought to myself. *We'll catch up later.* I didn't quite know what that meant but I breathed out the ache and it felt nice.

I drove to my parents' place after that. They too had moved to Vancouver into a tiny little house in the suburbs. When I walked into the living room, Dad was pouring spicy nuts into a bowl and Mom was asleep on the couch. "Trudeau is going to win the election tonight. Sit down."

"And then what?" I wasn't particularly excited about the election the way Dad was, and clearly, neither was Mom, but it was the wrong thing to say. He lectured me about what Justin's father had done for Indian immigrants and how this was a resurgence of the old Canada.

I told Dad his ideals for this new prime minister were lofty and ridiculous. It was a different time. The past was irrelevant. Immigrants would never have the same opportunities for all sorts of economic and social reasons. The world was melting with terrorist attacks and natural disasters. And we didn't even know at that time who was about to become President of the United States.

But Dad wasn't listening. He had a new bottle of whisky that he just opened and was pouring it into a nice, old tumbler from the eighties. He usually never drank on a Tuesday night. Then I realized his optimism sprung from a nostalgia that was perhaps more personal than political. It spoke more of celebrating his own past rather than summoning a broader, more uncertain future where the wild landscape stretched out too far to fathom. "It's good to hope," he said. "Hope supports desire, and desire changes the world. Well, it changes some things . . . sometimes."

I looked at my father with amazement. "Wow, Dad. How did you come up with that?"

"I read it on Facebook."

He laughed, and his worry lines and laugh lines all mixed up into each other. It wasn't his job to tame forest fires or even wonder about them. He had done what he came to do on this earth. He learned how to enjoy sculpted gardens and he earned the freedom to cut his hair. It was our job to balance the elements.

"Where's Sarika and Jeevan?" Sarika was visiting. She stayed in New York with her boyfriend as much as she could but came for big stretches of time when she wanted to write.

"They're upstairs playing."

I crept upstairs and stood in the bedroom doorway. I liked to spy on Sarika with my daughter because I knew she was the more natural mother between the two of us. I was okay with that. In some ways, they were closer. I expected a nice scene with the two of them cuddled up reading a book like they usually did. But not tonight. Tonight, Jeevan was throwing toys around. She did this quite deliberately so that no real mess was made and no one really had to clean up. It was just enough to assert her rebellion or make a simple point.

"I want to go to the beach." She pulled some fake, gooey, pink sand out of a bucket and threw it on the ground without really making an impact. "The beach, the beach."

"Babe, it's too cold out. It's raining."

"Why?" Jeevan was generally obsessed with weather and seasons, and she didn't understand why it ever had to be cold.

"It rains a lot in Vancouver."

"Why?" Jeevan was also in the "why" stage all the time right now. *Why does Sarika go away? Why does Grandma eat chillies with all her food? Why are bananas the same colour as taxis?* She was also obsessed with the colour yellow. Sarika pulled out Jeevan's book of drawings and opened to a page full of yellow objects. There was a taxi, a banana, a sun, and a yellow star.

"What can you add to this?"

Sarika was so good with her. I was getting stressed out seeing the fake sand all over the floor and the crayons splayed out everywhere. Jeevan sat down and looked carefully at the page with her big eyes. Then she drew a lemon, a duck, and a butterfly.

"Your turn." Jeevan handed her the pencil. Sarika thought about it for a moment and drew a moon. Jeevan grabbed the pencil out of her hand and drew in some eyes, a nose, and a mouth with a tongue sticking out. Sarika smiled with the truth of what sustained her.

In the spring, I went up to Prince George to sell the house. I probably didn't need to go all the way up there, but I wanted to. It was the last thing I needed to let go of. I had rented it out to a young family who was perhaps leading the life I had missed out on. They were a young couple in their twenties with a boy and a girl and a beautiful golden retriever. They wanted to buy it, and I could tell they didn't have a lot of money, so I gave them a really good deal. In the past, I might have said those two white kids knew nothing about struggle and probably would have increased the price instead. But now I knew the truth: no one knew anything about what was going to come. So, at the very least, we shouldn't squash each other's dreams with bitter musings of the past. It was better to stay soft so that we didn't break.

I brought Jeevan with me and we stayed at the Holiday Inn. I wanted to show her around that little town that I still loved so much despite what anybody said about it. I took her to my church when it was empty to honour the good stuff that happened in there for me. I had found a new church in Vancouver that was sort of hippie and cool. They often sang songs like "Wonderful World" and "Somewhere over the Rainbow" along with traditional hymns. I alternated between there and the Sikh temple. I told myself I only went back to my roots because I missed the food, but then I realized it was okay to be ambiguous. At a certain age, it was probably a gift.

We also went to our old house. I looked up at my brother's bedroom and greeted him in my mind, imagining him throwing my lasagne out the window at me. I told Jeevan stories about her uncle – like how he used to make root beer popsicles in ice trays and eat them as he sat on his windowsill.

Then I made her walk through the sludgy, melting snow in the meadow.

"There's dog poo and it smells like vomit," she said.

"I know." Then I told my daughter so many things there in that meadow. I explained the seasons – how spring wasn't all that lovely in some places – and when the snow melted it wasn't pretty or neat; it got hard and dirty, and was difficult to walk through. Everything got exposed – old stuff you thought you'd gotten rid of surfaced in your backyard – and you had to deal with it, or it would stay there.

"And then what?" she asked.

"And then you have to clean it up and wait for things to dry up. And then you have to nourish the soil and plant new things."

"And then what? It snows again?"

"Yes," I said. "Eventually. It always does." I decided at that moment to buy her a dippy bird. I wasn't sure what she would learn from it – maybe stuff about patience or magic, needing to refill your cup, or maybe just something about the simplicity of watching time pass in an orderly fashion without making a mess of things.

My sister forced me to make a "manifestation wish list" on a new moon. I didn't like her cheesy self-help strategies, so I changed it to a list of "goals and general wishes" that I decided I would achieve one by one in a practical, methodical fashion – not because I sat and prayed for them.

In the summer, I crossed off number three on my list (number one was to get my PhD and number two was get a condo in Vancouver). I stood in my polka dot red bikini at the edge of the ocean. Sarika had found it in some vintage shop and took it as a sign of course. My skin was pasty and flabby in the warm bright sun, and I didn't care.

My sister and daughter were next to me, and Mom and Dad were somewhere behind us in the distance. Who knows where my brother was. Maybe he was loving us, maybe he'd moved on, or maybe, like many other contradictions in life, both were true.

Perhaps wisdom has nothing to do with "cherishing the moment" or "living life to the fullest" or any of those banal statements. Perhaps it's enough to hold a moment or let it take hold of you – let it inhabit you – knowing there's nothing you can do about its strangeness or wickedness, or even its beauty. Somewhere out there, crocuses are wilting and ideas and humans are being born; wood that was once a five-hundred-year-old tree, so certain of its own constancy, is being burned. And none of it, really, is any of your business.

For the longest time, I was unsure of where my heart lived. I thought it was outside of me and I couldn't reach it. But I was half right. It was everywhere and nowhere. It was here right under my feet. I laughed and jumped in. The water was so cold it hurt. It hurt so much I was pulsing and wildly open. I won't say it was glorious, but it was good and real.

# ACKNOWLEDGMENTS

I would like to thank everyone who has supported me through the long, arduous process of writing this book. There are simply too many names to write here, and I'm certain I would leave someone out. I drew my inspiration from the courage I have witnessed from so many people in my life, including clients from my counselling practice.

When I started writing, I thought this was a story specific to the Indian culture I grew up with, but as I began discussing it with friends and clients, I realized this is everyone's story. Everyone has gone through something – loss, grief, trauma, and just the difficulty of navigating through life with all of its crazy obstacles. This book is a work of fiction, though embedded in the story and characters are the experiences and truths of so many people I have met along the way.
I thank you all for giving me the courage to write. I am deeply grateful.

Made in the USA
Columbia, SC
21 September 2019